OUT BEYOND THE VERRAZANO

By

Terrence Dunn

To Tom and Olivia, O m'anam

ISBN 978-1-105-22154-5

Angela
September 2009

My hospital room is stuffy and the walls are an oppressive gray. I am feeling some pain, but I'm relaxed. It was a long ordeal, as they said it would be. But that part is over. It was not that bad. Things don't hurt so bad once you've stopped hurting yourself.

I cannot see out of the window from my bed. But I know the ocean is near, I can feel it. I was not born near the ocean, or so I was told. My early history is mostly a mystery to me. But I live near the ocean now and every day I find the time to go to it; to walk in the surf, or sit on the dock and dangle my feet. The ocean is part of everything I am about to talk to you about - it is the beginning and the end. It is religion to the people in this story.

Today it is raining out, hard. I can tell from the way the rain is rattling against the glass that the wind has swung to the northeast. I'm not a real sailor, not yet, but I can tell you that this evening will bring us some nasty weather.

But they will all come out to see me, no matter the weather. I turn my head, my neck stiff and sore, to look at the closed door. Who will be the first face I see coming through there? There are some faces I wish I could see. I imagine if someone who is no longer with us came through that door, how lovely that would be.

I will tell you my own story as we go along. It is still a work in progress. But I am at a threshold now and perhaps this is the time to tell it. An ending and a beginning. The most important part of my story is how I became a part of the MacAfee family and the life of that family. Everyone in that family speaks to me, one way or the other. And please don't think I'm crazy when I tell you that I even hear from the ones who are gone. They have all reached out to me, for which I am grateful. Although it has not always been easy for them or me.

I hear voices in the hallway. Male voices, several of them. Trying to keep their voices down, but excited and loud nonetheless. Just then the wind howls at the window. There are frightening things out there, forces beyond our control. This new life of mine is frightening in its way. But I sit myself up and take a deep breath. There is no turning back now.

I think of my father-in-law on that day on the *Daybreak*. It was such a beautiful day, but different from any other. And he knew that. What do you think about when you realize your life will never be the same again? When everything is about to change? I sit still and try to breath and wait for the door to my room to open.

Contents

CHAPTER ONE
John Patrick MacAfee
October 2007

She is lovelier than anything I've ever seen. Long, sloping lines, movements like a dolphin. Her curves and her flow sometimes catch my breath and my gut like the shock of winter ocean water. Now I hold on tightly and feel her trembling lightly but powerfully beneath me. She has a broad, open back; a high, arching breast; a proud face. She is a fifty-two foot lobsterman's boat, called *Daybreak*.

Wintertime, the deck is crowded with lobster traps and other gear. I've run lines and traps for every fish and shellfish known to man and a few I've only imagined. I've trawled, cast, dragged, seined and trapped for lobsters and blues, fluke and junk fish, crabs, eels, clams, oysters. I've deep sea cruised for marlin and sword. Anything I can catch, that's my living.

Spring and summer, I take out charters, usually groups of loud, overweight men, drinking huge quantities of beer and fishing for whatever is running. Sometimes they even stay sober long enough to catch something.

I've had *Daybreak* for thirty four years now and I've fished every day I can. It's all I've ever wanted to do.

On the boat with me today I have two of my sons, as well as my 13 year old grandson, Patrick, and my daughter-in-law, Angela. The boy sits in the stern, trolling with a deep sea lure, always hoping to get lucky. It's a gorgeous fall day, although maybe not what you would consider beautiful: it's cool and cloudy, still a gray day. But I can feel that it will stay dry and the air is crisp. I believe the clouds will pass. The day is sharp and awake.

Angela stands next to me on the bridge, huddled in a huge blanket and drinking coffee. She leans on me slightly and I am a little embarrassed about the secret thrill this gives me. She is a lovely woman.

"You ready to fish, Angela?" I ask.

"No, I'll leave that to the fishermen, Pop," she says, patting me on the hand, "I'll stay up here and keep an eye on things. You've got a full crew. I'll just get in the way."

"Don't give me that. Afraid of getting your hands dirty?"

"No, I'm not afraid of getting my hands dirty, old man. I've cut my share of fish guts."

"Landlubber. Women don't make good sea dogs. They're just visitors on a boat."

She turns and leans forward and glares at me. I mean really glares at me. Her jet black hair falls over her forehead and those dark eyes are flashing. Then she smiles.

"Why are you trying to get a rise out of me, you old grump? Why can't you just be nice?"

"Because I'm not nice."

"Oh, bullshit. You're a pussycat. All bark and no bite. And I *know* my way around a boat. I can mate for you, you know that."

I lean into her slightly. "I sure do. You can skipper my boat. I'm just messing with you."

She looks ahead and says, "I've always loved this trip. I love shipping out on Eastchester Bay this time of day. Everyone's usually too sleepy to talk, so you only hear the sound of the motor and the rush of the water. It's so peaceful. You sneak out past the City before it wakes up."

And so it is this morning. We head down the East River past a sleeping city, into Upper New York Bay at first daylight. In the morning fog I can see Ellis Island, where many of my relatives had entered this country. Then the New York City skyline looms like Oz behind us as we cruise under the Verrazano Narrows Bridge, through Lower New York Bay and out into the Atlantic Ocean. I turn and watch the Verrazano as we leave it behind. Its lovely arch frames the world you're leaving and the world you're coming to, the troubles of dry land and the fear and the thrill of the open sea.

My youngest boy, Michael, climbs up to the bridge and stands by my side at the helm. He's already thirty-four, but I still think of him as a little boy in dirty jeans. Michael is taller than me, but not nearly as broad. He's a bright man, a lawyer, so smart it scares me sometimes. Michael has a family of his own, two little kids, but he seldom seems happy; he worries too much. I used to be like that sometimes, but I try not to anymore. He's a good man, with few mysteries, and gentle in a way that has nothing in common with me, a way that has frequently driven me crazy. I have tried to teach them all that sometimes you have to push people, or even fight, to get what you deserve. But Michael was always reluctant. Still, I suppose I admire him, for who he is. He has benefited, I hope, from the small wisdom I accumulated the hard way raising his brothers. In a different way from my other sons, I would say that he and I are friends.

I pat him on the shoulder and smile. He turns and looks at me with a surprised puzzled expression.

My oldest boy, James, Angela's husband, stands in the stern behind the raised engine hold, on the top of which he has laid a large board. When we have our catch he will clean it on the makeshift table. He is expert at it, the best fisherman I know, which I have never told him. He is forty-two and runs *Daybreak* most of the days now. He had been captain on much larger boats for years, since his teens, the big party charter boats that sail out of City Island with seventy-five on board.

I know James loves skippering the *Daybreak*, but watching her go out without me still saddens me; it's like sending a child off. But that's the way it is. I've started calling it "our boat" to James, but he cringes and says, "No, Pop, she'll always be yours."

James is everything I should've been, I suppose: calm and sober. No dreamer. He may be content, I think, but it is hard to tell. He loves Angela, who wouldn't? They haven't had children and probably can't, since I think that is something that both of them would want. But you can't ask James questions like that. If he has dreams, wishes, he keeps them to himself. He loves what he does and seems confident in his abilities. He seldom smiles, and I sometimes wonder if he is happy.

Since James was half my size, he has regarded me as an equal, as if he'd crack me one if I pushed him the wrong way. I took that seriously, there is something about him that demands that. And we've had our differences and fights. He's stubborn as a mule. I wasn't always easy on him. Actually, he was frequently in the right, although I don't have to admit to that, not in my house.

I watch him now and he looks up at me without expression, his eyes as impenetrable as the dark green-blue sea around us.

Since we boarded this morning, I notice there are hardly any exchanges between James and Angela.

"Things okay with Jim and you?" I ask Angela.

She looks at me, surprised. "Oh, sure," she says. "Yes. Everything's fine." She looks away and fusses with the blanket hem.

"But how are you, John? You look a little tired this morning. You never look tired."

"I'm fine. Always fine. Strong as a bull. I just think it's about time these boys started pulling their weight."

But I'm not fine. I should tell you now, get it over with: I am sick. I am dying, I've been told, and the way I feel I believe it. I have cancer in my bones, the worst of it in my spine. I didn't initially understand the medical discussions, but I learned. You learn very quickly about dying when it is happening to you. You tend to concentrate more. Within a few months I will no longer be able to walk and almost any movement will cause me great pain. After that, my doctor said, death is inevitable. I told him I already knew that, although I knew he meant inevitably sooner. He won't say how soon, but it does not feel like it will be long.

I haven't told my children or my wife, Ellen. This news is relatively recent. They know that something is happening; they sense that something is wrong. But they don't know how bad it is. The boys don't appear to want to ask too much. I'd like to think it's because they're afraid to ask, that they're used to me being indestructible. But who knows, maybe they're just waiting for something to happen, maybe they've had enough.

When the doctor told me, he flinched, as if he'd just lit a very large firecracker. I half expected him to plug his ears with his fingers. He has known me for many years and knows me well, as well as you can. I am a large, boisterous man, sometimes volatile, unpredictable. He could imagine the physical pain I will suffer and the pain of what I will lose-- I've worked my whole life outdoors, on the sea. A day will come when I'll never go on *Daybreak* again.

But I didn't react one way or the other. There will be, I'm sure, a great deal of pain, and anger, if I work my way through this. But it's not the dying that will trouble me, it will be thinking of how I've lived. I have wasted so much of my life angry and drunk. But I never get mad at the course of nature. You don't get mad at bad weather; you survive it if you can. So that's what I've been doing, just trying to get through this storm that will sink me.

Now I leave the helm to James. Angela and I sit on folding chairs facing back over the stern. I think about telling her about my illness. She would understand. But instead I tell her a story.

"I asked Ellen once, out of the blue, 'What would you do if someone told you that tomorrow was the last day of your life? Would you give up, go get drunk? Would you try to live your whole life in one day?'"

Angela looks surprised. "What did she say?"

"She gave me look. I don't usually have what she would consider great thoughts, you know, but I do have an odd enough imagination that such a question would not surprise her too much. She answered it like she always does, on its most sensible level. She said, "You can't live your life that way. Any day could be the last day of your life. Every day is your life and you make the best of it."

Angela smiles. "Just like James. That's exactly what he would say."

"Well, one thing about Ellen, she frequently says things that I can't disagree with in principle, but that I'm totally unable to apply to my own life. How come you two don't talk more?"

"Me and Ellen? Oh, Pop," Angela sighs, "I'm not sure. She doesn't exactly approve of me. I guess I can't blame her."

"Oh, bullshit. How could anyone not like either one of you?"

She smiles slightly and looks pensively out to sea. I follow her gaze out to the horizon, a distant end that can never quite be seen. These days the horizon always reminds me of death. Once someone has introduced, seriously, the subject of dying to your day to day living, it's hard not to focus on it all the time. But I've been trying to keep looking forward. Which is ironic, it's probably the first time in my life I've concentrated on the future.

But that's all I'm going to say about my illness. I will not dwell on it, I promised myself that I would not do that, that I would not become some helpless, crazed old person.

Ellen and I are no longer together. I left our home some years ago, when things got really bad with my drinking and other things. But Ellen is kind enough to let me visit, although she regards me warily, with the eye of a woman who has been betrayed. There are certain things you cannot apologize for. Years ago I started messing around with a younger woman who worked in a local restaurant. There are no secrets on City Island and Ellen found out before too long. It was several years before she actually asked me to move out, but that was always at the heart of all the disputes that followed. I killed something inside of her when I did that, some kind of ability to trust or love. Killed, that is not too strong a word.

I have stopped drinking now. Of course, I didn't stop until they convinced me that I would die if I didn't. And now I'm going to die anyway, having nothing to do with drinking. But I figure as long as I've quit I'll stay that way. I've wasted enough time drunk.

Ellen and I had five children. James first and Michael last. We had three other children: Jack, Catherine and Seamus, in that order. Catherine was Patrick's mother. Catherine and Seamus are dead now. Then there is my third son, named for me but always called Jack, who is not at sea with us today. I have not heard from him in many months. I think of him all the time.

Catherine, Jack and Seamus were lost to me in different ways. Catherine died in a car accident just a couple of years ago, but I lost her before that, we were bitterly angry at each other.

And Seamus? Seamus and Jack went off on the *Daybreak* one morning 26 years ago to catch a swordfish. An innocent beautiful day. But some very bad weather found them instead and only Jack came back. Some part of me was left out there with Seamus when he didn't come back.

Seamus was 14 when he drowned, frozen in time in my memory at that excitable happy age. Jack was the captain that day, but only 15. James, only 16 but every bit the man, was supposed to go out with them but he got an offer to crew on the *Mrs. Pearl*. Jack pestered me into letting him go with Seamus. They'd done it a couple of times, but not for the whole day, not out into deep water. I finally said yes. I should have checked with Ellen, she would have talked me out of it. She would have thought it was a bad idea. But she has never blamed me or Jack or anyone. Not outwardly. She knows the risks of a fisherman's life.

Jack says that a squall came up out of nowhere and they got hit by a rogue wave. He was on the bridge and almost got knocked overboard. The boat almost rolled. By the time he got back to the wheel, Seamus was gone. Jack won't talk about it. It still troubles him deeply, but he won't talk to me or anyone else about it. I've told him that freakish weather like that isn't anyone's fault, that it could happen to anyone and there's no predicting what can happen any time you go to sea. But he is very prickly about the subject, he was the captain and he feels responsible. I guess I might have said some things when I was drunk and angry to make him feel that way.

Whatever happened out there that day was probably out of their control. I tell myself that over and over and most of the time I believe it. But I really don't understand how it could have happened. The weather was foul for sure, but they were experienced deckhands and I do not understand how either of them could have gone overboard in a little rough water. I taught them how to take care of themselves and how to look out for each other. Jack says when they saw the storm coming; they beat it for the shoreline and hugged the coast, just like I taught them. They should not have gotten hit by a large wave that close to shore. James said the *Mrs. Pearl* was down the coast a bit and it was rough, but nothing that would roll a fifty footer like *Daybreak*. These questions gnaw at me.

I have to confess that when we lost Seamus, the loss I felt for him was more than the love I had for anyone else. He was special to me; I saw part of me in him. It wasn't right to think it, but he was my favorite. All of the rest of them felt it and it hurt them, I know that.

"It would be nice if Jack was coming out with us, wouldn't it?" Angela asks guilelessly. She is looking straight ahead as she says it, her mind somewhere else.

Jack is the one I miss now, because he's alive and he's not here. When Jack wants to, he can fish as well as any of us, even James. But he's only been on *Daybreak* once, maybe twice in the past five years. There have been times when he was all anyone in the family talked about, happily. He became our biggest success, Ivy League college, basketball star, millionaire stockbroker. But along the way we lost him, he pushed us away. And there were times that I actually told people, bitterly, that I had no use for him, that he thought he was too good, too smart, to listen to a simple fisherman from the Bronx.

"Arrghh," I growl.

Angela laughs, a lovely sound, and looks at me. "Was that a growl? A real growl! You're the only person I know who actually growls as a method of communication."

"I still get so mad at him sometimes, just thinking of him throwing this family aside, leaving us like we weren't good enough. Where the hell is he going? What does he want? Michael tells me they've all lost touch with him recently, since he and Frances broke up. Mike says he's been acting strange. But what can I do? We've never been able to talk. What do you two find to talk about? You're the only person he ever talks to now."

"Well," she says hesitantly, "We talk about drinking a lot. He's really trying to get clean and I had to go through that."

There's more to Jack and Angela than that, but I keep my mouth shut. Jack has got something going on in his head about Angela and it bugs the hell out of James. The only reason James doesn't blow up is because everyone trusts Angela.

The *Daybreak* clears the harbor and the engine hits a deeper note as James pushes the throttle into deep water. I look out to sea and say, to no one in particular, "I get pissed off sometimes, thinking of all these things that don't happen because you're afraid."

Michael stops working on a reel and looks up at me.

"What?" he calls over the roar of the engine, "You have to speak up, Pop."

"Never mind," I call. "You know what, Mike?"

He looks at me, his eyebrows raised expectantly.

"I never learned how to swim. Isn't that something?"

He gives me a quizzical look, then smiles.

"You know," he yells, "You've been making some pretty odd observations recently." His voice carries away with the wind. "But I guess if swimming became real important in your line of work, you wouldn't be much of a captain, would you?"

"Pop!" James yells from the helm, "Where the hell are we going? Fish have got to be running here. You taking us to France or something?"

"Then stop the goddamn boat and put some goddamn lines down," I yell, "You're the captain, you can do it."

James stares at me in mock surprise, rolls his eyes at Michael, then cuts back on the throttle, shaking his head. I know what he's thinking, that I'm a pain in the ass. Sometimes I am.

James brings the boat about. "We'll stay here for a bit," he says, "As good a place as any, right?" He looks at me expectantly. I'm surprised, again, that after everything he still wants to know that I think he's right.

"Right," I say.

Angela stands up and whispers to me, "Excuse me, I have to use the head."

I stand stiffly and walk over and sit next to Patrick. Now that it has stopped moving forward, the boat pitches much more, side to side. But to my legs it still feels as steady as pavement. I sit back in the folding chair, tilting back on its rear legs.

"Let's see you two make yourselves useful and catch some fish," I yell over my shoulder as I settle in.

Patrick unfolds a blanket that he is holding on his lap. He leans forward and drapes it over my shoulders. Only a few months ago I would have shrugged it off angrily. But I do feel a chill, a little shaky, and the blanket is warm.

The sky is clearing some, now streaked with blue, although it is still cool. The sun hangs directly overhead, but it is dulled by slashes of clouds. When it emerges, the day warms.

The lines that James and Michael have set run out from the poles, taut, like veins under the glowing sea. James and Michael stand on the other side of the boat, their backs to us, watching over the lines. There is silence except for the occasional murmur of their voices, the slap of water on the hull and the laugh of the lone seagull that followed us out this far.

Angela comes from below and climbs back up on the bridge. She sits facing forward and pulls another chair over to rest her legs on. She makes a pillow out of her blanket and settles back.

"I'm just wasting time on these pleasure cruises," I grumble, "I ought to be working, making a living."

Patrick looks at me seriously. His face is a wonderful mixture of boy and young man, like the waters of a calm sea rippled with the breezes of an upcoming storm. He doesn't remind me of Seamus, not at all, but as we have gotten closer there is something inside that eats at me a little less.

"Grumble, grumble, grumble," he says. "James says you're just a nasty old sea dog." He smiles uncertainly, his eyes fixed carefully on me for a reaction. He's just gotten the nerve to tease us.

"I am a nasty sea dog, you pup," I scowl at him. "I can be a very unpleasant person when I want to be." I hold my serious look, squinting at him. He waits a moment, then smiles and waves me off.

"You don't scare me, Pop." And I feel the strangest thing: delight at these signs of his growing up, and the sharpest sadness that he isn't the little boy hanging on my every word anymore.

"D'ya know, Patrick, a long time ago I told James to throw my ashes off this boat when I die, and he refused me? He said he wasn't going to be skipper of a floating funeral home. One small favor, that's all. I give him my whole life and ask him one damn favor, and he won't do it. I don't know how I raised such goddamn stubborn children."

"You're kinda stubborn, too, Pop," he says, tentatively this time. "A little," he adds quickly. "What ashes? You're never going to die."

I look over my shoulder at James and Michael. They stand side by side and look over the water. They watch and listen: good fishermen don't get distracted. Michael is taller by three inches, but seems much slighter; James is as solid as a tree trunk. They talk quietly. James is teaching Michael something about tying a line.

I turn to Patrick. "Look at this, Pat, look at this boat. And this day. Isn't this a beautiful boat? Isn't this a hell of a life? Jack always said this was a miserable fucking way to make a living, but I don't know. I think it's just fine."

"Feel this, Pat." I take his hand and hold it to the deck. "It's like part of the ocean, the skin of this boat. It's like riding on the inside of a whale."

"Like Jonah." He says eagerly.

"You talked to Jack recently, Patrick?"

"Oh, yeah. He called at Nanny's a couple of days ago."

"Really? Where was he?"

He looks at me curiously. "I don't know. At home, I guess. Maybe in the city."

"Sound okay?"

"Sure. Why not?"

"I don't know. Just curious."

"Angela's asleep," Patrick says, looking up at her wistfully. "She wanted me to show her how to tie a salt water fly."

"You'll have time, Patrick. She'll be down in a bit. What are you two always talking about anyway? Girls?"

"God, no!" Patrick whispers in shock. "Just stuff," he says.

"Stuff?" I say, smiling.

"Yes, stuff!" he shouts, looking flustered. He then starts reeling in his line as fast as he can.

"You just cast that line, Pat," I say mildly.

"I know, I know!"

I pat his shoulder. "Relax; I don't want to know your secrets."

I settle back and look out over the water. For some reason, I think of Annette, the girl I thought I was in love with when I was twenty. I remember meeting Annette and thinking, instantly, oh my God, life is never going to be the same again. That scared the hell out of me. But life has a way of surprising and unsurprising you. Ellen would probably be appalled that I still have such thoughts. Or maybe not. Looking out over the ocean, there is just the slightest roll to it. The sky on the horizon is deep blue. Huge fortress outlines of white clouds cover the sky to its highest reaches.

Still looking out, I say, "You know, if Jack just wanted to be a fisherman, everything would have been fine. If that's all he wanted, I wouldn't have pushed him an inch. Look at James! I never pushed him. We're like brothers. James and I never get along, but we're like brothers. Jack was always in such a hurry to go out and conquer the goddamn world. The rest of the world, not our world. Never saw anyone in such a hurry. Him and his dreams, he dreamed of being everything. He couldn't dream of being a fisherman? I mean, he ends up in suits and nice cars and a big house and piles of money and we've still got fish guts smeared on our hands, and the house smells of brine and water and cod. That makes him better? I had dreams, too, you know. But people depended on me. He's not the only fucking dreamer in this family."

I glance at Patrick and I see that my ranting has succeeded in washing away those traces of adulthood. There's only a boy left now, his eyes wide open, surprised. He doesn't say anything, and I continue.

More quietly, I say, "He's never asked me into the city to see his office or where he lived. Not once. Not that I give a shit, but he never has."

This is how it happens to me, this bitterness rises up and I don't know how to stop it. My hands are clenched, and my teeth are grinding together. When I used to be drunk, it would get much worse. Then, if someone said the wrong thing, I could just hit them, just like that.

Patrick touches my sleeve tentatively, and then lets his hand rest there.

"It'll be okay, Pop. He loves you; you're his Dad."

That's impossible, not after all these years, but I smile and somehow feel relief just at the thought. I sit quietly for a moment, then I nod.

"Yeah. You're right, Pat. You're a smart man. It'll be okay."

I look at him, and I see traces of other people in his face, the dead and the lost, Seamus and Catherine and Jack, especially his dead mother. I reach up to touch his cheek, then catch myself and pat him on the shoulder.

Now, on the gently rocking boat under a hazy noon sun, I realize it's too late for Jack and me. Jack will have to settle his life on his own` terms. I check the horizon out of habit to see if any other fishing boats have followed us. Our boat has a reputation for knowing where the fish are. Not information I ever want to give away. But there are no other boats in sight.

"Jack's okay," Patrick says again, nodding to himself. "Everything's going to be okay." He settles back and stretches and yawns. "Sun's making me sleepy," he says, as he settles drowsily into the chair.

The boy's eyes are closing, the warming sun willing him to sleep. The sun is alone in a blue sky now, the day is much warmer. There is a long silence.

"Life would be so nice if we were all together again," he whispers, "You'd see, Pop." And then he's asleep. I watch him and as I do, I feel slightly dizzy and nauseous. I put my head in my hands for a moment. When I look up the sky is discolored, like looking through a dirty window. I feel sick to my stomach. I close my eyes tightly, fiercely, and press my hands to my temple. I feel the wooziness pass and I open my eyes. I think it has past.

I sit and listen to the water--a steady sighing rush. I turn and look over my shoulder. James has dozed off in his chair, his head on his chest. Michael has lain down on the deck, his head on a rolled towel. He is also asleep. I feel an overwhelming sense of comfort being here, but it is laced with a trace of panic. I will not be able to do this much longer, I'll be trapped in a deathbed, as far away from the sea as you can get.

"Some crew," I mutter, as I watch them nap. Then I laugh. The two of them had gone out with several other fishermen last night and I had not heard them come in. It must have been after three. "You all are getting too old for these late nights," I teased them when we set out this morning. Although I can remember mornings, well after I was their age, when I came straight to the boat from the bar.

I remember Jack and me drinking one night, over at Moody's Tavern. It was some years ago, he was in his late twenties. On top of the world, just married, making huge amounts of money trading stocks. I told him a war story. I guess he'd heard plenty of stories from me, about me, at one point or another. But I wanted to give him one for real. I told him about a time I was in a jeep in Italy in 1944 that got blown sideways by a landmine.

When I finished telling Jack the story, I sat back, set my jaw and waited. I don't remember what I might have really expected or wanted him to say.

He just looked down into his beer, then looked up and nodded.

"Don't you get it? I'm lucky to be alive," I said irritably, "You're lucky to be here. Every day we're lucky to be alive. I could've died and none of this would've happened. Don't you think that makes all of this special?"

Jack looked around the dark, smoky bar with an impassive face. It was a seedy place and we were the only people there except for a couple of local drunks.

"I'm not sure I would call this special," he said.

"What is your fucking problem?" I said, too loudly, too angrily. "You get everything you want out of life and it's not enough. I spill my guts, tell you something that's been scaring the shit out of me for years, what do you expect from me?"

Jack squinted at me through the haze. His face was hard, suspicious.

"Why did you tell me that story, Pop?"

Why? Because I was looking for a reason to be grateful for this life, to make it remarkable as it passed, because I wanted him to appreciate it, and think it was special. I don't fucking know why. There'd been so much bad blood between us, so many arguments; I was just tired of it. I wanted it to change; I wanted us to be different than we had been.

"Because we could die anytime, you know? We shouldn't take that for granted and spend all our time fighting. We're not going to be here forever, Jack."

And for a moment, just a moment, he really looked surprised. "Have we been fighting again?" he said, "I thought we were doing okay." He laughed. "Anyway, you can't just wave a magic wand and make thirty years of disagreement go away, Pop. It's not that easy."

"Yeah, but we're still here, Jack. We lost Seamus. We should try to hang on to each other while we can."

"That has nothing to do with me and you, Pop," He said, looking down. "We can't save Seamus, he's gone. There's nothing we can do about that." He looked at me sharply, and whispered, "There's nothing anyone could have done about him."

"I know that," I said, "I know that. All I mean is we're all we have, at the end. Our family. Each other. Right?"

He stood with a sigh, placing his hand on my shoulder to lift himself off the barstool. He swayed slightly and left his hand on my shoulder.

"Be nice if we could go back and change some things, wouldn't it, Pop? It always feels like you know so much better further on down the road."

This last comment was in a younger, clearer voice, laced with its own regret, and I chose to find reason for hope in it. He moved slowly toward the door.

"You going fishing tomorrow?" he called over his shoulder.

"James and I," I said, surprised. "Six o'clock. Coming?" I smiled drunkenly, unsure. He had not been out for many months.

"Going to give me a hard time about wasting my time being a stockbroker?"

"No."

"About having grandkids?"

"No!"

He stopped at the door and looked at me.

"About why I hate fishing and don't have enough respect for the family's way of life?"

"No, goddamn it!" Now I laughed and he smiled.

"Sure I'll come. You can tell me some more stories."

And he was there; he'd never miss it once he said he'd be there. We all went out, even Mike and Catherine came. Everyone followed Jack. Once we were out, James and Jack would get everyone going, in the way only they had with each other. They'd be laughing and we'd all relax. I remember those days, their smiles and laughter, as clearly as I remember that doctor telling me I have cancer.

So now, on this perfect day, I sit on my *Daybreak*, watching and listening to the ocean, doing what I've done my whole life. I want to believe in Pat's hopefulness, but I'm thinking now that Jack really won't come back to me, that too many things have happened to pull us all apart. Just as I feel that the good days I remember of my life are past, maybe were never there. I am overcome by this now, this feeling of loss; it has come upon me like this disease in my bones, bending my hopes like this illness twists my spine.

And I won't be fishing this spring, or any spring after that. Soon I won't be able to make it through a rough day at sea. Where does that leave me?

I get up and climb to the bow. I sit, painfully, on the very edge, dangling my legs over the side. I am out of sight of the rest of the boat, shielded by the raised cabin roof.

My waders are here. I had left them up here a few days ago after I'd worn them on a particularly rough day. I had not thought of them until this moment, but I realize now that I have counted all along on their being here. I pull the heavy boots on, all the way to my hips.

I stand and look into the water. It moves into the hull of the boat in rhythmic slaps. The surface sparkles in the sun. Underneath, it is bottomless, eternity. Catherine and Seamus's ashes are there. I feel their pull every time I look at the sea.

I've felt for many days as if there is no time, as if things cannot wait. My bones are rotting and I must cast my lot and believe in something. I don't know what will happen to Jack, or Patrick, or Ellen, or any of them. I don't even really know what any of them think of me, how can you really know what people think? I've been impossible at times, many, many times. And there have been times when they've driven me to unreasonable rage, all of them, even Ellen. But I love them, I suppose, if I understand that word.

The only really terrifying thing is that I'm all alone in this. In six months I'll be on my back, unable to move and breathing through a tube, barely able to see or recognize their frightened faces looming over me.

The sun warms my shoulders and a light, salty breeze holds my face. I breathe in the sea and the lovely fish and oil stink of the *Daybreak*. And I think to myself, with bitterness, and gratitude, that this is as nice a day as I'm going to see again. I look down into the water, the sparkle of sunlight bouncing off a bottomless blue. I sit down and start to ease myself quietly into the water. I take a deep breath and drop, into the future, into my past, into the deep.

CHAPTER TWO

Jack
July 2008

Now I pour myself another drink and I walk to the window. I try to remember my father. I imagine what he saw that last day on the *Daybreak*: He lowered himself off the bow, careful not to make a splash. He held his head above the water and clung to the side of the boat. He listened: just the sound of water. But then he'd swear he could hear the breathing of Michael and James, his sons, my brothers, as they napped in their deck chairs on the boat, believing their father was on watch. And he'd think: when they were babies, their mother, but never him, sat in the dark at night and listened to them breathe, listened to their squeaky baby dreams, picked them up to protect them if they woke frightened.

He looked up and watched the sky and felt the water hold him. His boots were filling with water. He let go and walked, not fell, into the familiar rushing wet of the ocean. He had never been able to swim, but it did not frighten him, it splashed over him every working day of his life. He lived on it and now it embraced him.

The water flowed around his legs, soaking his clothes immediately to his skin, covering his face. His mouth and cheeks blew up as he instinctively held his breath, then he blew it out, releasing a cloud of bubbles. His hair floated. He walked, one foot in front of the other, down and down, his water-filled boots like stones. His arms lifted over his head and he moved towards the bottom of a dark liquid sky, light slowly disappearing. But before the dark there were colors: rays and flashes of light--gold and blue and streaks of midnight. And then black, the last color.

Then he could not hold his breath any longer. He took a deep draught and felt the sharp taste of brine, down into his lungs and his belly. His head clicked -- like the sudden and terrifying brightness of a lamp turned on in the middle of the night -- and his heart stopped. But not like you'd think, you don't die just like that. It's the opposite, he was alive, awake, and his pain was gone. Looking above, he could barely see the sky floating beyond the ceiling of the ocean, the hint of light blue nothingness. For a moment he could just make out the bottom of his beautiful *Daybreak*, where he labored for his whole adult life. Then it receded and he felt the bottom below.

He thought of us all for a moment. He might have thought that if Patrick, my nephew, were there, he'd say, hey, where's Davy Jones' locker? Patrick inherited his mother's fondness for bad jokes. And my father would have thought of his daughter, and our mother, and of my brothers and me and what he might say to us, what he should have said to us. What would he have said to me, what would he have thought of me? Not well, at the end.

Maybe he would have seen Seamus, long ago entrusted to the deep. What would Seamus tell him? What secrets does the ocean hold? Would Seamus tell him how he drowned, how his brother failed him?

Pop must have had the strangest sense of longing and relief. But he did not need to say goodbye, he convinced himself of that, I am sure. Certainly not to me. I rejected a life like his and we pushed and pulled at each other like the tides, he did that with all of us. But I realize now he always thought he was a fisherman, just a fisherman, and that he was going to where he belongs.

But sometimes I hate him for it. He passed judgment on me my entire life and never had to answer for his own. Then he just leaves, without a goodbye, without a chance to show him who I really am.

I angrily yank the window open and stick my head out. It is a beautiful day outside, summertime late Monday morning. I used to hate Monday mornings when I worked downtown, but there's no reason to hate anything anymore. I don't work; every day is like the other. I am living on the sixth floor of the Comet Hotel, a transient hotel on the Bowery, on the border of Chinatown. The windows in my room rise from just above the floor nearly up to the ceiling, seven or eight feet. It is a spectacular view; the street below is a constant din, people and traffic roaring by in a steady raucous stream, like refugees fleeing a fallen city.

My brother Michael is coming. I stand by the window and search the sea of Asian faces below for his wide-eyed innocent face. He is all I can think of now and I hum to myself, rocking unsteadily back and forth on my heels. I take a long pull from the glass of vodka I hold loosely in my right hand. I think to myself, I ought to stay sober for this,

I really should. But that little voice sneaks up again quietly: Why? And who am I kidding? I could not handle it. Anyway, I'll only drink just this once more. That's it. The vodka tastes awful, burning a hole in my empty stomach. I had just enough money for the bottle and some cigarettes, no tonic.

I stand by the window for hours during these days and imagine my life. My room reeks, the hall outside stinks of urine, but I have to keep the door open to catch a breeze. The peeling walls of the room are filthy and the mattress is rotting and damp. Somehow, there are few bugs. I am grateful for this, on my worst nights I dream of bugs. I shudder and take another drink.

Bouncing up and down on my toes, I try to hum a song, Jerry Lee Lewis: "You shake my bones and you rattle my brain, too much love'll drive a man insane..." But it doesn't catch, my spirit is limp. I haven't eaten anything for close to a day and I'm getting drunk fast. I have to, I can feel the anxiety rush towards me, leaving a cold emptiness in my chest, like the feeling we got when we were kids and swam in the ocean for too long.

Michael is coming to take care of me. I feel guilty, for a moment. Maybe I should slow down, behave. I will have only two more drinks, maybe three if I feel okay. He won't even notice, he'll think I'm fine. I'll tell him I need a little money, not much. A short term loan. I've never taken cash from him before, that's always been a matter of pride for me. I suddenly laugh to myself as I take another drink, hell; I think he owes ME money. I loaned him money for tuition when he was just starting college and I was in business school. So maybe it doesn't matter if I get a little drunk. He can give me a little speech.

I shouldn't say that, Mike's a good guy. I feel in my pocket for his card: Michael P. MacAfee, Esq. Booth & Gray, Attorneys at Law. I have a picture here somewhere, among my few remaining belongings, a childhood picture of Michael and myself, taken by our older brother, James. I move from the window and pull open some drawers, throw aside scraps of paper, unpaid bills, and unanswered letters. I'll find it someday. It shows the two of us, twenty-six years ago, curly-haired boys, me 15 and he 8, dressed by our mother in similar plaid jackets. In the picture, I have a big smile on my face and my arm draped over Mike's shoulder, gazing confidently into the camera.

What a funny little kid he was, so quiet. We both went to a small Catholic school on City Island in the Bronx. The high school and the grade school were in the same building. I remember seeing him walking home alone as I was on my way to track practice, or sitting alone in the stands watching me play basketball. Always watching.

But that's just what I remember. I don't trust my memory to be any more real than my fantasies of the future. Michael has done well. He's the athlete now, golf and tennis, and he has a big house in a pretty town in New Jersey, with a lovely wife and two kids I adore.

Michael tries to take care of me during these lean times, but I make it hard on him. He calls, he visits, and he invites me out. He and Angela are only ones who know how bad things have gotten in the past few months. He has ideas to get me back "into the swing of things". He looks at me with such hope and enthusiasm that I either want to cry or punch him. Besides Angela, he is the only person in the world who has stood by me and for his loyalty, I punish him.

I tell myself not to grow to resent or hate him; to let him in, to change. But that reasonable voice is the voice of mine I hear less and less. More often now, I hear my other voice, the angry one, telling myself that I don't know how or why I ever could change. I don't know what I believe anymore.

My cell phone buzzes on the table next to me. I watch it suspiciously; I do not want to talk to anyone. Then I pick it up.

"Hello?"

"Jack! Stan here. What's up, bud?"

"Stan. Hey, Stan. Oh, not much, just hanging out." Stanley Carter is a managing director at The Masters Group, the equities trading firm in which I was, until quite recently, a senior managing director. I cannot stand Stan.

"Jack, I'm not here to lecture you or anything, like some of the guys. I'm just trying to get a handle on the Spearing account. They're telling us they'll only trade with you exclusively. Did you ever do a written exclusive deal with them?"

"No. We just worked on a handshake."

"So if someone like yours truly can convince them to let someone else handle their equity side, you're not going to pop out of the woodwork and sue anybody, are you?"

"No, Stan, I'm not going to sue anybody."

"I mean, Robert's saying you've gone off the deep end and all these clients are jumping to other firms because they will only work with you and he's freaking out because the revenue is going to go way down if all these accounts really jump and I'm figuring that you won't mind since you're obviously dealing with other things; I man, I hope you're getting it together, but..."

I hang up on him. I walk out into the hallway and into the wretched communal bathroom, the smell of which makes me gag reflexively. I drop the phone in the toilet and give it a flush. I walk back to the window.

The day roars by outside. I take another drink and feel a warm, crushing glow. On the street below, people shine in the sun, horns blare, and trucks roar like jets, there are a thousand lives exploding at once within my sight. I lift my arms to the world, exhilarated; I want it to come to me. I watch and wait.

I have let Michael convince me to commit myself into a substance abuse rehabilitation and therapy facility out in Jersey. I have since decided this was a mistake, the result of a stupid drunken confession to Michael at a bar one night--a pathetic grab for sympathy. But now, he's coming to drive me there. He says they'll be able to help me there, to cure me. Anyway, that's what the brochure says.

Mike has worked so hard at this. He has been very positive and active, mailing me countless pamphlets and brochures, calling me to talk. Finally, I picked out a place and told him I would go and get better. Just to make him happy. I knew it would make him leave me alone for a while. The brochure I picked had sailboats on the cover. I have always loved sailing.

I am uneasy about the whole idea. Michael says I'm depressed and alcoholic. "No fault of yours," he says. He lectures me in well-meant, deliberately offhand comments, "It's a disease, not just a bad habit. It can be treated".

But I know it's not that easy. Everything I've fucked up is sure as hell somebody's fault, and I know who. I don't think I buy all this hocus pocus. I know my life is my responsibility and to a very large extent I am exactly where I ought to be, given the effort. I try to convince Mike that I am structurally sound, just having a run of bad luck. And he wants to believe me and frequently does. Most of the time, I feel quite content. Of course, I am also drunk most of the time, but so what? It's not forever. I don't feel like working right now, I feel like drinking. Everyone deals with life in their own fashion. When I am ready to fix it, I'll fix it.

But sometimes in the morning, when I am sober, I have this sinking panic that my life is something I will never control. I feel these ghosts looming over me: my father and Seamus, both drowned, and Catherine. Could we have saved each other? The people still living haunt me also, with all of their expectations piled as high as a summer thundercloud. And always with me are the dreams I was foolish enough to have for myself, all of that imagined life weighing down on me, pulling me down to the bottom.

Mike tells me that he and Anne and the kids will come and visit me. That would be nice. He also says he believes that, with time, he can convince Frances, my ex-wife, to come and see me. If I were her, you couldn't pay me enough money to visit me, but this whole family is compulsively sympathetic.

What I would really like to do is to go and live Mike's life in New Jersey. To be him, although I could not, would never, tell him that. There are lakes and trees there. Mike's kids have these rafts; we take them down to the lake and float in the sun. When it gets too hot, we just roll into the water like hippos.

They are still little, Rachel is 5 and Mike is 4, so I can hold them afloat with one arm each and float along. They like me. They think I'm funny. They climb over me like puppies and I hurl them into the water. They squeal with fake terror. To them, there's nothing wrong with me, I'm Uncle Jack, that's all. We don't expect anything more from each other.

I do worry about Mike and Rachel, though. They are growing up terribly fast. They will change. I remember the first time it occurred to Michael to tell me that he disapproved of what I was doing with my life. I remember the shock. It is a frightening thing when children grow older.

I hear a slight noise and feel a movement in the light behind me. I turn and see a figure passing in the shadow of the hallway. It looks familiar in its bearing and size. My heart rises and falls so hard I have to swallow. For a moment I think it's my father.

I see my father everywhere. He drowned last fall off the coast of Long Island, on the easiest day he ever took on the ocean, a fishing trip with Michael, James, Angela and Patrick on the calmest day of the year. I don't really mourn him, because he lived a long life, mostly the way he wanted, and because I'm angry that he left on his terms, without saying goodbye. Most of our time together I couldn't stand him. I guess I really ended up being able to stand him at the end before he died. But growing up with him was an endless battle.

Once, when I was sixteen, I watched a man go fishing on a rowboat, forty feet from shore, just beyond the Atlantic surf. This was only a few months after Seamus died. It was a rough day; whitecapped waves pitched the boat back and forth. He was dressed in a slicker and waders, large boots up to his hips. It was very early in the morning, just light. There was no one else in sight on the beach. I worried, watching him struggle with his boat and his nets.

There were clouds hanging over the ocean, black and solid as stone. The approaching waves grew larger in succession and washed over the bow of the boat. He struggled to pull the net up from the water. Then he slipped forward, just the slightest bit, once, and then again. He put his arms out to steady himself. And then the boat pitched back with a jerk and he went over and disappeared headfirst into the surf.

He came up briefly, his arms thrust into the air, holding his head back, his mouth wide open. Just at that moment I think he saw me, I'm sure he did, I remember his eyes. He raised one arm towards me, as if I could grab it to save him. I moved towards him, stepping into the breaking waves. I thought, "If I can get just far enough into the water, if I'm strong enough, I can save him."

Then he went under. I thought his boots must be filling up with water, dragging him down. The surf was too strong for me. It knocked me over twice roughly before I could wade above the level of my thighs. I yelled in terror and frustration. I was not strong enough.

I ran, what seemed like miles, to our house to get help. My father went to call the Coast Guard. He told me to wait. "There's nothing you can do now, boy," he said, "Stay here." But as usual, I did the opposite. I ran back to the beach, running so hard I became sick. I stopped on the beach where I was closest to the boat, gasping for breath. The sea and the beach were empty, just me and his tiny boat, rocking wildly at its anchor. I leaned over and retched.

I saw a dark form washing up sluggishly in the waves. I went to him and pulled on his shirt, his leg, trying to get him to solid ground. The surf pushed him with me. He felt as if he weighed three thousand pounds. My father told me later that dead men gain the weight of all of their sins. I kneeled in the surf next to him. I looked at his face. It was blue and looked as if it would explode.

His eyes and mouth were wide open and held an expression of pure surprise. He was drowned. I was the only person in the world who could have saved him. The water rushed up, washing over his face, coursing around us. I held his head up over the foam, resting it in my lap. Dark clouds rushed towards the shore and in the distance, I saw a blue jeep driving towards me, a flashing light on top. It began to rain.

My father said the man was a fool, fishing by himself on a day like that. He said life isn't kind to fools.

"You should learn a lesson from this," he said, "It's a hard world." I read later that he was a man named Ralph Neeley and that he had no family. He lived by himself and he died by himself. To which my father said, "Everyone dies by himself." He would not let me go to the man's funeral. I hated him when he said that, but I told myself to forget it.

"You said it broke your heart when Seamus drowned," I challenged him one night, "Don't you think that man dying broke someone's heart?"

He looked at me, his eyes like stone. "Maybe. But not mine. And you're a fool if it breaks yours. He had nothing to do with us and this has nothing to do with Seamus. Nothing can bring Seamus back. I don't care about the rest of it, none of it." And he got up and took his drink into the other room.

"You have to give your father time to get over Seamus, Jack," my mother said softly, patting my hand. There was no getting over Seamus in her eyes; I could see that, I could see the emptiness. But she had something left for us, he didn't.

And there was no getting over Ralph Neeley or Seamus for me, either. For a couple of years after that, I woke in the middle of the night, gasping for breath, sometimes with my mother by my side. Only she could hear the sounds I made as I dreamt the silent, open-mouthed cry of the drowning. And I remember hearing my father's voice outside my room at night, after I'd woken, whispering to her, saying, "Leave him be, Ellen. You can't protect him forever; you have to let him go. He'll have to learn to deal with things like this; he has to learn to be strong. He can't let the things that happen in this world bother him that much."

My mother's answer, whatever it was, was too soft to hear. But I felt her presence remaining outside the door, watching and waiting, as the clinking of ice in my father's glass of whiskey followed him down the hall.

I shake my head to get away from those memories. I take another drink and pull the shade down to dim the sunlight. Then I hear footsteps and a voice.

"Jack?"

I turn, startled. It's Michael, gazing at me uncertainly, waiting for me to focus, to say something. "Jack?" he says, his voice rising unevenly with uncertainty and excitement. "Jack, how are you?"

He strides across the room with his hand outstretched, his face beaming. He looks terrific, nearly as tall as me, lean and tanned, brightly dressed in a clean, crisp summer shirt and multicolored golf slacks.

"Hey, Mike," I say slowly, taking his hand. I realize I'm slurring my words. I feel completely off balance and instinctively attack. "That's a hell of a pair of pants. Just get off the links?"

Michael looks down at his pants in surprise and stops in his tracks, embarrassed. I had to slow him down. But why would I be mean to him now of all times?

Michael avoids my gaze and looks uneasily around the room. I don't know what he was expecting, but he is clearly uncomfortable here. I look at him carefully. I have now relaxed somewhat. People are usually on the defensive when I see them these days. Walking down the street, on the subway, with my bottle in a bag, I look them in the eye, and they look away, as if they had something to be ashamed of. I don't understand that, I'm the one whose life is a mess. But I test it, look them straight in the eye, talk right at them. They back up. It's a strange advantage.

"Have you packed up?" Michael says.

"There's nothing to pack," I say, "What you see is what you get." I laugh and wave my arms around, "I travel light." I stumble slightly. My head is swimming. I am drunker than I thought.

"I left some stuff in a locker in the basement, winter things. That's okay where it is. I can get it some other time. I have some clothes and some odds and ends in that little bag in the corner."

I motion towards the corner with my hand and slosh some vodka from the glass onto the floor. Michael looks at me with raised eyebrows, but holds his tongue. He looks concerned, but I can also see that he has relaxed a little. I know it kills him when I get like this, but I think it takes him off the defensive. He can take care of me, become my keeper.

As always, Mike works at being upbeat. "Okay," he pronounces, "Let's get this show on the road. Let's get something to eat before we head west. I think there's a great Indian restaurant right down the block. Sound okay?"

I suppress the suddenly cranky urge to make a snide remark about his enthusiasm. I am hungry and I know I can get some beer at the restaurant. Michael won't take me someplace that won't give me a drink. That would be an insult. Mike is intent on treating me with respect and, yes, I do take advantage of that.

"Sounds good," I mutter, forcing a smile, "Let's get out of this hellhole."

We walk out of the building and into the blinding day. We do not speak as we walk down the crowded sidewalk. Mike leads the way with his loping stride, looking over his shoulder with an anxious smile every few steps. The air is as hot and still as a sauna, and the noise at street level is maddening: horns, construction drills, the metal rattle of the loose joints of the city. The yellow glare of the sun reflects off the cars, street windows, everything. The city seems on fire. I fight the urges within myself to run, and to hate my brother.

The restaurant we enter is icy cool, silent and dark. It is still early for lunch. We sit in an upholstered booth and busy ourselves with reviewing the menu and ordering from a huge, menacing waiter in a turban.

"So, how are the little folk?" I ask, munching on some dry Indian bread. I take a deep breath. I feel dreadful. I look around casually. The place is empty. Four waiters in turbans are gathered in a corner, murmuring to each other.

"The kids are terrific," Michael blurts with his mouth full. His eyes light up. "They're going to a day summer camp. They come home and tell me all the details every night, their adventures, who their friends are, what games they play. They're having such a great time. They are so normal, you know? I never felt so normal, when we were kids. He stops and looks at a corner of the table, his mind somewhere else. Then, he jumps back. "But they're fine. Great!"

The remark, although normal, strikes me as an opening of some kind, but I do not feel like picking up on that. Part of my mind immediately starts to daydream about his kids, telling me their adventures.

That life, Michael's life, stands in front of me like a great mountain, and the impossibility of climbing it, or getting around it, leaves me so tired.

"Ann sends her love," Michael says. His look swallows me up. "She's really hoping for you to get better." He waits expectantly for a reaction. I say nothing still. Each comment is a drop in a well, nowhere near full. I just can't make conversation anymore. I don't know what people want me to say.

"Ann and the kids and I will come up and visit you on the weekends." Michael finishes this in an offhand way, not looking at me. I appreciate that, not making a big deal of it. I really like the idea of their visiting, as he knew that I would.

"That would be nice," I say, "I'd like that."

I would like to take care of them somehow: the kids, Ann, even Mike. I daydream sometimes about that. There was a time when I could have done that, or thought that I could. There was a time everyone in my family counted on me to do that. Take care of people. But for some reason there have been so few people to whom I felt close enough to do anything for. The last time I saw Frances, she said, "You kept your distance your whole life, Jack, to protect yourself, so that no one would need you. It was selfish. And now things have changed, now that's all you want. Too late."

Last winter, at Mike's house, I went outside at night into the woods out back. The snow was frozen on top and my feet crunched through, ice chips dropping into my worn shoes. I walked back into the black trees, the air frozen on my face, my breath enveloping my head in great clouds. I looked back into the house, a dark, hulking form with bright eyes, windows glowing with warmth. I could see Ann and Michael and hear the soft pitch of a child's voice or a light sing-song laugh. I felt protective out in the cold dark, as if I could save them. I could have stood guard there all night.

I know Mike means to help me now, but when I think of what he has to do for me, of what I've come to, it just pisses me off. I get so angry at myself sometimes. But I have learned not to think of it.

The waiter drops a beer in front of me and an iced tea in front of Michael. I lift my glass and say, "To your family, Mike."

He lifts his glass and says, unsmiling, "To our family, Jack."

I breathe a deep sigh and take a long drink.

They bring our orders and we eat, both of us chewing carefully, staring at our plates, and not saying much. The beers keep coming and keep my head buzzing. I am happy to sit there quietly, eating and drinking.

"Jack, are you ready for this?" Michael suddenly leans forward, serious and intent. I can tell from his hard swallow that he is nervous. I remain silent, watching him.

"This could be such a great opportunity, Jack. I know you don't want to hear this, but you don't have forever. Think about it, you could get back on track, get back to work, and get in shape. Everything could work out, you know? Man, the things you've accomplished when you wanted to, Jack, you'd be back on top in no time. You could be great again."

I look at the ceiling. Everything he promises has happened to me, everything has come my way once: money, success, and people around me. It must have been easy once, but I can't even picture how it would happen now. I look in Michael's face and I see worry, and hope.

I remember being with Mike at the hospital when Rachel, then just a baby, was in for surgery. He had so much of himself thrown into the hope he had for her, it frightened me, to care for someone that much. I wanted to save her, for him. And I as I look at him now, see his concern for me, I get just as frightened. And I can't save me for him.

I summon up a smile, "Well, Mike, I'll give it my best shot, I really will, I promise."

He nods, confused and frustrated. I can see that is not enough.

So I tell him a story about going to meet someone at a brokerage house about a job as a stockbroker, just like I used to do. Michael is thrilled by this, as I knew he would be, and I feel lousy for the lie. But it starts to develop a balance between us. Michael must have hope, it is what he lives on.

"It'd be a great start, Jack, I always thought if you could get things going again, everything would take care of itself. You know more about the market than anyone, you could make a fortune in your sleep. The firm was stupid not to stick with you. But it'll come together. Just like it used to. This program will take care of that."

"I need to go to the men's room," I say suddenly. I am half out of my chair when Michael grabs my hand. I haven't really thought about what I intend to do, but I can see from his look that my face has betrayed something.

"Don't you do this to me again, Jack. Don't you fucking run off on me again."

He is hissing these words through clenched teeth, now leaning forward, and half standing. I am astonished by the ferocity of his reaction. I have not seen him like this before.

I smile and spread my hands out. "Mike, what're you talking about. Hey, I'm not going anywhere. I'm right here." I sit back down and smile broadly. Mike shakes his head angrily, then sadly.

"You were going to run off."

"No." I shake my head, but I lose my smile.

"Oh yes," he says, "Yes." And he shakes his head with some finality, as if deciding something. "I used to count on you, Jack." He looks away and I see other feelings on his face, in his eyes: Anger, mistrust, even disgust. I don't recognize these things in him. I shift uncomfortably in my seat.

I reach across for his hand, "Hey, Mikey, it's going to be okay..."

He slaps my hand away, hard, and glares at me. I slump back, feeling as if I have been punched in the gut.

"Where have you gone, Jack? What happened to you? Ann and I took Mom to church the other day and she asked how come Jack ran away from Pop's service?"

"I don't want to hear this," I say, trying to show some anger of my own, but feeling none, feeling nothing but tired. I move as if I will get up and Mike doesn't stop me. But I stay in the chair, rigid, holding on to its arms as if I would fly out of it otherwise.

Michael shrugs. "So don't hear it. Fuck it."

I whisper, "Don't say that, Mike."

I think of Pop, of what he might think of this, of what his sons had come to. I have thought of him recently, feeling him looming up out of my blurry thoughts, jumbled flashes without any pattern: strong, young fisherman; tired old drunk; several different men, none of whom I remember clearly. Always angry with each other. Why? I can't even remember the reasons, although there must have been. Everything is so poorly remembered now. What is clear now is that I thought his dying would change something, lift some burden. But it hasn't. Everything's the same.

"Pop must have been proud of you," I say suddenly.

Mike looks startled, wary. "What the hell makes you say that?"

"Nothing." I shrug. "I bet he was, that's all. I wonder what he would think of me now." And I laugh oddly. I feel uncomfortable. I should not have brought this up. "Probably wouldn't even recognize me. Probably still be fighting with each other. Either that or we'd be drinking buddies."

"Neither one of you was ever half as mad at the other one thought he was. I never understood what either one of you wanted from the other. So goddamn stubborn. And you'd never be drinking buddies. Neither one of you wanted drinking buddies. You'd rather do it all by yourself."

"Fuck him," I snarl in a voice that startles even me. Michael's mouth is open in surprise.

"What? I thought you guys were okay at the end."

"He just ran out on us again, that's all. He let us get a little close for the tiniest bit of time, then he left forever. What kind of father is that? I never had a chance, never had a fucking chance to really connect with him." I put my bottle down with such force that I knock the sugar container over and it rolls to the floor. There is a slight hush as some of the other diners look at me.

Michael squints at me, playing nervously with his fork. "Sorry, Jack. I didn't come here to go over that again. I keep on thinking I could have done something, for you, or him. Maybe I could have changed things."

"You are doing something. You are." I take a long pull on my beer. I feel like I am being smothered, like the dark, veloured walls are wrapping themselves around my neck. "You are." I take another deep drink.

Michael says, "Jack, take it easy," but easier, with real concern.

I look at him, and my head clears for a moment. And there he is, my baby brother, his face as wide and hopeful as an empty June sky. I can almost see me mirrored in it.

"Do you remember, Mike, when I had all that money a few years ago, when things in the market were really hot? And Frances and I and you and that friend of yours, what was her name?"

"Lydia." He smiles.

"Lydia. Beautiful Lydia. We went skiing in Wyoming. Just came and swept you up out of law school and off we all went."

Mike laughs, nodding. "Crazy times, Jack."

"There should be someone to tell you when things are at their best, you know?" I try to force a smile, a laugh. "Someone should say, hey pal, this is the best day of your life. Wouldn't you want to know that? Why wait until three or four years later when you're drunk and getting divorced and your little brother is trying to work up the nerve to tell you he thinks you've fucked everything up. And you know what? It seems like nothing happened to go from there to here. No catastrophes. Some drinking, some gambling, some arguments, I don't know, maybe I just lost interest in living a real life, became a dreamer, you know? Who knows?"

I didn't know what I was trying to say. Michael listens and watches, his expression changing with every word, tensed, as if his life depended on it.

"Nothing seems extraordinary. It's all just life. Happens to everybody, everyday. Some people get through it, some people don't. But, Mike, things are going to change." I say this last thing with conviction, because now I am desperate and need to convince him that there is some meaning to all this.

"I'm going to turn it around."

I grab his hand and I smile the best I can. And I can see in his face that he believes me, despite everything, believes these words that even I have to force myself to swallow. Because he wants to, because he has to.

Michael says," You have a pen? I can write down some of the information they gave me on the phone this morning."

I reach into my pocket and hand him a pen. I accidentally pull out a post card with it.

"What's that?" Michael says absently, as he starts to write.

"Nothing."

It's a postcard I've been carrying in my pocket the past few days. I found it in a magazine stand on Canal Street. I collect bits and pieces like that. On this card, there is a young man and a young woman, dancing at night under a streetlight in the old part of Paris. They are both laughing. He is a little shorter than her. Her skirt swirls around her legs, her blond hair impossibly swirling around her head in the opposite direction. The street around them is dark and deserted. The back of the card says "Bastille Day 1955."

I am a stupid romantic. I pull the card out sometimes, on the bus, standing at a bar, and I think, what a wonderful thing, to be dancing on a street in the summer in Paris. Before this postcard, it was a picture of Michael's kids on a raft in a lake, wet and laughing. Sometimes I'd imagine they were mine. Before that, I don't remember, I think it was a picture of Frances I carried. I had a photo from our honeymoon, in Rome, that I carried around for ages, Frances sitting at a small cafe in front of the Pantheon, a beautifully serious look on her face. I stand behind her, the picture taken by an effervescent waiter who said, "You a honeymoon, ok!" I used to look at it and try to remember what we were like then, whether we really were happy. I think we were. But after a time our faces in that picture began to look unfamiliar: younger, more hopeful, unsuspecting of the many small disappointments that we would feel in each other, each of which passed only briefly noticed, until they finally welled up and washed us and our lives away from each other, like a spring flood suddenly rising and taking the houses of a small town.

"Do you ever run into Frances, Mike?"

He looks up and shakes his head, no. He frowns in thought.

"None of my business," he says, "But she gave up on things pretty quickly, you know? I mean, I'm sure you guys had some difficulties, but to just move out like that and not give you a second chance, that's not right."

"Well, I was pretty bad to her for a while there, staying out late and showing up at all hours. That's no way to live with someone."

"Yeah, but it's not like you cheated on her or anything, right? I mean, I remember how mad you got at Pop when we found out he did that to Mom. You'd never do that."

"No, of course not." I say quickly. I stare into my beer. Unwelcome images creep into my head. I take a long pull from the beer and try to turn my thoughts elsewhere.

Michael is leaning over the table and scrawling as intently as a schoolboy. I suppose he's always been a boy to me. Even though I've got no right anymore to think of him like that. I feel a sudden wave of affection for him and I tell myself, this time I'm going to give it a try for him. Try to slow down and pull it together.

"I do have to go to the men's room, Mike."

He looks at me steadily and I look right back at him. This time I don't smile, but he does. This time he believes me, and I feel okay. "I'll take care of the check," he says.

"Damn right you will, moneybags. I've got enough to live on for a week and that's it. I'll take you out when you and Rachel come out to visit me at camp on visitors' day."

He laughs. "I think I still owe you about $5,000 for college anyway."

I call over my shoulder as I walk towards the front, "I invested in your education? And you say I know something about investments?"

I wave over my shoulder and walk to the men's room, under the entrance stairway. I pause there, for just a moment, and then I walk out the front door without looking back. It is done before I can think of it, out into the sun and the heat and the noise. I shield my eyes from the sun with my hands. I'm pretty buzzed and everything swims a little. I can't do what he wants me to do. Not yet. I'll hate it, they'll hate me. I can still hear a slight voice that says I must go back, back to a real life, back to just trying to live day to day. I know that if I stop for a moment; catch my breath, that this panic will pass.

But that voice carries no weight and I cannot stop. I run down the street as fast as I can, helter skelter, barely keeping my feet, alarmed Asian faces scattering in front of me. A low, strange sound purrs from my throat, which I only hear after a time.

I stop at a corner, clutching my heaving chest, sweating through my shirt. My head is pounding. I will leave, I think. I'll go to the bus station. I have 60 dollars in my pocket. I'll go to Wyoming, someplace far away. I'll get better there by myself and come back to them. A long bus ride to sit and watch out the window at someone else's life going by. I can get better outside of New York, outside of this mean place. I'll write to them and explain. I'll send the kids funny postcards, they'll love it.

I stop at a liquor store on the corner of Canal and Bowery to buy a pint of vodka. I stand in the sun and watch the traffic coming off the Manhattan Bridge, honking angrily. I take a huge gulp from the bottle, tilting my head back, feeling the sun warm the bottle and my face, the liquor warming my throat and stomach. I stare down the street, a steady stream of strange bright faces bending around me like river around a rock.

Then I see Michael running towards me. He has not seen me. I duck into a doorway. He moves past me quickly, but carefully, glancing briefly in each direction, his eyes wide with alarm. As he leaves my line of vision, he calls my name loudly: "Jack!" Not a command, instead, a hopeful urging. Come back.

I wonder what I saw in his face as he passed. Maybe fear. And maybe it looked like he might cry. But I don't remember ever seeing anybody in our family cry. He was just pissed off, that's all. And who could blame him, all the trouble he went through. But he'll get over it and he'll be better off not having to deal with me.

I take another deep drink and start to forget what I have seen. I move down the street, dancing to a song in my head. This will be okay, heading west. Go west to find my life. But wait, first I have to go see Angela. Yes, I need to explain all this to Angela. She'll understand.

Then I hear my name called and I stop. My vision streaks as I turn my head too fast. It's not Michael calling. It's someone else. Seamus? Seamus! For a blurred moment I think I see him, a boy, standing alone in the shadow of a doorway. I move towards him, I want to tell him I tried to save him, but then he's not there, his voice is gone. It was just other voices, a car horn, nothing. Just the city, speeding past me, crashing down around me.

I tell myself Michael wouldn't have been crying. What does he have to cry about? His life is great. But I stand rooted in the noise and the heat, and watch for him and Seamus, and listen for my name. I close my eyes and I believe I can hear them calling me again and again in the din of the city.

CHAPTER THREE
Angela
July 2008

I stare out of windows and daydream about that last day on the *Daybreak*. I am awake as Pop walks to the bow, puts on his waders and steps off the boat. I say nothing to him, but as he disappears into the deep, I follow him. I dive in and swim down, far down, leaving the light behind and finding the dark sandy bottom. Large seaweed plants wave slowly and brush my face. Pop is there, on the edge of a deep ravine, with still further to go. He motions furiously with his hands for me to turnaround, to go back. He points at his watch and points at me and shakes his head emphatically: No! He reaches out and takes my hand, pushing me lightly up. Then he lets go and falls silently into the ravine, disappearing into a darkness that no eyes could see through. I slowly rise to the surface. I am gasping as my head finally breaks the surface.

I know why he did what he did. The idea of leaving, of running away, has always been a perilous attraction for me. For I have done it once before. I have to tell you my story from the beginning for you to understand.

When I was a girl, just 9 years old, I was taken out of an orphanage in the Philippines and placed into foster care with a large Irish family of small means in Addison, New Jersey. It was part of a Catholic program, which paid the family pretty well. Addison was a rundown town strung along the Erie Lackawanna train tracks. There were four children, two boys and two girls, one of them another foster child, from Belfast. Mr. Parnell treated us all the same, he ignored us when he was sober, which wasn't often, and smacked us around when he was drunk. Not hard enough to injure, but hard enough to hurt. Mrs. Parnell cowered when he was around and tried to be a nice mom when he wasn't, but she never seemed to know what to do next. The kids mostly resented me, the last to arrive, although I became friendly with Doreen, the girl from Belfast.

One summer afternoon, Doreen found me in the basement, where I was hiding, reading Pride and Prejudice for the third time.

"Angie," she whispered, "come with me."

We snuck out the back door and I followed her to the end of the street and up on to the train tracks.

"Where are we going, Reenie?"

She looked over her shoulder with a smile and held her finger to her mouth. Shssssh. Doreen was fifteen and I was thirteen. I thought she was beautiful and funny and smart and I would have followed her anywhere. I was skinny and I had crooked teeth and the boys called me china girl. Don't worry about them, Doreen said, they're too stupid to know what country you're from.

Doreen was considered a wild girl by people in town. She told me stories about all of the things she'd done and I used to lay awake at night dreaming I was her. She went on a class trip to the brewery in Unionville and snuck off to the tasting bar right after the tour started. She said it was just like a bar from a western movie, very dark with crimson red velvet walls and gleaming wood. She sat in a corner of the bar and flirted with the bartender. She convinced him she was a teacher. She looked older, but not that old. But she was very pretty and the bartender was no match for her. She got drunk and made out with him in the hallway. They suspended her from school for a week. But she told me, with a wink, that she hadn't planned on going to school that week anyway. I loved the idea of sitting in a dark and mysterious room, drinking what the adults drink to forget their worries, disappearing into a dreamy world. My foster father was drunk a lot, but I wouldn't be like that, he was just mean. I'd be like Doreen, or characters I'd seen in movies, sophisticated and funny and romantic. And I'd get swept off my feet by some handsome man, just like Doreen had.

She led me up to the top of a hill, on top of which stood the huge water tower that was the only sign of the town that could be seen from nearby Route 46. It was dilapidated and out of use, with "Addison" painted on the side in faded white letters. A frail ladder ran up the side to the tank, around which ran a walkway with a low railing. The tower was as tall as the ten story bank building in Passaic.

"Come on," Doreen said. She started to climb.

I could not climb up that ladder. No way. I was afraid of heights and even if I wasn't, no person in their right mind would go up that rickety ladder. But up she went, calling down to me.

"Come on, Angie, you can do it. Be brave!"

So I climbed, terrified every step of the way, gripping the ladder so hard my hands cramped. I looked down, I couldn't help it. The ground looked miles away before I had even climbed ten rungs. After several minutes, the ladder looked like a picture I remembered of a ladder running up into the clouds in Jack and the Beanstalk. It made me dizzy and nauseous. But I hung on and kept putting one foot up. I suddenly felt a hand grip my shoulder and I climbed up onto the walkway. I sat and pressed my back against the rusty tank. My feet dangled over the edge. The entire world spread out around us, miles and miles of trees and hills and buildings in the distance. Doreen stood up and walked around the tank once, yelling, "woo, woo, woo!"

She sat down next to me, breathless.

"We are one hundred and fifty feet in the air. You're scared to death, aren't you?" she nodded at me with a big smile on her face.

"Yes," I whispered.

"Don't be, Angie. What's the worst that can happen?"

I looked at her, puzzled. "Is that a trick question?"

"You fall, you die. You go to heaven." She shrugged. "Would you miss this place all that much? Would you miss Daddy Parnell whacking you on the ears? And those idiot boys? Do you know Roger told me he wanted to screw me? Like I would have sex with a slug like that."

"Sex?" I whispered.

"Why are you whispering, Angie? You can yell up here! No one can hear us!" She stood up and screamed, "I hate the Parnell's, I hate Addison, and I hate my life!!"

She sat down and put her arm around me. She gave me a small hug.

"I feel better, much better. Want to try?"

I shook my head, no.

"We could just jump off here, Angie," Doreen said, "we could hold hands and jump. Nobody would miss us. There's nothing for us here. We'd just be moving on to the next step, wherever that is." She looked up at the sky, then down at me. She held out her hand.

I was very frightened at first, but then I saw something in what she said. I had no life here in this world, nobody cared about me. And what if we jumped? You could die anytime; people die all the time, usually without any warning. You die or you live. Any day you could make that choice. I looked at Doreen.

"I don't want to jump, Reenie. I don't know why, but I don't."

She nodded and smiled gently.

"Hey, Angie," she said in a softer voice, "I want to show you something, okay? But you have to stand up, okay?"

I stood up slowly, both hands on the side of the tank.

"Look out there, way, way out on the edge of the trees. See that blue?"

I could see a thin, shimmering line, sparkling like a necklace with tiny blue stones on it.

"That's the ocean. See that water down there to the right?"

I looked down and saw a small river, disappearing into the trees.

"That's the Passaic River. Do you know where it goes?"

I shook my head.

"All the way to the ocean. Everything leads to the ocean. If you follow the river, you get to the sea."

It did not seem possible that the thin band of water below us, winding casually into the forest, could possibly find its way to that distant imaginary sea. I had not seen the ocean since I left the Philippines five years before. I felt a pang of longing and loneliness. I sat back down and braced myself against the tank again.

"Do you ever think about living in a real family?" I said to Doreen.

She sat down and looked out and sighed.

"All the time, Angie. You know, the whole thing, a dad and a mom and a little brother to play with. A dog. A cat." She laughed to herself. "It's pathetic how little it would take to make me happy. I have you, though, you're a good sister. But, I don't know, maybe someday. Maybe someday I'll live with someone nice and have kids and we'll always be nice to each other. That's going to be my only rule. You have to be nice to each other. I don't care if we have no money or anything, we're going to have each other."

She looked down and said quietly to me, "I have to run away, Angie, and I can't take you with me. I can't wait around for Roger to catch me alone. If I take you they'll come after me because you're so young. Then we'll both get in trouble. Do you understand?"

I nodded.

"I'm sorry," she said.

I stood up to look at the ocean again.

"Look at you," Doreen said admiringly, "you're standing on your own. We better get down, dinner's going to be ready and big daddy will be drunk by now."

She started to climb down the ladder, pausing a few feet down to wait for me. She looked up.

"You go ahead," I said, "I want to stay here for a little while."

Doreen looked totally surprised, then she smiled.

"Atta girl, Angie," she said softly.

I walked around the side so I had the best view of the horizon. I strained my eyes to see the ocean more clearly. Were there boats on it? Waves? I decided I wanted to get there. I leaned against the tank and watched the thin blue line slowly grow brighter, luminous, as the sun sank down towards it, then disappeared in a slow cascade of sparkles, as the sun pulled the daylight down behind the horizon. Then it was dark.

Doreen ran away from home two weeks later. We wrote to each other every once in a while, last time was a couple of years ago. She is divorced and living in California with two kids. She told me in a letter that she still thinks about jumping every time she gets to a high place. She wrote, "My shrink says people who talk about jumping all the time are just attention getters, they never really do it. Maybe I'll surprise him, the prick."

I ran away when I was fourteen, shortly after Roger decided that I was "turning out okay" and started showing up in my room at odd hours. And some years later I found a real family to be a part of, my husband James' family. In my daydreams I always imagined it would be just like this, a big family with a husband and his parents and brothers and sister and wives and children. Only everything turned out very different than in my daydreams.

I figured later that there ended up being four people from the same family I fell in love with: James, Catherine, Jack and Patrick. I loved James to marry, Catherine to talk to, Jack because he was such a great drunk, just like me, and as for Patrick, why do I love Patrick? I'm still figuring that out. Because he's the boy I might have had, the one I might have saved from all the troubles in this world.

Pop and I sat on the dock in City Island early one morning very recently, shortly before that last voyage, watching the boys get the *Daybreak* ready to take out.

"You coming, Angela?" he said in his raspy voice.

"Nah, you make this a boys' trip, Pop," I said, patting him on the shoulder, "I'll stay here and keep an eye on things."

He smiled at me and shook his head slowly.

"You're okay, Angela, you know that, right?"

"Oh, I don't know, Pop, I've had my share of trouble." I looked at him and smiled. "There was a time I could have drunk you under a table, Pop."

To my surprise he didn't even smile. "No," he said, seriously, "I don't know if you know what I mean." He leaned over and put his hand on my arm. He looked at me steadily.

"We're lucky to have you. We've all spent part of our time here trying to destroy ourselves, anyone who tells you he hasn't is a liar. It's part of the sin we're born with. All that matters is if and how you come through it. You are very special, Angela. Please don't ever leave us."

"Why would I do that?" I said, surprised.

"Because people should leave when it's time," he said, "but never before."

"What do you mean, Pop?"

"I have been dreaming about Catherine and Seamus recently. The Catherine dreams are nightmares, all anger and confusion and darkness. She left when things were worst and there is so much regret and sadness in that. But the Seamus dreams are different. They are clear and light. The dreams always go back to the days just before he drowned, that same summer, when the boys were coming out on the water with me all the time. It seemed like that's all they wanted to do, all they would ever want to do."

He looked at the horizon for a moment. I thought he was going to continue.

"I better go," he said, getting up slowly, "enough of this yammering. Take care." He squeezed my hand and stepped on the boat.

I did not think much about his words at the time, because I didn't really understand them. Except for Catherine, I had not suffered a death of anyone close to me and I was just then getting close enough to people to care if they left. I realize now that I have always been running away, my entire life spent with one foot over the edge, ready to jump. That's what alcoholism is, escape. Or a slow form of death, depending on how you look at it.

That morning, I stood on the dock as the boat moved slowly out of the harbor. There was still a night chill in the air, the sun just peeking out from behind low lying clouds. I finished my coffee and stared at the horizon as the boat got smaller and smaller. The sea was much closer now then when I was 13, not a distant shimmer of a dream, but a real body of water slapping casually at the dock beneath me. But the things I wanted in life still floated away on the farthest reaches, where sea and sky come together and disappear. Dreams so far away I could barely see them, just a hint of color or hope on the horizon.

CHAPTER FOUR
Jack
July 2008

I am stumbling down Mott Street. The streets of Chinatown are unbearably bright. The alcohol pounds in my brain. I feel a brush of cool air and follow it into a darkened doorway. It is a Catholic church, St. Augustine R.C., like the ones I was raised in, except the signs are all in Chinese. It is empty, cool and still. I sit in the back pew and rest my head on the back of the bench in front of me.

The last time I was in church was at my father's funeral. I sat by myself in the back row of St. Raymond's Church, an enormous Catholic church with pews running the distance of a football field up to an enormous altar topped with a twenty foot crucifix. I sat in front of the flickering lights of the rows of votive candles that lined the back wall, each wavering flame someone's sad or desperate prayer to the dead. I could not even see who was seated by the altar, a surprisingly large group of people. Mostly fishermen, I figured.

I was angry and uneasy. I did not want to be there, but I did not want to just not show up. Patrick came walking down the aisle with a sorrowful expression. I tried to wave him off, but he sat down next to me. He leaned up against me. I did not want to help him; I did not want to make anyone else feel better. I was completely separated from the world and that's the way I wanted it.

A priest's voice, deep and impersonal, called to us from the distant altar in the huge Catholic church. "We come here to celebrate the life of John Patrick MacAfee. All rise."

"Jack? Can I ask you a question?"

"Shhhh."

"What happens to you when you die?"

"I can't really answer that question right now, Patrick. We're not supposed to talk at a funeral."

"Just a quick answer? We can whisper. A teensy answer."

"You go to heaven. IF you're good."

"How good do you have to be?"

"I don't know. Pretty good."

"Like good all the time or some of the time?"

"Yes."

"Which? All the time or some of the time?"

"No one's good all the time, Pat. You just have to try and be as good as you can."

"What if you don't try? I mean, like once. Or maybe a couple of times. What if you're mean to a friend or you tell your teacher a lie? A little lie. But it wasn't really the truth."

"Are we talking about you, Pat?"

"No! I mean, it was just, I didn't want to get someone in trouble."

"Patrick, lean over here."

"What? Why?"

"I want to tell you something."

"What?"

"You're going to go to heaven, but not for a long, long, long time."

"How do you know?"

"Because you're asking me these questions."

"I don't understand."

"You will."

The priest again: "Please be seated and join us in the singing of Hymn No. 215 in your Hymnbooks."

"Jack, what do you write about when you write your stories?"

"Oh, all kinds of stuff. Whatever I'm thinking about."

"Do you just make it up?"

"I don't think you ever make anything up completely, Patrick, everything is partially based on what you know."

"Do you ever write about me?"

"Sometimes."

"Can I read it?"

"Someday, yes."

"At school they told us about writing a memoir. I think I'm going to write a memoir. It's what you remember. It helps you remember later, about what happened to you. Do you remember everything that happened to you?"

"No, but I'll remember this."

"This what?"

"You. I'll remember you, everything you say, everything you do, the way you look and laugh and walk and complain and won't stop asking me questions all day long. I will never forget that."

"I won't forget you either. I'm going to write my memoir about you."

The priest, loud, insistent: "These are the words of our Lord Jesus Christ. Please be seated."

"Jack, do you believe in God?"

"Yes. Sort of."

"How come you don't go to church?"

"Well, Sunday morning's my basketball game and you go to Sunday school. I'd probably go if I could sit with you."

"Don't you worry that God will get mad? Do you think you're going to go to hell?"

"No, God's not mad at me, buddy. I don't know why he isn't, I certainly don't deserve good luck, but he's not mad at me."

"How do you know?"

"Because he gave me you."

"Why does that make you lucky? Do you think you're lucky when I'm being a pain, like now?'

"Especially then."

The priest: "Please rise."

"Jack?"

"Pat, this isn't really a good time."

"Do you remember all the things that happened to you when you were a boy?"

"A lot of them. I remember being your age."

"Were you happy?"

"Most of the time, yeah."

"Sometimes when I'm not happy I feel guilty because I know I'm lucky."

"How do you know you're lucky?"

"Because everyone keeps telling me." In a fake low voice he says: "*You* don't know how lucky you are."

"Do you feel lucky, Patrick? Honestly."

"Yes. But I'm not always happy."

"Nobody's happy all the time, Pat."

"When is the saddest you ever were?"

"I remember I was very sad when your Mom died. I miss her."

"Nanny was sad when Mom died."

"Yes, she was. It's hard for a parent to say goodbye to a child."

"Do you always get better when you're sad?"

"Mostly, but I think that there are things that happen to you that you never forget. I mean, you can be happy again, but you always carry certain things around with you. Are you shivering?"

"It's cold in here."

"Come here, get under my coat. How's that?"

"I want to stay here forever."

He snuggled in further and I put my arm around him and pulled him close. I was holding him so tight I had to loosen my grip a little.

"You can stay here forever," I said.

"Jack, I was playing kickball at lunch at school yesterday and I hit a grand slam."

"You did? That's awesome." He looked at me and smiled.

"You know Michael Pierce?" he said.

"The big star athlete in your class?"

"Yeah. You know what he said when I hit it?"

"No, what?"

"He said, so what? You just got lucky." His smile faded and he squinted at the ground. "Why did he say that?"

Because he's a miserable jerk, I thought, but I held my tongue. "Patrick, how much better are you now at kickball then you were at the beginning of the year?"

"Oh, much better. I couldn't even reach the fence at the beginning of the year."

"So it's not luck, is it? You worked to do that."

"I practiced a lot. So why did he say that?"

"People get jealous of success, Patrick. Not everybody, but some people. Some people don't want anyone else to be able to do what they can."

I watched his face. That was not a good enough explanation, but I could not think of what else to say. I looked to the altar. The priest was giving his sermon, his voice an earnest drone. Patrick handed me a piece of paper. There were names written on it:

Pop.
Randolph Pierce - he died at the world trade tower.
My friend Sophia's Mom.
The soldiers in the newspaper.

Mom
Seamus

"What's this list, Patrick?"

"Those are the people that I know that died. How many people die every day, Jack?"

"Oh, I don't know, Pat."

"Can you guess?"

"Where? In the whole world?"

"Yes."

"I don't know. Millions."

"What?" He turned around and looked at me in shock. This was the wrong answer. "Millions? It can't be that much, that would be everybody soon!"

"Well, not millions just around here. Millions in the whole world. Remember, there are billions of people in the world."

He looked at me shaking his head in disbelief, and then he thought of something. "Oh, you mean in the whole universe, like every planet, right?"

"Well, yes, right." I had to change direction. "Patrick, how many people have you known that have died?"

"Just the list, I guess."

"So it doesn't happen all that often, right?"

"I guess not. Jack, when are you going to die?"

"I don't know, pal. Don't worry."

"Are you afraid of it?"

"Sometimes."

"Diane Pierce says her Dad never knew he was going to die."

"He probably didn't."

"Because it happened so fast that he was just sitting there and then the jet came and hit the building and then it was over so fast and he went to heaven even before he knew he was dead, and it never hurt, right?"

"Right."

"But Sophia's mom knew. She was sick for a long time. And the soldiers, they probably think that it might happen, right? And Pop knew, because he did it on purpose. What is it like when you know?"

"I don't know the answer to that question, Patrick."

"Can you guess?"

"It depends how long you know for. If it's real sudden, like the soldiers, you're probably afraid for a little while and then it's over. If you're Cynthia's mom, you have time to think about it and get ready and you have time to say goodbye. So that's okay. But then you have to be brave."

"I would want to say goodbye."

"Me, too."

"If you knew you were about to die, would you call me on your cell phone?"

"Yes."

"Then we could talk. What if people stop dying, what if they find a way for people to always live. That could happen with the new medicine and the geniuses in the world. Then we could be together forever. You could be old man Jack, walking around with a cane."

He wrinkled his face and hunched over, whispering "ho, ho, ho," like a very tired Santa Claus.

"You'd be an old man by then, too," I said.

"We could be old guys together! We could have no teeth and play chess!"

I had to try very hard not to laugh out loud. I looked at him and I wanted to hug him. He reminded me so much of Seamus at that point, bright eyes and a freckled broad smile. And then I felt this old familiar fear, this revulsion with myself, this understanding that I would fail him, that I had nothing to give him.

"Did you say goodbye to Seamus, Jack?"

"What? No. I didn't have a chance. He was just gone. One moment here, smiling and laughing, then gone."

"Do you ever pray for him?"

"No, Patrick. I never pray. Maybe I should."

"Yeah, if you prayed to him, maybe he'd answer you. Maybe you could hear his voice again. He could tell you everything is okay where he is."

The priest's voice: "Please rise for the Recessional Hymn."

And then I felt like I had to leave, like always. I physically could not stand staying so close to death, to Patrick's unyielding love, to the ghosts of Seamus and my father. As the crowd rose at the end of the service, we stood and moved to the aisle. I gently pushed Patrick forward. He turned and looked at me, waiting.

"Go ahead," I said, "I'm going to wait for everyone outside."

"Okay," he said, and then he moved down the aisle. He turned once to look at me again and I nodded at him with a smile. Go ahead. Angela appeared at his shoulder and greeted him with a hug. He turned to her. For a moment I felt drawn to her. I almost walked down the aisle to get closer to her. But then I saw James behind her, stern and unyielding.

I turned and eased out the back. I walked down the sidewalk away from the church, not looking back. I paused in front of a house on a corner, thinking about which way to go. From the yard I heard a radio playing Puccini, a scratchy Italian tenor soaring in some Tuscan field somewhere.

Overhead the sky was pale blue with wispy clouds flying across. The clouds gave the whole world a sense of motion. I thought of Diane Pierce's dad and Sophia's mom and Seamus and Pop and my friend Nicholas, who died of esophageal cancer last year.

Nicholas said you never believe you're going to die until you're dead. He said it with a smile one afternoon up in Boston, not long before he died, when he must have known he was going to die much, much sooner than he had ever thought. He shrugged and said, "Now I'm alive. That's what matters right now. I'm not dead yet. Remember that Monty Python bit on the plague, where they toss that guy on the wagon and he says, 'Wait a moment, I'm not dead yet.' I feel like saying that to people when they talk to me. But sometimes I look at my girls and I get very, very sad. That I won't get to see them grow up. That I won't walk them down an aisle."

And I thought of Seamus, of his laughing face just moments before the ocean took him away from me.

I turned and looked at the church down the block. It was quiet now, no singing. The radio in the yard had been turned off. But there was the slightest sound in the breeze, something musical that I could barely hear. I looked up and saw tiny forms in a tree across the street. Birds, hundreds of them. They were singing, in unison, a sound so light and sweet you could barely hear it, unless you stopped and didn't move, didn't think, didn't even breathe.

CHAPTER FIVE

Seamus
August 1993

"Seamus MacAfee! Goddamn you! Get back here, you little bilge rat!"

I scramble up the stairs from the galley and down the gangway. I run, panting and laughing, out into the parking lot. My father stands in the stern of the boat, waving his sandwich at me. "Get back here!" he roars. But there is the slightest smile on his face and it is very early in the day, so I know he's still sober and I'm safe. He throws the sandwich into the bay and waits for me, hands on his hips, as I saunter back.

I had taken the kippered herring he favors off his breakfast roll and put two live bait fish on it, heads and tails still on them. I crossed my fingers that he would bite the head end first and he did. I let James and Jack in on the gag ahead of time and they roared when Pop spit out the two fish heads!

I walk slowly up the gangway to the boat and Pop grabs me by the collar and rubs the top of my head.

"God, you are the devil, boy." Then he laughs. "Jesus!" he exclaims, wiping his mouth, "that's the worst thing I ever ate!" He pushes me gently toward the steps to the bridge. "Get the helm and get us out of here."

I hear James and Jack yelling below as I scramble up to the bridge. "Why does Seamus get to take us out? We're older, why is he captain?"

I'm the captain because Pop says so. I slowly nudge the *Daybreak* out into the channel. I look around proudly. I am the only 14-year-old who gets to take a boat this size out on his own.

I look hopefully at the dock behind Angelo's Seafood Restaurant. There she is, leaning on the railing behind her father's restaurant. Annabel Sorrentino. Even from a hundred feet away she gives me a breathless feeling: slender and blond, with long tanned legs. I told her I was going out this morning with my dad and two older brothers, hoping that she might look out for me. But this is working out so much better than I could have dreamed: I'm at the helm!

Suddenly James and Jack come bounding up the steps, laughing and shouting incomprehensible commands to me. "Full speed! Hard alee! Bring her about!"

"Leave the captain alone!" Pop bellows from below. Never disturb the man at the helm!"

We are directly abreast of Annabel now. She waves shyly at me. James and Jack look at her, then at me, and then explode into a cacophony of shouted accusations.

"So THAT'S what this is all about!" Jack yells. "Pop! Pop! He's just showing off for a girl. He's not even watching where he's going! Pop, we're going to crash!"

James screams in mock terror.

"Hello pretty girl!" Jack yells at Annabel across fifty yards of water. "My weenie little brother loves you!"

I put my head on the wheel, wishing I could hide, wishing I could kill the two of them. They are now jumping up and down, waving their arms wildly at Annabel. Pop stomps up the steps, shouting.

"Shut up, you fucking idiots! Do you want everyone in City Island to think I've raised a bunch of retards?"

But they don't stop. I look over cautiously and see Annabel still looking at me, a broad smile on her face. I give her a small wave and a shrug. She has been leaning on the railing, but now she stands up straight and tosses her lovely blond hair over her shoulder. She looks right at me and blows me a kiss. Then she turns and strides back into the restaurant.

For once in our lives together, my father and my two older brothers are stunned into collective silence. They all turn and look at me, incredulous. I smile, shrug, and turn to look out to sea. But my neck is tingling.

When I think about things all day, whatever it is I happen to be thinking about, I always see her, sometimes in the background, sometimes very close, her smile and her hair and her slender brown legs.

Today is a regular kind of day, cloudy with a wet breeze blowing from the northeast. Whitecaps are on the water even this close inland. But it all looks so beautiful, smells so wonderfully salty and fishy, that I feel like singing. I have always loved it out here, every minute of it. There are gulls trailing us, swooping back and forth over the stern, hoping for bait fish. We pass through the sleeping city and out into the main harbor. As we enter the main channel I push the throttle forward and feel the engine roar. The Verrazano Bridge passes by overhead, like the giant mythical statues from *Jason and the Argonauts* or *Lord of the Rings*. I imagine I am an ancient warrior, at the helm of a ship being rowed by a hundred Vikings. I pull out my sword and hold it against the sky so that its polished steel glistens even in this dull light. We are heading to a distant island, to do battle and rescue Annabel from evil captors. I'll fight them on the beach, three and four at a time.

An egret flies directly in front of me. A rare bird, with its U shaped neck and long stick legs. In flight it coasts on wide white wings, effortlessly. I watch it glide low to the water towards the tall grass on the shore.

Soon there is nothing but open water ahead of me. The waves almost instantly get larger, more rhythmic, as we pass the shoreline on either side of the Narrows. The *Daybreak* moves into the swell with ease, rising up and over the white capped crests, sliding down the other side with a thrilling rush. I look behind me at the Verrazano Narrows Bridge, the doorway back to everything common. And I turn to the sea, which could rise up and crush us in an instant. But it chooses not to, it rises up and carries us along. A wave crashes over the bow and salt water smacks me in the face.

"What are you laughing at?" Jack shouts as he comes up next to me.

I shrug, shaking my head.

"You are always laughing at something Shay," he says, but with a smile. "Give me the helm and go down and get something to eat. Pop brought some egg sandwiches. Check them for fish, though!"

It takes a while, but James and Jack get back to the subject of Annabel. We're fifteen miles out and fishing for swordfish, each of us with a big deep sea rod. James has been grumbling all morning about why a "fucking brain dead fourteen year old gets to helm the *Daybreak* out to sea." Pop appears to be ignoring him, but I'm guessing that he's letting him stew on purpose. Pop had told me not too long ago that he thought James was getting a little uppity, starting to act like he was captain of the *Daybreak*.

But Jack is past all that. He sidles up next to me and says, "So what's this sweetie's name, eh?"

Jack has girlfriends, even though he's just 15. He's had girlfriends since the seventh grade. All the girls like him. "You know," he says slyly, "I'm not sure she blew that kiss at you. Could have been me. I am the handsome one, after all."

I just smile and tilt back in my chair.

"Look at you," he says admiringly. "You cocky son of a bitch." He pokes me in the side, hitting me exactly at my tickle point. Then he knocks me off the chair and wrestles me to the ground, tickling me at my sides where he knows I'll scream.

"Stop! Stop!" I gasp, "I'll do whatever you want, I give up, I surrender!"

We both sit back against the hull, laughing.

"Boy, that girl's pretty," Jack says. "She's in your class?"

I nod. "History. I helped her with medieval history and we got friendly."

"You helped her with medieval history? What do you know about medieval history? I thought you were on permanent academic warning."

"Yeah, well. I read a lot. Just not what I'm supposed to be reading. Is James really pissed at me?"

Jack squints up at James, who is cleaning the one fish we've gotten so far.

"It is a mystery, Shay. What James is thinking, why James is pissed off, it's all a mystery."

He says this loudly enough for James to hear him, but James ignores him.

"All we DO know, with certainty, is that gorgeous girl was not blowing a kiss at James. Maybe you, maybe me, but definitely not James."

James stops and looks up at Jack, casually flipping the scaling knife up and down in his palm.

"What makes you so sure about that?" he says.

"You don't even talk to girls. You do not acknowledge their existence." Jack stands up and approaches James. "You know, I could introduce you to some girls. Some of the many, many, many girls I know have commented that you're not too bad looking. You could actually go out with someone if you wanted to."

"Maybe it's not that easy for everybody," James mutters, going back to work.

"Oh, it is *so* easy, Jimmy. It really is." Jack wraps his arms around James from behind and hugs him. "They want you, Jimmy, they want to hug you and kiss you." Jack puckers his lips and pretends like he's going to kiss James on the cheek.

"Jesus, get off me," James yells, shrugging Jack off. But he's laughing.

"Jesus Christ!" Pop yells from the bridge. "Are you three going to fish or not?" He throws an empty beer can at us and stomps back to the helm.

"Jesus Christ! Ya idgits! Catch some goddamn fish!" James says under his breath in a fake deep voice.

"You three are the worst fisherman in the world!" Jack says in a whispered rasp, stomping around and waving his arms in mock outrage. The two of them grab each other by the collars and pretend to throttle each other. I am laughing so hard I trip over a chair and knock one of the rods over. The explosive clatter of the equipment makes all three of us break into convulsive laughter.

I look up and Pop is pretending to ignore us, his gaze fixed forward over the helm. But I can see a smile on his face.

An hour or so later I am idly spinning my rod when the line suddenly rips out to sea, straight out, running so hot that I cannot shut it down.

"Let it run for a bit, Seamus," Pop yells as he hops gingerly down the stairs. "James, take the helm." James nods and quickly moves up to the bridge. "Jack, get behind Seamus." Jack nods and moves behind me without a sound.

"Okay," Pop says, "Now try reeling it, just a bit."

There is fierce resistance, like getting your line stuck on a log. Then the line pulls away from me, fast, cutting back and forth, hard, then down.

"What's it feel like?" Pop asks.

"Sword. But big," I say.

"Excellent!" Pop says.

Then all of a sudden Jack's line pops and starts to run. He scrambles around and jumps in his seat, firmly grabbing the rod in both hands and wedging it between his feet.

The rest of the afternoon is a thrilling blur. After I finally get my fish in, my hands blistered and bleeding, James gets a marlin on his line. All three fish are huge. We gather at the helm on the way back, the sun setting over the approaching landline. Pop has given each of us a beer, only for special occasions, he says. We are singing and laughing. We pass another charter coming in, *Debbie's Dream*. My father yells at her captain, "Ricky, you should see the fucking fish my boys caught today!" Ricky waves back with a smile.

James' marlin is the biggest fish in the harbor all summer. But mine is pretty big, too. There's a crowd gathered around at our mooring in the early evening, admiring the three fish hung up across the stern of the *Daybreak*. Someone has brought a cooler full of beer and it's become a party. Annabel appears at the edge of the crowd. James walks over to her and escorts her past the boisterous group of men. He takes her elbow and leads her up the gangway right to me. She turns to smile at him, but he's gone.

"Hi!" she says.

"Hey. Sorry about all of that yelling and screaming this morning."

She laughs. "That was so funny. I love your brothers, they're so goofy." She looks at me. "You're pretty goofy, too. But you're not all goofy, are you." That didn't sound like a question. I look at the ground, desperately searching my muddy brain for something to say.

She laughs and touches my elbow. "Which fish did you catch?"

"The big swordfish over there." I walk towards it, the spot on my elbow tingling where her fingers rest.

I look towards her. "You know," I say quietly, "I'm never silly about things that are important to me."

She looks at me seriously. I am not sure exactly what that means or what she thinks it means, but then she smiles and says, "Show me the rest of the boat?" Her hand stays on my arm as we walk to the bow, where the moon is floating gently on the mirror still harbor.

CHAPTER SIX

Jack
July 2008

Think, Jack. Where are you? What are you doing? Angela. That's what I'm doing. I am going to find Angela. I am going to tell her how I feel. I am going to give her the letter. I reach into my pocket and touch the folded piece of paper, the letter I wrote to her one sober morning two weeks ago. I am going to give it to her.

It has been hours since I ran off from Michael, but I don't know how many. I am sitting in the Port Authority Bus Terminal, blearily trying to make out the schedule for Greyhound's national bus routes. I feel sick, but there's a beer in my hand and I take a swallow from that. I am sitting in the last seat of a row of plastic seats. A boy, about 12, stands ten feet away from me and peppers his mother with questions. When will we get to Chicago? What does Chicago look like? Can we go to Wrigley Field as soon as we get there? His mother murmurs responses as she roots through their bags for something. He is practically hopping with excitement.

"Will Daddy meet us at the bus station?"

"Yes, Paul, Of course, you know your father, he'll probably meet the bus halfway. He wouldn't miss you for the world."

The boy sits down and looks up at the departure schedule, a perfect smile on his face. Drunk or not, I recognize a truly happy person when I see one. His father is waiting for him. That's all we want, is someone waiting for us.

An announcer's voice drones over the PA system, calling off the names of destinations: Binghamton, Glens Falls, Utica. Towns too dreary to travel to by any means other than by bus. Busses reeking of diesel and littered with wrappers from Hostess cupcakes and Slim Jims. The voice reminds me of a priest at mass, doomed to repeat the same message day after day after day.

I get up and start walking and eventually find myself in the bar by the bowling alley on the third floor. I sit there in the mid-afternoon, nursing a beer. I am just this side of being too drunk and trying to stay right there. I have a sense of where I am sitting, but the specifics of how I got there are very blurry. There is just me, the bartender and an older drunk at the end of the bar, who appears to be unconscious. The sounds of the bowling alley come through the half-opened door: the hard clatter of pins and the grind of the bowling machines. Bus announcements drift up the empty corridor outside, "Buffalo boarding in five minutes, Utica boarding at two twenty four."

"Not working today, huh?" the bartender says, absentmindedly drying glasses.

"I'm retired," I say with a smile.

"Good for you, I should be able to retire in thirty years or so." He says this without a smile, but he looks seventy, so I take it as a joke. I laugh.

"Married?" He says.

"Divorced."

"This is my hobby, trying to figure out what brings people in here in the middle of the day."

"What's the answer usually?" I say.

"Well," he pauses, then sticks his hand out, "Sam, I'm Sam."

"Jack," I say.

He nods. "Let me ask you a question, Jack. What would it take to make you content?"

"Content?"

"Yeah. Not happy, not delirious, just content. I've been standing here for twenty five years and I get no contented people in here. What's it take?"

"Content, don't know what that means, exactly," I say. I took a long drink. "Angela would make me content," I say quietly.

"Who's Angela?"

"My brother's wife."

"Oh, ho! Now that's trouble. What in the world makes you think you're going to find contentedness stealing your brother's wife?" He laughs as he says it, amazed.

"I'm not going to steal her," I say defensively, "you can't steal her, she's a person, not silverware. And this is a fantasy, isn't it? This happens in a world where nobody gets hurt by it happening. I mean, I don't really care if my brother gets hurt, but let's just say."

"Well, okay," Sam says, "nobody ever established rules to this question before, people usually say they want a billion bucks and leave it at that. But you want Angela, so you can have her. But you wouldn't care if your brother got hurt?"

"Oh, you know, he's my big brother and always knows better and never smiles and doesn't understand why I've screwed my life up. Like there's a one paragraph explanation. He bugs me. Fuck him. Give me another beer."

"Please give me another beer," Sam says with his eyebrows raised.

"Sorry. Please may I have another beer?"

"So what about Angela," Sam says quietly, handing me a beer. He starts wiping down the bar.

"She's different than everyone else. She's a drunk."

"She's a drunk?"

"A beautiful, beautiful drunk. You'd never know it. She went straight a while ago, right when she got married to James. She's funny and smart and lovely. Filipino. Her eyes are the color of the ocean just when the sun is going down, you know the water gets darker and darker until it's that purply black color? She's a great listener."

"Your wife didn't listen?"

"Oh, my wife is okay. She's just too straight. I do not understand how a person can stay sober and serious all the time. I'd blow my brains out. Angela understands. You know how people say they haven't had a drink in three years? Angela says she's been waiting for three years for her next drink."

Sam laughs. "She sounds okay."

"You know what," I say, "I'm going to go see her."

"Oh, wait a fucking minute," Sam says emphatically, holding his hand up, "now there's a really, really bad idea."

"No, it'll be fine. She teaches in the Bronx. I'll just swing by and say hi. I have a letter for her." I pull the folded piece of papare out of my pocket and wave it at Sam.

"It explains everything," I say, "Everything that's in my heart."

I get up and leave a wad of bills on the counter, not even counting them.

"You should go home and sleep it off," Sam says as I walk away, his voice rising in warning. "Nothing good can come of this."

I stand silently by the door, squinting down the corridor. A scratchy announcement says a bus for Atlanta is leaving in five minutes. Atlanta, I think, I've never been to Atlanta. It would be very easy to just go downstairs and hop on. I smile at Sam and say, "I have nothing to lose at this point." I turn and walk out the door.

"You could break your heart, Jack," Sam calls out, sounding genuinely upset. "You could lose your heart, that's still something, isn't it?"

My heart? I stagger down the brightly lit corridor, the falling bowling pins like distant thunder down the hall. I have no heart. I have nothing to lose there. How can you break something that never worked in the first place? Sam is wrong, anyway. Angela could help me, help me find my way. There's got to be a way out of this hell, I thought, who better than an angel to help you find your way out of hell? She'll know what to do. I'll go to her school. We can talk. I'll give her the letter. She'll understand.

I grip desperately to the escalator rail as it pulls me down to the raucous, teeming main floor of the Port Authority. I blurrily watch the mass of people as I slowly descend into them, like a strange being floating to earth for the first time. Would they greet me or tear me apart? I shake my head to clear it. I better get another drink and find out. I stagger into the crowd at the bottom of the escalator and look around in a sudden panic. I raise my arms to ward off the swarm of people around me. I must find Angela. I will find her and she will save me.

CHAPTER SEVEN
Angela
July 2008

You are going to hate me after I finish this story, but I am going to tell you anyway. When James proposed to me four years ago, down on his knee with a ring in his hand, I spontaneously swore to him to quit drinking. I knew my drinking was an issue for him. He pointedly told me many times that he loved me sober. Which I took to mean that he didn't love me so much drunk, but I had long ago convinced myself I was a charming drunk and I thought I could get away with it. But I was so surprised when he proposed that I blurted this promise out. Stupid, stupid, stupid. What was I thinking? But from that day on, he never saw me take another drink. Oh, I did not stop drinking, not even for a little while. For four years I kept on drinking but hid it from James and everyone else. It became my secret and in doing so, I grew to love drinking even more.

I became a genius at hiding my drinking. Everything revolved around my drinking schedule. Most alcoholics will tell you that they're "functioning" alcoholics or some other term that is intended to slyly indicate that they're different and better than all the other fuck-up alcoholics who can't hold a job and live in the gutter. I was even worse than that, I took enormous pride in standing in a group of people, sipping a coke, knowing that they believed I was composed and sober, when I was actually smashed.

Here's how I do it: I get up, go to school, teach all day, drink coffee, sneak cigarettes at lunch. I stay after school and prepare lessons for the next week, grade homework, do my job. I don't stop working until there's nothing left to do, because once I leave the school building, my day is shot. I never drink during the day and thereby convince myself that I am functioning. I try to ignore the throbbing hangover.

Then I leave school. I drive from school in the opposite direction from my home, up into Pelham where nobody knows me, to one of the Irish bars on the Main Street. I go to a different bar each day so my appearances seem a little less obvious. I drink vodka on the rocks; it's quicker and doesn't give me such a bad hangover. I chain smoke. I talk to the bartender, tell him a fake name. Leave the bar at 6:00 and go to a liquor store. Buy four little airline vodkas. Stop at a Deli and buy two beers. Drink the beers on the way home. Hide the vodkas in my bag. I greet you when you come home. I am friendly, outgoing. One of the advantages to coming home half in the bag is I always make an effort to be nice, so I don't attract close scrutiny. I drink Seven-up at night and drop a vodka into a mostly filled glass every once in a while. I keep my glass where someone won't pick it up or knock it over by accident.

James either takes the boat out with customers on a night fishing charter and comes home after I've gone to sleep, or he goes to bed early for a 5:30 start. I stay up, sitting alone in the dark. Drunks are chronic daydreamers. I spin elaborate fantasies in my head, imagining a life in which I am special, famous, where men can't help themselves but to fall in love with me. I go to bed around midnight. I wake up with a hangover, but I'm used to that. I get up, take a couple of Advil's, go to work, repeat.

It was easy. The years flew by in a blur. Then one day I was sitting in B&B's Pub in Pelham, 5:30 on a Tuesday, sipping vodka on the rocks and lighting a Kent, when Jack sat down next to me and I got an adrenalin surge of fear that almost knocked me off my chair.

James has given up on Jack, but I still hold out hope for him. I've tried to stay close to him, although he is elusive, like most drunks. Jack is the most dangerous kind of drinker for me: secretive, charming, never out of control. And I will tell you now, I will admit to you, that I've always been drawn to him for what I've known are the wrong reasons. Something else I've hidden from James.

Jack knew why I was in that bar. He said he'd driven by the school on a whim to see me, and then followed me on my secret rounds.

"Where were you coming from?" I asked.

"Long story, Angie. Michael came into the City to rescue me. He wants to take me to a rehab place. I thought about it, but then I took off. I don't need that kind of help; I can get a handle on this by myself."

He put a hand on my shoulder. "You can help me," he added brightly. I was annoyed at all of this, I felt exposed and ashamed having him find me in this bar. I wanted to deal with him from a position of authority, as a former drinker, a rescuing angel, not a fellow drunk. I became flustered and left.

I walked to the car and sat in the front seat for half an hour. I started to cry and then I could not stop. I put my head on the steering wheel and hung on to the wheel tightly with my hands. It started to rain, the drops pounding on the windshield. I saw Jack leave the bar and walk down the street in the other direction, oblivious to the rain.

I flashed my headlights at him. He turned around. It is possible on very rare occasions to look at someone's face and for just a moment to see exactly what they feel, in that fleeting moment before they realize you are watching them and draw the curtain on that open window. It is a glimpse into the heart that can be absolutely lovely or heartbreaking. Sometimes when I'm out on the boat with James and he is at the helm and doesn't think I am watching I see who he is and what he feels: serenity and purpose. That night Jack turned in the rain and looked at the car with a look of such hopefulness, such relief, that I nearly started crying again. What was it that he wanted from me? There was no way I could give it to him.

I waved at him and he walked over and got in the car, absolutely drenched. He looked at me and for a moment I saw that look again, this look of unguarded hopefulness.

And then he kissed me lightly, tentatively. It did not surprise me. Drunken people will do things like that. But I kissed him right back, because I was drunk and lonely and I always had a thing for him and he seemed to care very much about me. He froze in surprise and then kissed me harder. We sat there for a while doing that, his hands gently on my face and nowhere else. It felt very nice and I started to disappear into the feeling. Then I sat back and took a deep breath.

I told him I couldn't do this, that I loved James and that I had to get my life back in order. I told him that he and I were alcoholics and we needed to do something about it. He said tell me something I don't know. Jack said he had very powerful feelings for me. I told him he might think that, but he did not know his own feelings, his true feelings. He could not know those until he got sober.

He got annoyed and said blah, blah, blah, he'd heard it all before. Then he was instantly contrite and became upset with himself. I told him that one of the main reasons I wanted to get sober was because I did not want to end up like him, alone and afraid.

That was an awful thing to say, but it was the truth. He just smiled that Jack smile, the easy bemused one that just blows me away every time, and he said that I was never going to end up like him, because I had James. He said he loves his brother; he's the best part of who he is.

I started to cry, which really pissed me off. I hate crying in front of men, especially in front of James or Jack.

He reached into his pocket and handed me a letter. He said he'd been meaning to send it forever but hadn't worked up the nerve. He motioned for me to read it, while he opened the door and stepped out into the rain.

"Where are you going?" I said.

He shrugged. "To my mother's. I want to see Patrick."

He pointed at the letter and walked away.

I am going to let James read it, he should know everything, but I hope he can forgive Jack for his feelings:

Dear Angela

This is not a love letter, I won't do that. Love letters are pathetic if the other person doesn't want to get it and I don't think you do, not from me, anyway.

I find myself thinking about you at certain times. Like when it's a summer afternoon and everyone has finally turned off their lawnmowers and I walk out back and all I can hear is a breeze in the trees and a bird singing and a far off child calling; I think of you then. I think of your face when you lean forward to listen and you wrinkle your forehead just a little. I think about your eyes: dark, impenetrable but alive, like looking into the heart of a forest. And I wonder if there ever could have been a way that I would have been the man that you fell in love with and placed all of your hopes on.

There are other times; sitting in traffic when it rains, the light drumbeat of the drops on the windshield makes me think of that day we ran down 42nd Street trying to make a train, clinging together under a broken umbrella. Your laugh sounded like it floated out of the clouds with the rain, falling lightly all around us.

I cannot escape you. But that's okay. Maybe all we ever could have been were drunks together. And I would not wish that on you, even if it could make me have you all to myself. I really want to say goodbye, I need to, but I don't know where else to go.

The letter ended there. I did not see him again for three months and by then things were very different. But right then I just sat in the car for half an hour, staring at the rain on the windshield.

I went home that night and fell asleep. James was out on a charter. I woke up before him the next morning and sat in the kitchen drinking coffee. I was being crushed by a black mountain of despair. I felt like dying would be a relief, like there was nothing, nothing, in the world that mattered even a little bit. And I knew what this was, this feeling. This was me actually deciding not to drink anymore. Kissing Jack in a drunken stupor was the last straw. I had to do this or everything I cared about was just going to shrivel up and die. I would have to leave behind all of these drunken daydreams I had subsisted on. I would have to put aside Jack's letter, which I had read a hundred times and which described something that I craved, the idea that someone could fall head over heals for me. I would have to wander out into the real world, colorless and drought stricken, a world where the only real love I might get would have to be from James, a man I was about to give every reason not to love me.

I went out to the yard and lit a cigarette. I was very frightened, I did not know if I could actually do this. And if I failed, that could be the end of me, I suddenly saw that. I walked in circles, telling myself it was going to be okay, I was going to be okay. But I knew it wasn't going to be okay.

Out of the corner of my eye I could see James looking at me from the kitchen window. I realized I had been talking to myself, out loud. I stood in the middle of the yard and looked up at the sky, which hung there like gray stone, without a hint of sun or life or pity.

I put out the cigarette and turned to walk into the house, to start this new part of my life. The steps felt heavy and slow, as if I was walking on the bottom of the ocean. I could not see a way that I could possibly get through this. I walked through the door and looked at James, standing by the kitchen table, looking at me expectantly. I am going to have to tell him all of it, the drinking, the hiding, the kiss with Jack. I'm a lying bitch, I thought, how is he ever going to care for me anymore?

Do you know what I said? I have something I need to tell you, James. I said it in a whisper; I could barely get the words out. He looked at me with a half smile, truly puzzled. Another face with a heart revealed. We had talked about having kids and buying a bigger house and all of these other dreams and I hadn't been sober through a single moment of it.

I motioned for him to sit down. Sit down, my love, I thought. Sit down so that I can break your heart.

CHAPTER EIGHT
Patrick
July 2008

My Grandmother sits on the front porch of her house in the Bronx, waiting and praying. She prays for all things, with absolute faith and without regard for result, for the coming of good and the passage of trouble. It is six o'clock on a summer evening. It has just stopped raining and there is a chill in the air. She draws her shawl around her shoulders.

I call to her through the screen doors.

"Nanny, you'll get a chill. Mrs. Cronin's expecting you to walk her to seven o'clock mass. She'll want you to visit after."

"But Jack's coming to visit. He said he'd be by in the late afternoon when he called before. I haven't seen him in months!"

"Uncle Jack will get here soon. Anyway, I'll be here. He'll wait for you. You'll see him when you get home from Mass."

She comes in to get her coat.

"What'll the two of you have for supper?" she says, "I've nothing on."

"Don't worry, Nanny, we'll take care of ourselves. We'll fix up something."

"It's not like him to be late," she says, glancing worriedly at the door. "I don't like to leave you alone here, Patrick."

"Nanny," I say sternly, "I'm thirteen. I'll be fine." I stand up straight to my full five and a half feet. She looks up at me, her eyes wrinkling in surprise.

"You've grown up so fast, Patrick."

"Go on, Nanny. I'll be fine. And don't worry about Jack, nothing bad could happen to him. He must've gotten stuck somewhere or something."

I kiss her on the cheek. "You look terrific, Nanny."

She smiles, with a touch of embarrassment, and she leaves her home. She pats her hair and looks about carefully, at each corner of her life, the small rooms dotted with pictures of saints and two generations of first communions. She says quietly to the walls, "Goodbye."

I sit by myself and wait. Nanny's house is as quiet as a church. I can sit by myself and just daydream, my mind has no trouble flying off on its own.

At 7:15, there is a pounding at the door that brings me to my feet with a jolt. I run to the door and let in two Emergency Medical Services ambulance attendants, who carry Jack into the living room on a stretcher.

"On my shield," he mumbles in slurred speech, "returned from the fray." He smiles sloppily and throws an unhinged look around the room, his eyes swollen and squinted shut against the bright lamp light.

"Jack!" I say, "What happened?" I look at the drivers. "What's happened to him?"

"Seamus!" Jack yells at me, "Hey, Shay!"

I lunge forward awkwardly. I ask one of the drivers, "Is he okay?" My voice cracks.

The smaller one shrugs. "How the hell does he look?" the larger one says sourly.

He looks dreadful. His shirt is stained and disheveled and his hair is a mess. When he smiles he looked like a madman.

They place him on the couch. The large driver says, "I'll tell you, this guy's something else. We thought he was going to croak in the van, he gawked up two or three meals worth. He passes out for a few minutes, then his eyes pop open and he's fine and dandy. He's out of control."

He turns to me belligerently and pokes my shoulder for emphasis.

"We've got better things to do, pal, then drive around drunk stockbrokers."

"What're you talking about?" I say, "he must be sick or something. He can't be just drunk; I've never seen him drunk."

The larger one rolls his eyes. "He told us he was a stockbroker," the smaller driver says in a slightly more good-natured tone. "His eyes pop open and he says, go long, my friend, go long on wheat. Wheat and cotton. Take your little pennies and buy. What the fuck does that mean?"

"Commodities, you twit," Jack says, quite clearly. "Futures. Get rich quick."

His eyes remain shut. He has folded his hands over his chest as he lays on the couch. He looks like a body at a wake. The two drivers and I stand over him silently for a moment, like mourners.

"You want to spend the rest of your life being a goddamn fisherman?" he mumbles, "Get into the market! Everybody's making a fortune."

The larger driver stamps his foot impatiently and says, "Come on, Ronny, let's go." The smaller one ignores him and says to me, "What is he talking about? We're not fishermen."

Jack opens his eyes and looks blearily at me. I sit by his side on the couch.

"Pat. Oh, it's you. I can't convince anybody of anything, Patty. Nobody listens." He closes his eyes. "No one ever believes me."

"Are you...drunk, Jack?"

He opens his eyes wide and they water. He smiles and says calmly, "Don't be silly, Pat. I've been in the city all day, busy. What kind of man gets drunk in the middle of the afternoon?" Jack looks at me steadily. They are all looking at me now, as if the next move is my decision and as if I have some sense of what to do. I feel my ordinary fear and uncertainty. Then I have a clear idea of what to do.

"Take him upstairs," I say. "There's a bedroom up there."

The two drivers carry him upstairs, as I direct them, to the front room over the porch. Nanny says that's where her children had all napped as babies: Jack, James, Padraic, Michael, and my mother. Then me, my brother, sister and my cousins. They lay him down gently on the bed.

The large driver turns to me and says in an surprisingly quiet voice, "Your Dad, kid?"

"Sort of. Well, no, my uncle. He's okay, you know. He's a great guy."

He nods thoughtfully and pats me on my shoulder. He stands for a moment at the door, shakes his head sadly, and they leave, clumping down the stairs. I sit on a small chair at the foot of the bed. I remember my Mom and, at different times, Nanny, sitting there as I woke up when I was younger. I watch him, feeling as if I am guarding him from whatever has made him sick. He turns to the wall, clutching his arms to his chest, and he sleeps.

What had happened to him? The ambulance driver had said he was drunk, but that didn't make any sense. I'd never even seen him drunk, not like I thought drunks looked like. Not like some of our other relatives and people you saw on the streets of New York. He drank some beer, like all the men in our family, but there was never anything wrong with Jack, he was always fun, always said the right thing.

I think of a time a couple of years ago, when my Mom and Dad were fighting late one night, before he left. They had been talking, fighting, about how he couldn't find work. I listened through my closed bedroom door.

"How did I get <u>stuck</u> with you?' she asked in a bitter whisper, "my child is supposed to look up to you as a father? You can't even support yourself!"

"<u>Our</u> child," he said quietly. Always quietly.

"At least he has some people to look up to. Like Jack."

"Why him? Because he makes a lot of money? Is that all it takes to make you happy? He's got his own problems, you know.

"What's that supposed to mean?"

"He can drink a fair amount when he feels like it..."

"Come off it, Roger. That's nothing and you know it. You <u>like</u> him."

A brief silence. "So? So I do. Stop waving his successes in my face. I am trying, Catherine."

"Trying is not good enough. Not for us."

I helped my Dad move when he finally moved out, down to Point Pleasant, in Jersey. We packed his stuff into a van at our house on City Island in the morning and he gave me a ride back the next morning. Mom made herself scarce. She didn't want me to go at all, but she let it go when I insisted. That wasn't like her.

He and I talked about a lot of things that day, but not about what was happening. I told him stories about school. I stretched the truth some and told him I was very popular, even though I didn't feel that way. It seemed to cheer him up.

"You're going to be okay, Patrick," he said, "I've got faith in you. Maybe your Mom's right, maybe you should be looking up to your Uncle Jack, and Michael, they're successes. They're good men, too. So is James, for that matter, although I don't think your Mom's ever going to tell you to admire a fisherman. I'm never going to be rich. I never wanted to be. I just want to be an artist. It's hard to make a living in art; you end up designing other people's wall paper. I always felt stupid when I talked to your Mom about it. It sounded like something a child would say, you know: I want to be an artist, an astronaut, a fireman."

We were sitting on the front steps of the small development he had moved into, eating ice cream bars.

"You know," he said, "I like to hang out with Jack sometimes, he's fun. But he makes me feel...he doesn't mean to do it, I don't think, but he makes me feel inconsequential. You know what that feels like? To feel...small?"

I nodded. I did, but I didn't want to hear this from him, from my father.

"Would you like to be like someone like that," he asked casually, "like Jack?"

"I guess," I said. I thought for a moment. "I'd like to be like you, too. I like you."

He turned to look at me and I thought maybe I was sorry I'd said it. It was what came to me, but it didn't seem like nearly enough. He looked a little surprised, and sad. Then he smiled.

"You're okay, Pat, you know that? We'll be okay, you and I."

But I hardly ever saw him after that, just a couple of visits and a couple of calls. Even those times, even when Mom wasn't around, he seemed distracted, edgy, like he was visiting a place he hadn't wanted to come back to. And then I never heard from him again.

I stand by the bed where Jack sleeps for a while and watch out the window, wondering where each passerby is going, who they are, what their lives are like. I want to step into and out of their lives. I only want to be me some of the time. Jack stirs and turns to me. He opens his eyes suddenly and smiles, a natural, funny grin.

"Hey, Pat," he says, sitting up, "Whoowee, I had a rough turn of it there, didn't I?"

"What happened, Jack?"

"I didn't read the prescription right on this medication the doctor gave me for my knee. You know the injury I got skiing?" He leans over and rubs his knee gingerly. "I thought I was supposed to take four pills at a time. It's four pills a day. I figured it out when I started to feel woozy a couple of hours ago. Then I lost it! Those stupid drivers thought I was drunk, like I'm going to be wandering around midtown Manhattan drunk in the middle of the afternoon like some bum. I've got better things to do, thank you very much. Anyway, I'll never do that again."

He stands and puts both hands on my shoulders.

"Give me a second to clean up, sport, and then you and I are going to figure out what's going on."

"Okay!" I say. Doing anything with Jack was the best. He is back in a few minutes, looking as if nothing has happened, just a little worn around the eyes. He has changed into a new shirt and pants.

"Left this stuff the last time I was here. How do I look?"

"Great!"

"You hungry, little dude?"

I nod.

"Well, let's get going here," he says, raising his voice and clapping his hands together. "Let's go, go, go, Patty. The world is ours for the taking. Hey, let's go to Louie and Ernie"s."

Louie and Ernie's is my favorite, a little pizzeria on Waterbury.

"Where's Nanny?" he asks.

"She's at Mrs. Cronin's."

"Well, I'll give her a buzz and tell her we're eating out. Let's go!"

We eat a whole sausage pizza at Louie and Ernie's, or actually I eat most of it, Jack doesn't seem very hungry. He has a couple of beers and I have a soda.

"How are the girls coming along, Pat?"

I feel myself blushing. "Oh, I don't know. I feel really stupid around them."

"Anybody you like?"

I pause. I have secrets I don't tell anyone.

He looks at me with a sly, crooked smile.

"C'mon, Pat. It's me."

"Ginny Bailey," I say quietly.

"She pretty?"

"Yeah, I guess."

"You guess?" He leans over and pokes me in the arm gently. "Now don't go overboard, buddy."

"Yes she is," I blurt, "She really, really is. I ride my bike by her house all the time. Sometimes I see her outside, or through the living room window. That's pretty weird, isn't it?"

"No, Patrick," he says thoughtfully, rubbing his chin, "No. That's perfectly damn normal."

"I fell off the bike one day, right in front of her house, I wasn't watching where I was going, I was trying to peek into the garage and I ran into the curb. It sounded like a jet crashing. They must've heard it; they were probably all laughing at me in the kitchen."

He laughs so loud that heads turn.

"I'm not laughing at you, Patty, I've done much worse. Ever talk to her?"

"God!" I say in shock, "No!" I shake my head emphatically. "I mean, why would she?"

"Oh, you'd be surprised, Pat. You're a smart, good-looking kid. She'd probably be happy to know you."

I didn't believe that for a second, but it makes me happy to hear Jack say it.

"I don't know, Jack. I never know what to say to girls."

"Oh, come on, what do you talk to Angela about? You two always have some private conversation going. She's the loveliest woman on the planet and you've totally got her attention."

"That's different," I say quickly. I can feel myself blushing. "That's way different, she's my aunt." But deep down I feel a thrill that anyone might think that Angela thought I was special.

As we head back to Nanny's, Jack asks me how things are going with Nanny, and if I have heard from my father. I tell him I haven't, not for a while. He puts his hand on my shoulder as we walk.

"Think much about your Mom, Pat?"

"I try not to. I feel...guilty, sorry. Sorry the way things happened, the way they ended. I wish I could re-live things."

"Not your fault, Pat. Your Mom and I were close, but that was just the way she saw me, she couldn't be like that with everyone, she... she was what she was. I don't know if she had it in her to be the kind of mother she wanted to be. What you needed." He sighs. "Maybe she took after your Grandfather too much, although God knows they didn't get along." He is quiet for a while, as we walk along.

"Catherine MacAfee," he says quietly. "When we were little I called her little Katie Mac." He smiles down at me and squeezes my shoulder. "Boy, she and Pop used to fight. And Pop and I... I think people would treat each other differently, would live differently, if they knew they weren't going to be around forever. I never thought there'd be a time when they weren't both around anymore."

"I get scared sometimes when I think that everyone's going away," I say. "That I'll be by myself someday."

"Don't worry, Pat," he says, "I'll always be around."

We don't talk the rest of the way. As we walk up Puritan Avenue towards Nanny's house, the entire block is dark, except for a light like an island from her kitchen window. Jack holds his finger to his lips as we tiptoe in. She is sleeping in her chair by the kitchen table, her head tilted slightly to the left, breathing slowly and deeply. Jack leans over and kisses her lightly on the forehead, whispering her maiden name, "Hello, Ellen McGuire." She opens her eyes slowly and smiles with delight.

"Hello, Jack, dear."

I am directed gently to bed not to long after that, since I have school early the next morning. Jack follows me up, teasing me a little along the way.

"Couple of years and you'll be staying up to all hours, Pat. Don't mind Nanny, she just wants you to do well at school."

"I know," I say with a grudging sigh.

Jack stands in the doorway as I crawl under the covers.

"Will you be here tomorrow, Jack?"

"You bet, chief. I'll see you when you get home from school. Maybe we can shoot some hoops."

"That'd be great! You don't have to work?"

"No," he says with a small smile, "Not tomorrow."

He turns off the light and walks over to the side of the bed. He leans over and gives me a kiss on the forehead, which surprises me. As friendly as he is, he usually keeps his distance.

As he walks out the door, he says, "You take care of yourself, Patrick. And you take care of your Grandmother."

"Okay, Jack."

"Good night, buddy."

I listen to his footsteps down the stairs and then, as I try to settle in, to the sounds of the traffic on Tremont Avenue. I think of my mother and Jack and Ginny Bailey, and then my father, and then everything and everyone else, spinning around in my head, uncatchable. I try to start a dream as I fall into sleep, of being on a big, beautiful boat on the ocean, my Grandfather's, with everyone on it, together and happy. I even put Ginny Bailey there, impressed by me, the first mate. And my Mom is there, by my side, as I sail us all away.

But I cannot sleep for long. After tossing and turning for a while, I sit on the edge of the bed, rubbing my eyes. I hear Jack and Nanny's voices downstairs, wordless murmuring. I get up quietly and walk to the top of the stairs, and then I tiptoe down the stairs to the lower landing. I am still around the corner from the kitchen and can not be seen, nor can I see them. I sit down. I can hear the voices clearly.

Nanny is laughing quietly, a childish giggle. "Stop teasing me now, Jack. You're a devil."

Then Jack says, "Tell me some more, Mom."

"I dream about him sometimes, Jack. I see him clear as you here. I can see him in the yard, cutting the lawn on a summer's day, with one of those shirts on, you know, the white sleeveless t-shirts."

"A guinea T, he called it," Jack said.

"Yes, but he meant no harm. He called everyone by names: guineas, micks, polacks, wops. We all came over here together. When I see him in my dream, he's pushing that old rotary mower we had, you know, the ones without power. He had to push it with all his strength and I watch his arms, so strong, and his skin is shiny with perspiration. I always liked to watch him work, he'd lose himself in it. He was always strong enough to take care of us all."

"I know," Jack says quietly.

"He's smiling up at me on the porch and his smile, Jack, it looks just like yours. And in the dream the houses on the block are bright with fresh paint and the trees are full of leaves. Not like now. The street is brand new, everything is beautiful, and the sun is shining like it never does now. Coming down the street is your Aunt Lucy with all of you: James and Michael. Seamus and Catherine, God bless their souls. And you. You are all so young, such beautiful tiny creatures. You're all calling out Pop! in your little bird voices, and he is standing there, waving at you slowly, his arm over his head, as if you are far away, just beaming, as if his heart will burst. That's my whole dream, Jack."

"He would have liked it. That's him," Jack says. I hear the refrigerator door open and the hiss of a can opening.

"There's chicken, Jack, and potatoes."

"No, thanks, we ate plenty, Mom, I'll just have a beer."

"Does it bore you to talk about these things, Jack?"

A silence. I lean forward anxiously. Say no, Jack.

Then she laughs. He's done something without speaking, a face, a smile with an eyebrow raised.

"Tell me more." Then I hear a chair scrape a little, and imagine her settling herself in.

"Your father told me, when we were young and just here from Ireland, that this place would be a whole new world for us. He said that anything was possible. He was so enthusiastic when he was younger that you couldn't help but believe him. Sometimes on a Sunday we would walk through the city and pass through a dozen countries- Chinatown, Little Italy, Russians, Jews, everyone. The whole world had come to this place with us. The first time we saw this house, long before we could even dream of owning it, he said this is where we'll live, Ellen, with our family, and we'll grow old here. We were eighteen."

There was a silence.

"You had a good life together," Jack says.

"For a while we did. But things changed, Jack. It's easiest to remember what happened last, the hard times. Now I think about those first times as something I dreamed. I feel like I dreamed my whole life and now I look out the window and the houses are old and worn and the streets all broken up. I don't recognize anyone on the streets anymore. It's like my connection to that old world was cut off when he left."

"But you wanted him to move out, didn't you? I thought you insisted."

"Oh, yes, I've no regrets about that. Except I wish we could have talked more before he died. I wasn't about to live out my days with him, with the way he was getting, drinking and chasing women half his age. And all that bitterness, that cynicism. You know, he was a dreamer, too. But his life swallowed all those dreams up."

A small laugh from her.

"He was just afraid to get old, that's all it was. I think he figured that out at the end. That was the funny thing, he picked the worst time to go, we were just starting to talk again."

A pause.

"Look at that, Jack. Your First Communion picture. Look at that smile."

"I'm missing three teeth. I like that other picture."

"Din and Daniel."

The pictures are on the mantle over the stove. Nanny has explained all of them to me. The picture of Din and Danny, my great-uncles, were taken at the family home in Kerry, called Malnahone.

"You visited Malnahone, Jack. In college."

"That's right. I stayed with Din. We went on a tour of every pub in Kerry."

"Oh, Din. Always trouble. He was the youngest. There were fourteen of us. Can you imagine? Danny was the strongest and Din the shrewdest, but they called me the wildest one!" She laughs.

"Your father used to call this house our Malnahone," she says, "He thought we should give it a name, but somehow we never did. So many things we meant to do. Sometimes I feel like we just got here."

A chair scrapes as someone gets up.

"Can you imagine living with someone in a place for 52 years and then having to get used to everything all over again? Jack, do you remember the time you and Frances took me to Saint Raymond's to Pop's grave?"

"Yes."

"You and Frances had already split up then, hadn't you?"

"Yes, Mom. I'm sorry."

"You don't have to be sorry to me, Jack. How come I'm always the last one to hear anything around here?"

"We didn't want to upset you. I knew how much you care for her." A pause. "I didn't stay at his funeral. I didn't go to the cemetery."

"That was a strange day, Jack, when we buried him. It was sunny, but it was chilly. The hedges and plants had all just been cut back for winter; they looked like bare arms, reaching up. Everyone was there, but I felt so much by myself. I felt so calm, so...nothing. Like I didn't believe it. Do you think that's terrible?"

"No, that's how I felt. But more...I don't know. Relieved. Do you think that's terrible?"

"No. But then that day Frances and you took me out to the cemetery, that was our secret trip, we didn't tell anyone. And you seemed so happy, I thought, the two of you. And on the way back, you were telling your stories about Pop, and Frances and I were laughing so hard we couldn't breathe. It didn't seem like a bad thing, to be thinking about him, about the happier times, and laughing. That's when I finally missed him. And I remember I was sitting in the middle between the two of you and Frances smelled just like my garden does after it rains. You are both such lovely children. I thought you were going to be happy forever."

There is a pause. "You're not going to leave us, are you, Jack?"

There is another silence, then, "Now what would make you worry about that?"

"It's like your father...I see it in you sometimes, Jack. Don't forget to look around you here, Jack. He always thought there was a better world someplace else. And he just got mad when he never got there."

"Oh, don't worry, Mom. I'm not that complicated. Hey, maybe we'll all be happy forever yet. Nothing's final in this life, as long as we're all still here together. Right? It'll be okay. Now we should turn in. Tomorrow could be a big day."

Both chairs scrape and I move quietly up the stairs. I climb under the covers and keep one eye half open. They both peek in.

Jack is right. Tomorrow might be a big day. Jack is around and we are going to do something together. I lay in bed and wait for sleep, listening to the house settle down around me. I feel happy for the first time in a while, with them around me and the comfort of the things they'd said to each other.

The next morning, as I run down the stairs, I see Nanny through the open front porch door, standing there looking down the block with an oddly startled look on her face. She holds a piece of paper in her left hand. As I open the door, she turns and sees me and in an instant wipes the expression from her face. She smiles, although something in her eyes remains far away. And I know, without knowing why, that Jack is gone, that he has disappeared like everything else in this life. I step forward, feeling like my dreams when I'm falling, falling, falling out of the sky, watching for someone to catch me. But I take her hand and smile my best smile and say, "So what should we do today, Nanny? Today's a big day."

CHAPTER NINE
James
October 2008

I am on the *Daybreak*, out on the ocean alone. I have stayed out of sight of shore the whole night, but still unable to escape my anger and sorrow over Angela. Now I am coming back on a morning that has a strange feeling to it. The wind is blowing in strong gusts from every different direction; cloud cover is low and moving fast. The water is rough, ten foot waves breaking at angles to each other. I push the boat in at top speed. I look over my shoulder and see an enormous black cloud rolling down the horizon, filling the sky in front of it. It is going to be a squall, as big and nasty as the one that blew Seamus away. There is a shoreline to run to, somewhere near Atlantic Highlands, I could make a run for a small harbor that I know there. I look at the sky; feel the rain start to splatter against my face.

I remember the storm on the day that Seamus drowned. I was on the *Mrs. Pearl*, but probably no more than two miles from where the *Daybreak* was. I look down from the helm and I can picture Seamus down there on the deck. Once again, I imagine I was there, like I should have been, and I try to measure if I could have gotten down there in time to get them into the cabin and safety. I wasn't really that concerned when I was on the *Pearl* at the time. The storm didn't seem that bad. They were both experienced deckhands who knew their way around a boat better than the people we hired. Jack not as much as Seamus. Shay could have sailed this thing right through the storm. I wasn't worried about him; I was more worried about Jack.

But that was a long time ago. Now the wind is blowing hard and it is time to make a decision. "Fuck it," I say to myself, and I turn the boat away from the shore and right into the teeth of the storm. This makes little sense, to choose to ride this storm out when there is safe harbor within reach, but I do it anyway. The waves start increasing in size instantly, huge whitecaps blowing off the top of waves that are now fifteen, twenty feet. The boat pitches wildly to either side as it rides up the side of one wave and down the other. I am drenched. I can barely see through the wind and the piercing rain. I hold on to the wheel as hard as I can and ride it out for an hour. I look back and watch the waves crash over the stern, submerging the entire boat at times.

I think my father blamed me partially for Seamus drowning. He never said so, not to me or to anyone else that I am aware of. But I know his feelings on who is responsible for what happens on a boat at sea. I should have been the captain that day, I was the eldest, but I chose not to go and I think he blames me for that.

Jack blames himself; he has a way of punishing himself. But he shouldn't; I've told him that. How could he? I'm sure it happened so fast, he says he didn't even see Seamus go overboard. I try not to blame myself; I know that there really isn't anything that could have been done. But I still feel responsible in some way.

I sometimes hate the way I am perceived in this family. All the rest of them imagine they are these tortured souls and I am this stolid, pragmatic person with no emotions. What the hell do they know? I am every bit the dreamer of Jack or even my wife. But no one has left me the time to daydream; I have been expected to carry the weight since I was a teenager.

I have these dreams, almost every night. Dreams in which my family float in and out like wraiths, cursed and haunted. I see Seamus and Catherine and Pop. The dead. I am usually sitting at a bar, with Roger working as bartender. Roger was this old deckhand I had who worked for me for years. He kept showing up drunk and I had to fire him. One night he wandered into traffic on Route 95 and was killed by a car. Another lost soul, another one washed out to sea. Anyway, he's the bartender and he's none too happy. He's slopping whiskey into shot glasses and I'm throwing them down. Seamus and Pop don't stay, I follow them to the door and they just float away. Catherine sits with me and asks me if I'm taking care of Patrick. Yes, Katie, I say. I am. But then she snarls, liar, you're a liar. I can't trust him with you. You don't want him. Look what you did to Seamus. And she floats away. Then Jack and Angela appear, hand in hand, laughing about something that will never be explained to me.

I think this qualifies as a nightmare. The dream won't go away. I wake up uneasy, nervous, and regretful. Fearful. I work strenuously to create an appearance of fearlessness. My family depends on me to be strong. But I don't feel that way.

I turn the boat away from the wind. The storm has become unmanageable, I cannot fight it. I run the boat in front of the weather, riding the waves as they come up behind me. The wind and rain flattens my hood around my face. The wind is howling. I am gripping the wheel with both hands, holding my course for dear life. As always during these moments, I think of Angela.

When I walk down the street next to Angela, I see men look at her with frank admiration, well-dressed, successful men. I don't understand how I can compete with them, with my hands reeking of fish and my muddy boots. Of course, they don't know her. She's a hell of a lot more than they can handle. She's more complicated then they'll ever know, a drunk who broke my heart, an unreliable vision. She is so beautiful that still I feel the blood rush to my head when she walks up to me. But it's all a mirage.

She says she's changing; she's not a drunk any longer. So she says. She told me everything that had happened to us for the past five years was a lie, a drunk lie. She told me that she kissed my brother in a drunken stupor. And I just accepted that and told her it was going to be okay and told her I believed her when she said she'd stop. Because she was crying and clearly heartbroken and that's the way I'm supposed to be. But I don't know if I'll ever believe her again. She says the kiss was nothing, but what really lies behind it? Will she really be able to stop drinking? Those are crushing doubts. I had so much hope placed in her. That hope is scattered to the wind and I don't know what will remain when this storm passes.

As for her, she remains by my side for reasons that cannot be understood, because I don't understand what attracted her to me in the first place. But will she wake up one day and come to her senses? That's the real fear, that the marriage I imagined we had was a dream, a pleasant, passing dream, and that we are waking up to a more believable but terrible reality.

Years ago, two weeks before Seamus drowned, our entire family, all seven of us, went out to dinner at Lou and Earnie's, Seamus's favorite pizza place on Waterbury. It was a late birthday party, his birthday had been two weeks before, but Pop had been out fishing the whole prior week on a charter that paid especially well. So there we were, Catherine next to Michael, who she guarded like a hawk from his mean older brothers, Seamus next to Pop, me and Jack sandwiched around Mom, who actually hung on to our shoulders after we sat down, as if without her gravity we would just lift up and fly through the roof.

"Mom, loosen up a little, will you, my shoulder stings," Jack said with a smile.

She put her hands nervously in her lap. We all watched each other warily. There were certain friendships here, couples between whom peace could be expected to remain. But there were combustible combinations here as well. There hadn't been any screaming arguments in the planning or execution of this evening, so it was not certain what was likely to happen.

"A toast to Shay," Catherine suddenly said.

"Yay, Shay!" blurted Michael. At ten, he was four years younger than Seamus and adored him, adored his humor and reckless spirit. Seamus high-fived Michael across the table.

We all nodded and raised our glasses. My mother started singing in a curiously tentative, tremulous voice: "Happy birthday to you…" We all joined in, roaring the words out by the end, then pounding the table as we chanted, "are you one, are you two…"

"Make a wish!" yelled Michael.

"Make a wish?" Jack said with a laugh, "We don't even have a cake yet."

"We don't even have a waiter yet," I said, looking over my shoulder.

"Grumpy, grumpy James!" Michael yelled. Everyone laughed, including me. Michael looked elated. He tried it again, "Grumpy James! Make a wish for James, Shay!"

Seamus looked at me and smiled. "Oh that's easy," he said with a sly smile, "I wish for James to meet a girl."

"That's not happening until James learns to smile," Catherine said dryly.

"I know how to smile," I said.

"I know what's going to happen to you, James," Catherine said, leaning forward with her usually intensity, "You're going to meet some beautiful girl who will absolutely flip for you and all she'll want is for you to open up and you will be so muleheaded about being a tough guy that you won't do it."

She looked across the table at me intently. "But I'm going to <u>make</u> you do it."

"Can we just back up for a second?" Jack said, stuffing some recently arrived garlic bread in his mouth, "This part about a beautiful girl flipping for James, now exactly how is that supposed to happen?" He winked across the table at Michael, who laughed.

"That could happen," Mom said.

"Mom," Jack said, "I know he's your son, but come on." He leaned over and smiled at me, trying to disarm everyone. But there was an edge to his look.

"Catie's right," Seamus said, nodding, "it'll happen."

"Why?" Jack demanded, "What do you know about girls, anyway, you're fourteen."

"He knows about Annabel Sorrentino," Catherine said, with raised eyebrows.

"Look at him blush!" Jack yelped.

"I'll tell you why Catie's right about James," Seamus said, "because he'll take care of that girl, whoever she is." He looked at me steadily, "Just like he takes care of us, without asking any questions, without making us change the way we are, just because he's James."

Jack rolled his eyes and looked at Pop, who sat impassively. "Pop, can I have a beer? I'm almost sixteen; I need a beer to get through this."

"Quiet, Jack," he said gruffly, "let them dream. There's no harm in dreaming."

"Dreams?" Jack sneered, "Dreams are nothing. If you don't live in the real world you might as well be dead."

"Jack!" Seamus said in amused alarm, "You have to dream, don't you? How could you stand all the terrible things that happen otherwise?" He looked around the table. We were all, for once, silent.

We are all dreamers in this family. But there is harm in it, dreams can tear you apart. Dreams can break your heart. I run the *Daybreak* out by myself sometimes now. I'll tell Patrick to stay home and I'll take her out myself. The old-timers tell me I'm crazy, you need a mate, what if something happened out there? But I like it alone. Sometimes, recently, when things have gotten colder between Angela and me, I've taken the boat straight out to sea and slept on her overnight. I do this in bad weather, when there are no charters to be had. It is possible to lose yourself completely in a dream world while at the helm in the open sea, especially at night. The engine and the rush of the water are hypnotic. I daydream about Seamus and Catherine, imagine what our lives might have been like together. I think about sitting down and having a conversation with my father where I just tell him what I think. I imagine a world where Angela reveals herself to me and solves all of her mysteries; where she somehow, in a way not possible even in a dream, explains everything so that I believe she loves only me.

Now the *Daybreak* breaks over a cresting wave and comes back to the water with a crashing rattle that shakes my legs. I pull off my hood and look around me. The wind has slowed slightly and there are streaks of light in the dark gray cloud cover. The storm is subsiding, although you wouldn't know it unless you'd been through many of them. I set the wheel on a course and walk back and sit in the stern. Looking out over the wake of the boat, there is nothing but miles and miles of rolling waves, whitecaps blowing off the tops like feathers. I walk into the cabin and pull out a bottle of Glenfiddich. My father always liked to carry a nice bottle of scotch for bad weather. I sit in the stern again and take a long pull and then another. It warms me all the way down, very pleasantly.

I start to cry and I cannot stop. This has happened to me recently out on the water by myself, this feeling of terrible loss and hopelessness and anger. Jesus Christ, what the hell is wrong with me? If Pop could see me, blubbering on the deck of his boat, he would just explode. Well, fuck him anyway. Fuck everybody, Angela and Jack and these goddamn dreams. I test my voice by saying their names, Seamus, Catherine, Pop, Angela. My voice comes out dry and raspy. There must be some kind of ending, some kind of goodbye, but that isn't going to happen. The dead are always out here, waiting for me in the clouds and the waves whenever I go to sea. And the living wait on land and haunt me just as much.

I think of the first time I brought Angela home to the Bronx, five years ago at Christmas. Pop was still living at home. Everyone was at the house when we walked in: Mom and Pop, Mike and Ann with the first baby, Catherine and Patrick. Before introductions were even over Jack came sweeping in with bags of presents. Michael and Patrick looked out the window to admire Jack's BMW sedan.

"Big bonus at Dean Witter this year, folks," he announced with a wink to Angela, "It's a Merry Christmas!"

He had a diamond necklace for Mom and expensive earrings for Catherine and Ann. Ann was visibly pleased, she adored Jack. He had special deep sea fishing rods for Pop and me, models I'd seen in West Marine that cost hundreds of dollars. I was bothered by the fact that I was thrilled to get it. And for the grand finale, for Patrick there was a new pair of skis. Patrick had just joined his school ski club. Patrick hugged Jack and there was no mistaking the real bond between the two of them.

Then Jack walked over to Angela and held out his hand, saying "I'm sorry for the spectacle, I just love Christmas. It's nice to meet you, I'm afraid I don't have a present for you."

He put a hand on my shoulder and said with a big smile, "But you've got James, so you probably don't need anything else."

She smiled warmly and shook his hand. I could tell she believed him, but I wasn't sure, I was always looking for a trace of sarcasm in

Jack's occasional compliments to me. There was always an edge between us. And I could not put my finger on it, but there was a connection right then between the two of them and I would never be comfortable with them together.

But that was a long time ago and many things have changed. I steer the boat through calm waters into Lower New York Bay, then underneath the Verrazano Bridge. I find myself reflexively looking behind me at the Bridge's span, framing a clearing sky and sparkling deep blue water. My constant invitation to leave the dreary world of the landlocked. I head into Upper Bay and up the East River to home. As I cruise into the harbor at City Island, I see a figure standing at the end of a pier. It is Angela. Recognizing her gives me an electric jolt of excitement, anger, sorrow, longing. She starts waving at me wildly, jumping up and down. I can hear bits of her voice carrying over the water, "James! James! Are you alright?"

I wave back. Part of me wishes I could just turn the boat around and go back out. Part of me feels a little foolish for having worried her so. Part of me cannot wait to get closer to her. She runs down the dock along the boat as I make the turn, still waving madly. I feel like waving back, just as madly, but I cannot let go, I cannot open up to her.

"Did you hit that storm?" she calls, "Are you okay?"

I give her thumbs up. "No problem," I yell.

She looks at me, now twenty-five feet away, with an anxious look still on her face.

"I'm fine," I call to her.

"You better be," she says, offering up a tentative smile.

She grabs a line that I toss to her from the boat, expertly tying it to the dock. "Don't you go sailing off without me, James MacAfee," she says seriously.

"Where else would I go?" I shrug and look away.

She stands up and looks at me steadily, only five feet away, but still separated from me by water. She holds a line in both hands.

"James?" she says, with the softest questioning in her voice. "You will be careful out there, won't you?"

"Oh, hell," I say and I cough to mask the slight break in my voice, "Nothing's going to happen to me. I couldn't drown out there if I tried; I'd just pop back up like an old lobster buoy."

I look at her and I cannot help it, I say, "Little late to start worrying about me, isn't it?"

She grimaces and nods. "Yeah, sometimes I think maybe it is too late. I think that all the time."

She offers up another smile. "Coming home? I can make some dinner."

The evening has become silent and cool after the storm, the silvery blue sky fading to sunset. Gulls call over the bait shop and a distant outboard motor hums. Her voice and her question hang in the air.

I hesitate for a moment. "Sure, why not?" I stand up straight and offer a salute.

She drops the line and holds out her hand. I take it and I cautiously, gratefully step on shore.

CHAPTER TEN

Patrick
October 2008

It is only when Jack disappears that I actually realize how much I had counted on him. I counted on him to fill in the spaces in my life. To give me a normal life. Now that he is gone, what am I going to do?

I daydream about having a normal life. Like other kids, a mom and a dad and sisters and a dog. But my night dreams are different. When I hear people talk about their dreams, they always go to imaginary places that are lovely, strange or frightening. That's not how I dream. In my dreams I always travel to the same place, over and over, to revisit a real day in my life exactly as it happened. On a chilly spring day three years ago, my cousin Robert appeared at the door of my math class. He was my dad's sister's son, a college student. He was dressed in a suit and looked like someone else's father. After a whispered exchange with Sister Joan, she motioned for me to come to the front. I approached carefully, certain that my family had conspired with the Sister for something dreadful. Robert was never nice to me and I could not imagine what he was doing here. But as I approached, she looked at me with the strangest forced smile and then she reached out and squeezed my shoulder.

"You must go home with your cousin, Patrick. I'm sorry."

Sorry? I moved out the door quickly, before she came to her senses.

"What's up, Robert?" I asked excitedly in the hallway.

And he, too, passed completely out of character, putting his arm around my shoulder and walking me slowly to the door of the school. He let out a deep sigh.

"I don't know how to tell you this, Patrick." He stopped and faced me. With a firm set to his jaw, he lifted his arms, placed both hands on my shoulders and looked me in the eye, cocking his head oddly to one side.

"Your Mom is dead. She was in a car accident." His eyes became moist and his voice shook a little. He watched me and waited.

"Huh?" I said. I repeated the words to myself: Mom is dead. Mom is dead. I suddenly couldn't even picture what she looked like. I was lost. I stared at Robert and for a moment I felt a wave of something not quite recognizable, but what I guessed was my hatred for him. To have to share this, go through this, with him and everyone else, who all felt so distant. And what was it I was supposed to feel? No one had told me about these things. I broke away from Robert and ran out the door, outside into the cold and down the road, my breath following me in tiny clouds.

Eventually, I did go home. I knew that sooner or later I'd have to go there. Robert and his mom and dad were there, waiting for Uncle James and Angela and everyone else. Someone said Angela had been able to see my mom before she died, but no one else had, there hadn't been time. They were all crying and hanging on to each other. It didn't seem right to me, like that could be how everyone really felt. I didn't think my mom and I ever got along very well, or showed any real feeling for each other, except when we got mad. I couldn't imagine where this deep grief came from and I didn't trust it. Or maybe I just didn't understand why I didn't feel the same way. I understood that I should feel terrible, but I didn't. Ever since that moment when Robert had told me, I had waited for a wave of grief, sorrow, anger, something. But inside I was as calm and flat as a summer sea. There was only something that I recognized, with some shame, to be relief.

Everyone watched me and asked how I was feeling. I couldn't think of what to say. I think they mistook my lack of reaction for shock. After a while, I went to the only place I felt safe, to see the one person who couldn't stand her. I went to see Pop. I asked Jack if he could drive me to Atlantic Beach, where Pop lived. We hardly spoke the whole way there. Jack was distraught and I did not know what to say to him; he loved my mom and I was always angry at her. He said he was going for a walk on the beach when we got to Pop's.

Pop lived in a house on a hill by the ocean. This is the house he moved to after Nanny asked him to leave. The house was gray, tall and narrow, and clung to the edge of a bluff, high over the whole world. As I walked the broken pavement that wound up the hill, the ocean spread out below me to the right. There was no beach, just rocks tumbling down to exploding surf. On the left the road was bordered by a stand of permanently bare trees, dead from an ancient blight. The air was sharp and salty and there was always a wind. Many days, winter and summer, it was sunny and both sea and sky were bright blue. But some days a storm would sweep up angrily over the plain of the ocean, spitting rain or sleet, shoving the white capped ocean in front of it into the shore.

It occurred to me as I walked up the hill that I would have to tell Pop that she had died. I daydreamed as I walked, imagining the attention and sympathy of people at school when they found out what had happened.

It had turned into a rough day, the ocean so incensed, so raucous that it was hard to tell where the spray and surf ended and the body of the sea began. The dead trees bent before the wind, groaning sadly. An occasional seagull flew by, blown wildly before the wind, as if tossed to the horizon.

Pop stood at the door, waiting for me as I struggled up the hill. He could see down the road from the kitchen window and always came out to greet, or confront, a visitor. He did not like to be surprised. He was dressed, as always, like a working fisherman. His short was torn, his boots frayed. But the combination of what he wore would keep him dry in a gale. He knew that with a certainty.

"You're just in time, boy," he called to me, "I was just about to catch dinner. Maybe I'll let you try."

We walked down the long wooden stairway to the dock that he had built on the rocks. As we walked, he rested his hand lightly on my shoulder. I couldn't remember so many people touching me in one day. We sat on the metal bench that was set on the end of the dock. I always called this our spot and that was one of the few things I knew that could occasionally make him smile.

The spray of the surf washed over us. Even though I was quickly soaked and cold, it felt delicious. I licked the salt off my face. I knew that we would sit in silence for as long as I wanted. I started all of our conversations. The sea wind washed my thoughts clean, swept away all the debris, down to what was in my heart and mind and would not leave.

We fished in silence for some time. Pop got up eventually and walked to the water's edge. I called loudly to him over the surf and the wind, "Pop?"

He turned to look at me.

"Mom died," I said. I didn't know how else to say it.

"I know," he said, walking back towards me. I couldn't hear his voice, but I could read the meaning in his face.

"I was coming to tell you," I said, "I didn't think you knew."

He stood in front of me. "Policeman came by this morning. Friend of mine. Thought he was doing me a favor."

There was something in his voice, a slight tremor that made me feel uneasy. I felt unanchored all at once, as if the dock was floating out to open sea, out of sight of shore.

He sat down next to me and leaned in close, so that I could hear him. His voice hung in the air, a tiny, raspy whisper.

"Patrick, I've said some harsh things about your mother. Now you forget them, you hear?"

I shook my head. No, that wasn't right. I felt betrayed.

"Pop, it's not our fault she's dead. You said you didn't have to love a person just because you're related to her. What about all the things we talked about, about her?"

"That was all...nothing. It meant nothing. You forget about all that. You listen to me now."

"But what you said about her, you meant those things, I know you did. I know you."

"You listen to me, boy!" He slammed the rod on to the deck, kicking it away angrily. "You have no idea what I meant and what I know. I never told you a single blessed thing about love or anything like it, because I don't know a goddamn thing about it!"

He gripped my shoulder and looked at me, hard, closer than I remember him having done before. "Don't even begin to base what you believe on what I say," he said, his voice lowering, "or what any other one person says. There's too much to understand to believe in one person, except yourself. You have to measure things by looking at them from every side. You have to figure things out for yourself, and it's not always clear. I made some bad, bad decisions, Patrick. Don't you repeat them."

But I didn't understand. I didn't know what his words meant. I didn't understand the fear in his usually hard eyes, the catch in his voice.

"Think kindly of your mother, boy. I let you dislike her because it was convenient. But never mind her temper, she deserved better. Better than the father she had, that's for sure. You go back to your family and mourn her, and hope that someday someone does the same for me."

He stood stiffly and picked up his rod. He walked to the edge and cast a line out roughly to sea. He said aloud, more to himself, "I always thought I'd be the one dying first and she'd be the one to feel this."

I timidly said to him, "Pop?" But he ignored me, staring straight out to sea. There were questions that would bring out the answers I wanted, but I could not think of their words.

I walked back up the dock on unsteady legs and climbed the steps to the house. I stood over the ocean and saw him, a tiny figure at the end of the pier. He cast his line out, over and over again into the sea, much more than he had to. I turned to walk down the hill to our house, then I turned to walk back to him. I stopped and sat on the top step.

I had thought that I was right and she was wrong, and that someday things would be evened out, somehow. I had counted on Pop for that. Now there was nothing. She wasn't wrong; she was just dead, gone. And I would never see her again to see what might have happened. I looked out over the broad expanse of wild ocean. I though of what Pop had said, about being caught unprepared at sea, and the shock of realizing you might never reach land.

I stood, feeling as if I should cry, but I had never done it. I looked to the dock and saw Grandpa standing, holding his head in both hands, like she used to, and bending to the wind like the dead trees.

That's what happened when my mom died; that's what I dream about over and over. And now Jack is gone, too. Not dead, but gone in a way that showed he meant to leave us behind.

With him gone, Nanny and I are left sort of stunned. After that, we do not talk about Jack leaving. We both try to be cheerful to each other, but I know that the vacant sorrow I see in her eyes is what she is seeing in mine. When I go to bed at night, I leave her sitting at the empty kitchen table. I kiss her on the top of the head and she squeezes my hand. I look back from the stairs and she sits looking down the hall, not moving for I don't know how long.

I walk through the days in a fog, thinking about the ghosts in my life. My Mom died and I always feel bad about not feeling bad enough about that. My Father lives down south somewhere. I never hear from him. Pop is dead. I miss him. But there was always Jack. Jack was always so cool, so fun. He could really listen to me. I used to daydream he was my Dad. He told me and he told Nanny that he'd be here forever. And I thought things would be okay for us because of that.

From the moment Jack left all I can think is I have to go get him back. I have never thought about anything so strongly in my life. I will rescue him, and everyone, dead and alive, will see me as someone special.

Just a week or so after he leaves, Jack sends me a postcard from Chicago. All it says is:

"Heading west, Patty. Maybe Denver or maybe I'll just keep going. I expect some people are not going to understand (Especially you-- you're the least likely candidate to run from anything). I'm going to have to turn & face that someday, I suppose. I don't expect you to understand. I'll explain it all to you someday. I promise. Jack.

p.s. I thought of you, of all of us, when I saw this card. I found it in an Irish book store."

The card is a picture of a medieval manuscript page, with a black and white drawing of a fisherman in a small boat, over the words: "Muir Speir is Fuil". I carry the card around with me. I ask Don Connally what the words mean. Don is one of Uncle James' occasional first mates on the Daybreak. He still speaks Gaelic. He says it means "Sea, Sky and Blood".

One afternoon a month later I call information in Denver. The operator has a listing for a John Padraic MacAfee. I walk around for a few days with the phone number in my pocket, afraid to call for some reason. Then one night I call and a woman answers.

"Is Jack there?" I ask, almost whispering.

"Yes, Jack MacAfee lives here," she says. She sounds nervous, even afraid. "Who's calling?"

"I think I have the wrong number," I say, "I'm sorry."

I hang up and sat and look at the phone for ten minutes.

Nanny and I live quietly side by side after Jack leaves. I get up every morning and eat breakfast with her, then walk down the block to get the bus to school. We never mention Jack. I think of talking about him five hundred times, but I hold back. There is something about her that worries me, a deep, tired sadness that I see when she sits in her chair and looks out the window. When my Grandfather died she had been shocked, but you could see her gather her strength and move on. Now she floats through the house like a ghost, silent and untouchable. The voice I had heard as I hid on the stairs when she was talking to Jack that last night, a voice light and happy as a girl, that voice is gone.

I decide that I have to follow him out west, that I need to see him if I am going to try to find out what has happened to him. I think I might scare him off if I tell him I am coming. I need to bring him home to Nanny. They need each other, I can see that.

And so one day I take the subway to the Port Authority, carrying a backpack and a transistor radio. I have $398, the money Nanny has given me and some money I have earned babysitting the next door neighbor's three year old over the past year. I buy a ticket to Denver and get on a bus. No one asks me why I am travelling alone. I am pretty tall and can pass for 14. I am very, very nervous, with the stomach ache I get whenever I get nervous, like for a big test or when I have to talk to a girl.

The bus pulls out of the terminal and into a gray day. We head west. As we drive down the overpass leading from the Port Authority, I look down on Eighth Avenue, on hundreds of cars and trucks and people streaming every which way. It looks like one of those science fiction movies I watch in the middle of the night after Nanny goes to sleep when the giant monster is invading the City. I suddenly think about what I am doing and feel so frightened that I almost scream at the driver to stop the bus. I grab my head and press it down against my knees and say over and over to myself, like two people talking back and forth, "This is crazy. I have to do this. This is crazy. I have to do this." I sit back and close my eyes as we plunge into the Lincoln Tunnel and I think this is what people feel like on a plane when it points straight down and they know they're going to crash. I have to do this. I have to do this.

Time passes, minute by minute, and I settle down a little. That's what my Grandfather used to say to me all the time, "settle down, boy, settle down." I have all these voices in my head telling me what to do: my Mom, Pop, my Father, Jack, Angela, my teachers. I've heard them all argue with each other about me. I don't know who to listen to and sometimes I just close my eyes and try to listen for my own voice. I'll stop and say, as calmly as I can: "What do you want me to do, Patrick?" I am waiting for an answer.

But this time the voices all seem to say the same thing. Take it easy. So I try. I spend my time listening to whatever I can find on my radio. Everything sounds lonely on the highway. It rains most of the way, the bus moving endlessly on a straight, shiny, slick road through crowded suburbs that through the hours turned to bare fields. I try to sleep but can't. I become very uncomfortable as the night wears on, getting more and more antsy. The bus stops for gas in Bucks County, Pennsylvania. The gas station was on the only hill we'd seen for miles, a brightly lit oasis in the early evening in the middle of this huge, dark ocean of fields.

I decide at that moment to get off and try a different way of getting there. I just can not stand another minute on that bus. I figure Pennsylvania is a safe place, you never hear of people getting mugged or anything there. I have this idea I will hitchhike, but first I really, really want to sleep in a bed.

Right next to the gas station is a small motel called the Lancaster Inn. In the lobby, a young couple waits nervously for the manager to give them a key. They can't be more than a few years older than me, and they both look really scared. I don't know why they should be scared, they have each other and so many people don't have anybody. I wait until they leave, then I tell the manager a story so he'll let me stay. I tell him that I am meeting my mom in the morning. That I had come to visit from my dad's and that she is driving down from the country to pick me up. I tell him that she will call in a little while to make sure I am okay. He smiles and says, "Well, son, we'll take care of you for your mom." I am getting good at making up these stories. I am making up a life for myself.

I think for a moment about what it would be like if my Mom really was coming to meet me. Then I feel what I always feel when I wander into that part of my mind, this suddenly breathless empty feeling like I just stepped into a hole. I don't know why I talk about her like she's alive. My Mom is dead. She follows me around and I guess she always will, like a life I'm not going to get to live. I feel very strange, lying in a dimly lit motel room in a state I'd never been to before, all of those feelings about her dying suddenly washing over me again, this desperate feeling that you are all by yourself and that all of your life is contained within something you can't control. But then I think of Jack, disappeared, and how I am going to bring him back to HIS mother and make everything better. I turn on the television, but then turn it off. I feel a little better with the room quiet. I turn off the lights and watch the lights from passing cars reflect off the ceiling. I imagine each light floating by is a ghost, first my Grandfather, then my mother, then Jack. Jack isn't dead, but I am beginning to feel like he is a ghost, someone I have only imagined.

I fall asleep and dream of my Mom, dying again. I wake up with a jolt, sweating even though I have kicked the sheets off. I suddenly realize that I need to go home.

But where is home and how would I get there? I fall back asleep. I feel the beginning of a dream, the one I always have. But no, this one was different. In this one, my mother is coming for me. I am sitting on a beach on a brilliant day. She is walking towards me, shielding her eyes, her light dress flowing around her in the ocean breeze. She is smiling. She says, "Hey, Pat," in a sing song voice. I stood up and took her hand. But when I wake up, she is gone and all I can think of is how that never, ever happened.

I look at the clock by the bed. 5:25. I get dressed and sit by the window. I know James would head to his boat at 6:30. I wait until 6:35, then I cannot wait another moment. I call, desperately hoping to hear Angela's voice.

"Hello?" Soft, sleepy, melodic.

"Angela?"

"Pat, hey. Everything okay?"

"No, not really. I ran away, Angela."

"Oh, God, Patty." A pause. I hear a deep breath. "Okay," now her voice was cheery and sweet, "Okay, you crazy teenager. Where are you?"

"Pennsylvania."

"Wow." I hear the slightest sound in the backround. The swoosh of a match lighting. Another deep breath in and out. "Pennsylvania! Well, could be worse. Tell me where, love, I'm on my way."

"You shouldn't smoke, Angela."

"Hey, who's rescuing who here?"

"I don't want anything bad to happen to you."

"Okay, I'll put it out. I'm leaving, Pat, I just need to get some money. You're right off 80, right?"

I hear rustling in the backround. A coat being put on.

"Pat, why did you run away?"

"I wanted to bring Jack back. Nanny can't stand it."

"We'll take care of Nanny. You have to let Jack go. For now."

"I don't know if I can do that. I had to say goodbye to Mom and Pop. I don't want to do that again."

"I know, honey. I know. It'll be okay, it will. I'm on my way. Go to the coffee shop and have breakfast. I'll be there in 3 hours."

I sit in the coffee shop. I cannot eat. I drink a milk shake and stare nervously out the window. I can see the highway in the distance. I watch the entranceway to the parking lot. If this was one of my dreams, she wouldn't come at all. I'd sit here until dark, surrounded inside by empty booths and outside by endless, deserted fields. In my dream world I am always alone.

Newspaper and cups blow across the lot. It looks like the end of the world. At ten o'clock, three hours later, no one has come. I start to feel sick to my stomach.

She isn't coming; why would anyone come for me?

A beaten up pickup truck pulls into the lot and a man in a rain coat steps out. He spots me through the window as he walks towards the building and waves. He is the manager from the night before. He walks in.

"Hey, fella, your mom didn't come yet?" He walks behind the counter and pours himself a cup of coffee. He sits down across from me in my booth. He looks older in the daylight. He wears glasses and his hair is thinning, he has it brushed over the top from the side. He is thin and his skin looks worn.

"Not yet," I say, "she must be running late." I play nervously with my milkshake glass.

"She *is* coming, though, right?"

"Oh, sure. Yes." I nod firmly. I look at him and see, to my surprise, a glimmer of concern or sympathy or something in his eyes. I sit back against bench seat.

"It's not my mom," I say quietly. "Someone else is coming." I look at the manager, who nods slightly, as if he knows what I am going to say.

"My mom is dead," I say.

"I wondered what was going on with you, son. You looked lost. I came back early to see if you were still around. You run away?"

I nod.

"Who is coming to get you?"

"Angela. She's my aunt. I might stay with them. Only my Uncle James might not want me to."

"Why not?"

"I don't know," I look out the window and shrug. "I just get the impression I get on his nerves. He's very organized and knows what he wants and he's a fisherman and I never feel like I know what I'm doing when I'm out there with him."

"Where were you heading last night?"

"My Uncle Jack, my other uncle, ran away and I was going out after him. My grandmother is really sad he took off. I thought I could bring him back."

The manager looks into his cup of coffee and smiles slightly.

"So why's your aunt coming out if your uncle doesn't want you?"

"She's like that. She's special. She could rescue anyone."

"She didn't rescue your uncle who ran away, did she?"

"Well, no, but that's different."

"Maybe, maybe not. You going to stay with them?"

"I'd like to do that. But I don't know if my Uncle James wants me to."

"Look, son, you seem like a good kid. I'm guessing your uncle who took off is going to do what he's going to do and there's no one who's going to make him do different. And I'm guessing your aunt's coming out here because she cares about you. And as for your other uncle, well you can't change who you are just for him. The way I see it, you gotta rescue yourself before you can rescue anybody else. And if your aunt wants to help, I'd grab that chance and not worry about your other uncle. You know what I mean?" He smiles.

"I never had kids or a wife or anything," he says, "I didn't get the chance to give out much advice in my life. But I think you just got to take care of yourself first, you know? How's that advice sound to you?"

I smile at him. "Sounds good," I say.

At 10:30 a Toyota pulls into the lot and a woman jumps out, seemingly before the car has stopped. Her long black hair is blowing up and over her face. But I can see her smile as she spots me through the coffee shop window. I run for the door and nearly jump into her arms.

"Hey, hey, hey, Pat," she whispers, holding my face in her hands to look at me.

"I'm sorry I dragged you all the way out here, Angela."

She looks out into the desolation surrounding us. Low flying clouds slide along the horizon, which is as flat as the ocean but dull green.

"Picked a hell of a place," she says, mussing my hair.

I turn to the manager, who has gotten up.

"Nice to meet you, ma'am," he says, remaining at a distance. "Just keeping an eye on him for you."

Angela looks at him carefully and then smiles warmly, a radiant event on this dreary island. She walks over to him and kisses him on the cheek. "Thank you for looking after Patrick," she says, squeezing his arm.

Even under his leathery skin I can see him blushing. He looks down. He looks at her as if he is about to say something, but then he looks down again. Angela walks back to me.

The manager looks up and says to me, "I bet things are going to be okay for you, son. You're not an old man stuck in the middle of nowhere; you've got a whole life ahead of you. But I was wrong about just looking after youself. You take care of your aunt, too, you hear?" Then he smiles and waves slightly and walks out of the room. There is something indescribably sad about watching him go. I start to cry and rub my eyes furiously to try to make it stop. Angela gently drapes her arm over my shoulders and guides me to the door. We stand in front of the motel and squint into the dusty wind.

"No water in sight," she says, "It feels strange to be so far from the ocean." She takes me by both arms. "You have no business being so far from the water, sailor!"

I cannot think of a word to say.

She looks carefully into my eyes. "Don't run off on me again, Patrick. I need you, you understand?"

I nod yes. Although I do not understand, not really. But it is a wonderful thing to hear.

"C'mon," she says, heading for the car, "let's go home."

CHAPTER ELEVEN

James
November 2008

"Jimmy?"

It is my mother on the phone. Past midnight, well past her normal bedtime. No one calls me Jimmy anymore, but every mother lives in her children's past.

"Mom? You okay?"

"Yes, of course I'm okay, why wouldn't I be okay?"

"Don't get testy. Just asking. It's late."

"You treat me like an old woman. Jack wouldn't ask me a question like that."

"Did you call me at midnight to compare me to Jack? Again?"

A long pause.

"Jimmy, I need you to take Patrick."

"What do you mean, take him? Take him where?"

"Take him to live with you."

"What? Why? He's okay with you. What's wrong, Mom? Look, let me drive over there and we can talk."

"No!" With surprising sharpness. There is another pause. Then, softer, "No, Jimmy. This is going to be tough for me. You know how I feel about him. I'm just going to get all blubbery if you come here now and you know I can't stand that."

"C'mon, Mom. It's okay to show a little emotion."

"Oh, *please*, look who's talking."

"Hey, I show emotion."

She snorts derisively. Then she softens, "James, he needs you. He ran away from me! He'll do it again."

"He was chasing after Jack, he was just confused. He won't do it again."

"It's worse than that, James. He's looking for a mother and a father and he can't find anything like that with me. He was running away from me, too, James. He can't live in my past."

"No, no, Mom. He just needs time. Anyway, he needs a hell of a lot more than I can give him. I can't help him; I've never raised a child. And he drives me crazy; his head is in the clouds. I can't reach him. I've tried. You can do it much better. I know Angela wants to take him, but it's for all the wrong reasons. He's not the baby we can't have, Mom. He'll never replace that. It's just going to break her heart, one day she's going to wake up and realize that he'll never be our son and it will break her heart." My voice is raising and I'm afraid it will crack.

"James!"

I take a deep breath.

"What?" I say heavily. I am suddenly very, very sad.

"Jimmy," and now her voice becomes soft and firm, the voice that sat at the edge of the bed at night a long time ago and convinced me that, somehow, everything was going to be okay.

"Jimmy, I keep calling him Seamus. He's not Seamus. He's haunting me. He needs to move into the future, not get stuck in my past."

"Jimmy, look, I know things are sometimes a little bumpy between us, but... listen to me. I have sprinkled the ashes of two children off the Daybreak. I know all about replacing what you can't have. I want to keep Patrick so badly; I want to feel like I had a chance to finish raising Seamus. Or finish my life with Catherine. Or bring Jack back. I sit in church on Sundays and curse God for stealing my children. I don't care if I go to hell. Curse him. What kind of a God would drown Seamus at 14? Catherine and Seamus should be here alive! Jack should be here, a beautiful, talented boy, he should be here, not drinking himself to death in some faraway place. What kind of a world is this? Sometimes the weight of all this heartache is so much I can't breathe. I could have a child in Patrick. He could be mine. He could become what was taken from me by this horrible world. But James..." She pauses. I hear a sharp intake of breath as she tries to stop herself from crying.

"Yes, Mom?"

"He needs a man, a firm hand. And a young, lively woman to be like a mother. And a table to sit at for breakfast and dinner, a place to tell two grown-ups about the world and have them tell him everything is going to be okay. And Angela needs someone to take care of. You won't let anyone take care of you. You won't let anyone that close.

Don't you know what that does to her? Patrick's not the baby you can't have. He's Patrick, that's all, and he needs you and you two need him. And you're the only ones who can do it. I won't put him in Michael's house. I love Michael, but his wife won't put up with Patrick and I won't let that woman tear him down. I'm sorry, I know that's harsh."

"Mom, I was going to go to West Virginia."

"West Virginia? Why?"

"We think Jack is there."

"Oh, Christ, James, are you out of your goddamn mind?"

"Jesus, when did you start cursing so much?"

"Oh, don't be squeamish; I've lived around fisherman my whole life. Your father was such a prude; I used to curse around the house to keep him on his toes."

"Well, you don't sound like yourself."

"I don't feel like myself. I feel pissed off. Why are you going after Jack?"

"I thought you'd want me to. For Jack."

"No, no, James, we need you here! We have to let Jack figure things out for himself. I want to go get him too, but he'll just run away. It's really hard, but for now I think we have to wait. There are people here who we have to help."

"I don't know if I can do it, Mom."

"Oh, Jesus Christ, James, don't you get weak on me. You're the one person in this family that never went to pieces. And that's not it, anyway. You don't want Patrick, isn't that it? Why don't you want him?"

"That's not true."

"It is so true, Jimmy and you know it!" she yells into the phone.

That is the truth, spoken plainly. And there's no denying it with my mother.

"I don't know, but I don't. He'll come between me and Angela. He'll realize I'm nothing special. He reminds me of Seamus sometimes, which makes me sad. I don't know if he can make Angela happy. It's not what we daydreamed of, a little baby in a stroller."

"You daydreamed of a little baby in a stroller?"

"I daydream about Angie and me being really, really happy. And I know that would do it. But the doctors told us that's a million to one shot. I don't know if I can raise a thirteen year old, Mom, he is so goddamn complicated. I could fail. I could fail him and you and Angela."

"You can do anything, James. Don't you understand why it's come to this? Don't you understand why Angela is with you, that lovely woman? Don't you understand why we all turn to you?Don't you know why Pop gave you that boat, the one thing he truly loved in this world? Don't you know who you are yet?"

"No, Mother, who am I? I thought I was James the fisherman."

"Oh, don't be such a wiseass."

"This family doesn't do philosophical discussions very well, Mom. C'mon."

"Jimmy."

"What?"

"What are you afraid of?"

"More than you know. I don't know what I want, Mom. Okay?"

"Then find out, damn it. Come over and get Patrick in the morning. Please. And don't make me cry when you do it. Let's make it seem like a vacation for him, something temporary."

"It is temporary. I don't think he and I are right for each other. I think..."

"Jimmy!"

"Yes, Mom."

"Do it for me? Just try it? For me?"

I take a deep breath. "Yes, Mom. We'll try it. But Mom?"

"Yes?" Hesitantly, her voice breaking. I know as soon as we hang up she will start crying and she will cry well into the night.

"You have to make me one of your blueberry pies or it's no deal."

She laughs softly. "Okay, Jimmy, you'll get your blueberry pie."

"I'll see you in the morning."

"I love you, Jimmy."

"Okay."

"Okay?"

"I'm John MacAfee's son, Mom, you know I can't answer that out loud."

"Oh, I know. If one of you ever said 'I love you' to me I'd just keel over and meet my maker."

"Don't meet your maker yet, Mom, we still need you."

"Oh, I'm just an old woman."

"We need you."

"Is that how men say 'I love you?' They say I need you?"

"You finally figured us out. Night, Mom"

"Night, love."

After the phone clicks on her end, I sit for a while at the kitchen table, hearing her voice. It suddenly dawns on me that she is an old woman and someday soon she'll be gone. When Pop got the *Daybreak*, I had voted to name it after her. Because she had carried me through all those early storms I had to weather by myself. I pick up the phone and I dial her number.

Her voice is soft, but wide awake and mischievous. "Is there something you want to tell me?"

"You know, you're not the helpless old lady you pretend to be."

"Oh, I know that."

"I love you, Mom."

"I know you do, Jimmy, I know you do. And I need you, too. I'll see you in the morning."

So I lie in bed and wait for sleep. Angela is next to me, her face soft and indescribably lovely at rest. But nothing like rest comes for me, only a crowd of faces, Seamus, Catherine, Patrick, Jack, Pop, Mom. And the last one is Angela, coming over the horizon fast in a beautiful array of clouds that are lit from behind by the setting sun. Lovely, pink and gray clouds towering high into the heavens. What would they bring? A cooling evening breeze or a squall that would blow me clear over? What would this boy Patrick do to my life with Angela, when our marriage was already a voyage that was turning into a tricky crossing?

I finally fall asleep to the sound of rain falling gently against the window, rain with no wind. A comforting sound for a sailor, promising nothing in the morning but still waters.

*   *   *

One day, not long after Patrick arrives, I stand on the *Daybreak* and watch Angela on the dock as we head out to sea, watch her growing smaller and smaller, finally blocked from my view by an incoming night-fishing boat. She stands stiffly against the morning chill, her cup of coffee clutched to her chest. Her long black hair blows up occasionally against her face. She brushes it away slowly, patiently, like she does everything. I am constantly sniping at her for being so damn slow. But then I wake up in the middle of the night and think that's the way she is and why would I change any part of her? In the distance, I think I see her wave, just before she disappears from view. But I am not sure. I feel a kind of sadness every time I leave her, a sadness tinged with a fear that I might never see her again. I don't know why I think these things. That's just stupid. I shake my head and went to work.

We have just had an argument about my going to West Virginia. I have been thinking that I should go to find Jack. How or why I would do that is beyond my ability to explain, I just feel like I have to do it. Patrick got a postcard from him a while ago saying he was heading to Denver. I called information in Denver and there was a Jack MacAfee listed in the phone book. I spoke to a very angry woman on the phone there and she said that she had gotten a card from an address in West Virginia, with a phone number. I called and, to my astonishment, Jack answered. Startled, I hung up without speaking. But then I decided I would go get him. Angela asked me a million questions about the practical aspects of all this, but I could not explain it to her. I decided I would fly to West Virginia and find him and talk to him and beat some sense into him if I had to. I am going to bring him home.

My mother says that I am the only person she ever met in her life who is more stubborn than my father. I didn't agree with her when she said that, but I can see what she means. But that fact is misleading, because we were never, ever alike, my father and me. He was blind to what other people wanted or needed. All he ever thought about was himself. Everyone thought I was the only person who got along with him, but by the time he got sick I had really grown to hate him, for the pain he inflicted on my mother and Catherine. But then he got sick and he changed, little by little. I wanted to let up, to find a way to forgive him. I wanted peace, some kind of peace. I really did. But then he killed himself and we had a different kind of peace, for a very little while. But Catherine was gone by then and she never got to enjoy it. I miss her so much.

"Fuck me!" I hiss to myself, as I slash my finger open on the side of the boat. I grip my right index finger. Blood spurts through my fingers. The cut is deep and the blood splatters my pants. I scramble below and rummage around in a drawer for a bandage. I find one and put it on. Inside the drawer is a notebook with Patrick's name on it. He must have left it here the last time we went out. I pick up the notebook with one hand and flip it open. There are notes written from the top of the page to the bottom. Page after page. I close it, feeling that it is private, and go up top to check my course.

I do not know what to do about Patrick. I don't feel like he and I have ever clicked, I just cannot think of what to talk to him about. He asks a million questions and none of them are on the subject at hand. How the hell should I know who is the happiest person in the world? What a stupid question. I wonder if he pestered Jack like this. He adored Jack, they were like father and son. But what good did that do him? Jack took off on him. I can tell that hurt.

I bring him on the boat to teach him something useful, something that is part of this family's history. I'll give him this much, he doesn't complain about it and doesn't look for ways out of it. At first, while he was on the boat he was pretty worthless. He had no instincts for what to do next to get a job done. I thought he would grow into that, but I doubted it. Then little things started to happen.

One day, we're coming back in a pouring rain and he turns to me and says, "I better stow the new reels, they'll rust."

I hadn't thought of that. So I let him handle the boat for a little bit and he doesn't do too badly. A few days later he very hesitantly suggests a place to stop and fish. I find myself wondering if fishing is in his blood after all.

One day as we were loading the boat he turned to Angela and said, "Why don't you come out with us?"

She never comes out on the boat. When we first started going out she did, but then she stopped. "You're too bossy on the water," she said with a smile. Then she grabbed my arm and said, "I'm just teasing." But she wasn't, not really.

But this time she smiled and said, "Okay!" Which bothered me a little. I wanted her to come, but not just because Patrick asked.

They sat in the stern and talked the whole way out and back, laughing uproariously at times. I started feeling mad, kind of jealous. Then they came up and joined me on the bridge on the way back.

"Patrick says you don't let him drive. You never let me drive, either."

"It's not called driving, Angie, we're on a boat."

"Oh, boat, shmoat. What's the big deal, you just use the wheel to aim it."

"Patrick, you've driven with your aunt, would you let her aim the boat?"

"Well," Patrick said, clearly weighing the impact of his answer, "Sure, I mean, you can't really floor it on a boat, so..."

"What do you mean floor it?" Angela said in mock outrage, "Are you saying I drive too fast?"

"Well," Patrick said seriously, "No. I mean, once I got used to the screeching tires and the bloodcurdling screams of the other motorists, it was fine. I think of it as a free roller coaster ride, like Disneyworld."

I laughed out loud. She made a face at him and smacked him on the arm.

"Take the wheel, Angela," I said.

Her smile disappeared. "For real?"

I nodded.

She hesitantly took the wheel in her hands and stood up very straight to look ahead, smiling proudly. I glanced over at Patrick, who watched her with unabashed fondness.

I think to myself I should get them out here together again. I go downstairs to get a chart and stop, again, over the notebook the boy left behind. I open it to the last page and I do not stop myself, I read it.

My Mom dropped me off at school one day and I never saw her again. I keep coming back to that. She was alive and we were arguing, about how I'll never amount to anything if I don't do my homework. And I slammed the car door and stomped into school, waving like mad over my shoulder at her nagging voice following me up the school walk, finally rising to a shriek, "You listen to me! You must listen to me!" And then my brother came to school two hours later and said she was dead. Now I can't remember what she looked like, I really can't. I know what her pictures look like, but when I close my eyes and try to see her for real, like she's standing in front of me, I can't. She's gone, like she was never here, like I've always been alone. And I get so pissed off, at myself, for treating her so rotten, and at her, for always being so mad, and at everyone else because they all still have each other. I am angry at everyone, at Nanny for putting up with Pop, at Jack for running away, at James for treating me like some useless child he got stuck with. Like James has a clue how I feel, what I think. Like he gives a shit about anything other than his fucking boat. He stands there and looks at me like he just wishes I would go away, drop off the side of the boat and disappear like Pop did. Sometimes I feel like doing that. Except I really don't think it would bother him much. But then sometimes I start thinking differently about it all. I start thinking about what life could have been like, with a little luck. I heard a little boy talking to his mother the other day on the street. "Mommy!" he kept saying. Mommy this and Mommy that. I do love the sound of that word. I say it over and over again to talk myself to sleep sometimes at night. Mommy, Mommy, Mommy.

I stop and think again about that day we were together on the water. On the way back, we saw a breaching whale. Paatrick spotted it first. He yelled, "Whale! Starboard side! Mom, look at that!"

We all pretended he hadn't said mom. But Angela looked at me to take the wheel and took his arm and led him to the side of the boat. The whale breached again, only fifty yards away and they watched it in silence, her hand resting lightly on his shoulder.

I find myself smiling as I remember that. When I get back, I will ask them to come out with me. I look out over the sea. It is overcast, the gray sea and sky blending into nothing at the horizon. A lone seagull followed behind, separated from land and hoping I know where I am going.

I try to think about Jack, about what to say to him. I realize that part of me just hates him and has nothing more to say to him. But another part of me cannot let go. As I listen to the boat's motor and the rush of the water past the sides, I realize that I will go to West Virginia. That I need to find Jack and somehow settle things and and get on with my life. Whatever that is. I push the throttle of the boat back to let it cruise slowly and sit down to read the notebook again. This voice in this notebook is different than anyone else I have known, so openly angry and wishful. I am trying to think of who the voice reminds me of, when I realize that it sounds like me.

I pick up the notebook again and leaf through to the last page. There is a poem written in a scratchy, uncertain hand. There is a stain on the page that looks like oil. It occurs to me that he has written this right here on the boat.

> Cruising home after midnight
> the boat's wake
> is fluorescent green in the lights
> a sparkling trail to the horizon
> leading to a lone star rising
> Wish on a star, James says,
> Fisherman's luck
> I wish for my mother
> to rise from this sea
> with her mermaid smile
> to pull me down to rest with her
> I try not to think of her much
> But then I see a child
> running in a playground
> towards a warm embrace
> calling
> mommy mommy mommy
> and I think

that I would sink like a stone
to the bottom of the sea
with no hope of return
just to see her once more
to try to make her happy

CHAPTER TWELVE
Patrick
November 2008

A few days ago, Nanny tells me I'm moving to James and Angela's. James comes and gets me, throws my stuff in the truck with barely a hello. And now here I am, tucked away in a little room with one window in their house. A nice house for the fishermen's community, because they have two incomes, but not a big house. Angela makes me feel welcome, but James barely acknowledges me. She says he's like that with everyone, but I think he really doesn't like me. I cannot get settled; I'm irritable and difficult. This isn't my home. But there really isn't such a thing.

Sometimes I feel like everyone who has ever cared for me is dead or gone, but then I think I'm just feeling sorry for myself and what the hell do I know? I do know this: Lately I wake up nearly every night with dreams, usually scary, violent dreams. Not the quiet ones I used to have about my mom. Now I wake lunging to a sitting position, breathless, sweating, and sometimes yelling. It is the feeling of pulling yourself out of water just before you drown, almost not strong enough to get your head out of the water. Angela is usually there almost immediately, sitting quietly by my side, talking in a warm, quiet voice: there, there, it's okay, everything's okay, you're home, you're safe and sound. I put my head on her shoulder and she wraps her arm around me. She smells like flowers. I've had these dreams my whole life, but this is the first time that anyone came for me.

One night Angela wanders out into the back yard as it is getting dark. I am back there by myself, holding a wiffleball bat and slugging wiffleballs off the back of the house, imagining game winning home runs and World Series victories. She sits on the picnic table bench and lights a cigarette.

Angela has long, lustrous, black hair. Actually, it's not just her hair, all of Angela is lustrous. I love that word. Lustrous, I looked it up especially for her. It means luminous, shining and radiant. I think I must be in love with her, whatever that means. I try not to let myself think that, she's my uncle's wife and it must be wrong to think these things. Besides, how could someone like her ever think of marrying someone like me? But that's what I daydream about, as ridiculous as that is, about us living in a house by the ocean somewhere, with a big boat, walking on the beach hand in hand. I have these terrible fantasies of men and women kissing and grappling with each other naked, like I've seen on television, images that make my dick hard and leave me out of breath. And I play with myself in the bathroom with those visions, stroke myself until I make a mess and sit there in shame. But I force the image of her face and body out of those pictures. She doesn't belong there, in a place that soiled. But sometimes her face comes to me in my sleep, when it's too late to stop it.

She sits on the bench and crosses her legs. Her shorts leave them bare up to the middle of her thighs. They are brown and smooth. She has on a T-shirt that clings to the curves underneath. She smiles at me and raise her eyebrows as she pulls on her cigarette.

"Don't tell James how many of these things you see me smoke."

"No. I wouldn't."

"What's wrong, honey? You look pale."

"Nothing. Tired, I guess."

"You woke up again last night. We have to stop meeting like that." She smiles. Then the smile fades and she looks away.

"How come you wake up when I do?" I say, "You must not be sleeping very well, either."

"I don't. I don't know. I wake up and think about things and then I can't go back to sleep. James would sleep through a nuclear explosion. So I stay up and read or think or walk around. Do you know what I was thinking about last night? I looked after another teacher's kids last weekend. Last night I thought about what it feels like to walk a baby around in the middle of the night. One of the kids I watched is a baby. My friend says it's terrible, waking up at all hours to a screaming child, always exhausted, frazzled. But last night I walked up and down in our bedroom, holding my hands like this." She cradles her hands so the baby's head would be on her shoulder. "I imagine he starts crying and then I calm him down and he falls asleep. I hear his breathing in my ear, these tiny breaths, shhh, shhh, shhh. And I talk to him." She whispers. "There, there, sweetheart. Go to sleep. Everything's going to be alright. Momma's here."

She drops the cigarette on the ground and gives me a wistful smile. "Oh, well, maybe someday."

"You would like that?"

She nods, then stands up quickly. "But never spend too much time wishing for things you can't have, Pat. Just makes you miserable. Life's pretty good for us, you know? We're all healthy and we've got each other. That's a lot more than a lot of people have."

"I'm very happy to be here, Angela. You know? I like it here."

She walks over to me. She puts her hand on the back of my head and kisses me on the forehead. "So stick around, already. What's all this talk about leaving? Stay with us." She keeps her hand on my shoulder and looks me in the eyes. "Right?"

"I don't know if that's what James wants." I shrug and grimace. "I feel like I'm crowding him."

"He wants you here. Take my word for it. And what if he didn't? Screw him!" She laughs. "I'm the boss around here! Right?" I smile. I want to give her a powerful hug but instead I move out of her reach.

"Okay." I say.

"Now you come inside and eat some Girl Scout cookies with me so I have a partner in crime." She leads me in gently by the arm. "And tell me about this Ginny Bailey girl."

"How did you know about that?" I ask, startled.

"I saw the post card on the front hall. Post cards are fair game, that's what I always say. If you don't want people to read it, put it in an envelope." She squeezes my arm. "I didn't read it, though. I just happened to notice the address."

"She's a girl who goes to Saint Raymond's. She's in the eighth grade. She was in my class when I was staying at Nanny's. I think she went away with her family for the summer. I just thought I'd send her this card I bought in Pennsylvania. It's a stupid idea; she probably doesn't even remember me."

"Oh, I bet she does, I bet she does. Who could forget a handsome man like you?"

So here I am on City Island, because of Angela, I guess, and because I want to be home somewhere. And the mornings I'm not at school James and I head out to sea on the Daybreak, under the Verrazano and through the Narrows. I stand at the back and watch the wake dreamily. That's one of the reasons I like the boat, it gives you the chance to slip into your own dream world. I imagine I am older, married. Successful. I am at a family party. Nicely dressed, shiny shoes. I am holding a tiny baby in my arms, my child, my own son, listening to his sleepy baby dreams as he nestles into the crook of my neck. And everyone gathers around to ooh and ahh: Pop and Jack and my mother, telling me how beautiful he is and how well I've done. I know I can protect him against everything in the world and I will, forever.

"Pat!" James calls from the wheel, "Wake up!! C'mon! Get some lines down!! If we're on the water, we're fishing! I've got a living to earn and if you're going to help me you better start working!"

I sigh. James was put on this earth to work. The last time we went out it was to bury my grandfather at sea. My grandfather walked off this boat on the prettiest day you ever saw, with James and Michael and Angela and me all dozing on deck. Just walked right off on purpose with his waders on. A tuna trawler picked him up in its net two weeks later. They cremated his bloated body. This was all months ago, before Jack disappeared and I ran away and all of that craziness. Then one day James says Pop would have wanted to be buried at sea. Like he'd know, or anyone would know better than me. Pop would have wanted to be buried by his house by the water, the house they couldn't sell fast enough after he died. But nobody asked me. And now that I think about it, I don't remember ever saying I wanted to help James fish. But here I am and where am I going to go after all of this? So I start to run some lines. I know what to do, mostly, and even with all his grumpiness I know James will teach me the rest. It is starting to feel like home, here on Pop's boat, stinking of fish and filled with ghosts.

*　　*　　*

One morning, I wake up with one arm dangling off the side of the couch, tingling, and the glare of the sun lighting the inside of my eyelids. The front door is open and a soft sea breeze comes through the screen door and brushes my face. I turn on my back and heard voices in the kitchen. James and Angela.

"Then what?" he says.

"Then you can put some flooring down and insulate it," she says. Her voice had a lovely lilt to it, a trace of her childhood in the Philippines. "We can paint it. It'll be a little chilly in the winter, but it'll have its own entrance, which any teenager I know would die for. We can make it a place he thinks of as home, he can pick the color and find some furniture and make it feel like home. . . he doesn't have a home, James."

"Then I don't have a mudroom anymore. Where am I going to put all my fishing gear?"

"You've been talking about building a shed since we moved here."

"I don't know," he says quietly.

"What is it that you're unsure about?" she says calmly. Patiently, but there is an edge of excitement to her voice. "Do you want him here?"

"Permanently?"

Then for a few minutes there are only the sounds of a kitchen being readied for breakfast, the slight clatter of plates and pans. The refrigerator opening and closing. A sizzle of something cooking. I smell the air. Bacon. I love bacon.

"What if we're lucky? Forget what Dr. Anzio says. Anything can happen. What if we do have a child someday?" he says.

"Then we'll have two," she says firmly.

"But he's not ours," he says, "do you understand that? And I'm not saying I wouldn't treat him like a son. But he can never be ours. His heart is with Pop and Jack and his Mom. His heart's all over the place. I don't want you to get hurt, Angela. Thinking you can just become his Mom."

A pause. Then, "I'm sorry, I didn't mean it that way. I meant, we can never be his parents. It's past that point. Way past that point."

Another pause. Then she says very quietly, in a trembling voice, "I know that." Now the excitement has been drained from her voice, in its place is a sad resignation. Then there is a very quiet sound, the slightest rhythmic singsong. Someone sobbing.

Another pause. I lay there, my body rigid so I don't make a sound. I get up and straighten out my t-shirt and shorts. I have to go to the bathroom, but I feel the need to walk into the kitchen at that moment. I feel like whatever I do or say at this moment, at the moment I walk through the door, will be very important. I take a deep breath. My knees are shaking. I feel frozen with fear and uncertainty, but I make my feet move, one in front of the other.

"Hi." I say, too loudly.

"Morning," James says, moving to the stove, not even smiling. But he never smiles, or hardly ever. Angela walks up and gives me a peck on the cheek, like usual. Her eyes are a little red.

"Morning, Pat," she says calmly, "hungry?"

"Very, very, VERY." I say. And a smile that I didn't know was there breaks out on my face, even as I try to suppress it. I sit at the table and look at James, who sits looking into his cup of coffee. Then he looks up right into my eyes, with a very serious expression on his face. I am smiling at him like a crazy person, I can't help it. I am terrified. I am hoping. I wait.

James looks at me quizzically. "What the hell's gotten into you?"

I don't answer, but it doesn't seem as if he expects me to. He nods slightly and takes a deep breath. He glances, ever so briefly, in Angela's direction, then back to me. Then he nods again, more firmly, as if to himself.

"Hey, Pat," he says.

"Yes?" I say, holding my breath.

"If you were going to paint a room, your own room, someplace you were going to live for a while, what color would you paint it?"

CHAPTER THIRTEEN

James
December 2008

Everybody wants to know what happened to Jack and me in West Virginia. So here it is.

Jack and I were drinking in Mickey's Magic Inn, outside of Parkersburg. It was about two in the morning. We were talking about Dad or Mom, or maybe I was trying to get him to stop drinking, which I always mean to do, but then we go out and start drinking. Then this guy stumbles up and starts yelling at me.

"Hey, hey! You must be him, you have GOT to be him."

He was shaking me by the shoulders, pounding me on the back. He was drunker than me, if that was possible, and he was a big guy, six two or three, nearly as tall as Jack and taller than me, but broader than both of us, with a huge red beard. He looked to be older than us, maybe early fifties. He turned to Jack.

"Am I right, Jack? Am I right? This is the guy, got to be."

"Right, Eamonn," Jack said, smiling calmly, "That's my brother. James, meet Eamonn Donovan."

He sat down on the stool between us.

"I heard a lot about you, James. Yessir!" He gave me another slap on the shoulder. "The good guy of your whole fucking family, eh? The white sheep. You're a fucking fisherman, right? Right."

I agreed that I was a fisherman.

"You come to get Jack out of this hellhole, Jim, or what?"

"Well, no, not exactly. Just, you know, visiting."

"Yeah, well, someone ought to get him the hell out of here. What the fuck you doing here, Jack? Smart goddamn stockbroker wasting his time teaching goddamn junior fucking high school in West fucking Virginia. Jesus, man."

He grabbed Jack by the collar, yelling "Jack, Jack, Jack!"

The bartender, an especially surly sort, leaned over the bar. "You guys keep it down or you're out."

Jack motioned to him in a soothing manner. "Hey, Eamonn, he said, "lighten up. Here, have a drink. Just relaxing here, E. Just taking a break in life, you know? Can't go ninety miles an hour all the time. Got to stop and look around sometimes."

Eamonn looked into his beer, nodding thoughtfully.

"Well, okay, Jack, that's okay. You got to do what you got to do."

He didn't stay calm for long and the bartender threw us out about fifteen minutes later, after we all started yelling about something or other.

"Well, fuck him," Eamonn bellowed in the parking lot. "I hate bartenders. I hate authority." He spat out the word as if it were an obscenity.

Jack put his hand on Eamonn's shoulders and guided him away from the building. "No you don't, Eamonn. There's good people around. Lot's of 'em."

"I don't hate this guy, Jim, I'll tell you that," he said to me, hanging on to Jack's sleeve, "I love this guy. Your brother is A-okay."

We agreed to go for a ride with Eamonn in his car, a huge, beaten Olds 88. This was not a particularly bright idea, I thought, but I was feeling like, what the hell? We drove away from town, up a country road marked Old Winslow. Jack sat in front and I in back. There were beers in the back and I opened one for each of us. I felt very comfortable for some reason, very happy, content. Eamonn lit a joint and passed it back.

"Hey, Jim," he yelled, "Jack says you was in the Navy. Were you in the Gulf?"

"No. No, I wasn't."

"Well, I fucking was, man. And I tell you, it was like Disneyland compared to life in the real world. People there were shooting at you, trying to waste you, but at least you knew what their gig was, you know? They were just pissed off we were wasting their fucking country. I can dig that, you know? I was hip to that, I would have done the same thing. But man, come back home and people are still trying to fuck me up, and for what? This world is a dangerous place, Jim, I'll tell you. How in the world did I end up in West fucking Virginia? All I wanted was a little peace and quiet. And some bread, man, some real bread. I'm from L.A. I should be a movie star or something. But I know what Jack's doing here. I'm hip to that. Old Jacko's hiding from his fucking life. And that includes YOU, Jimbo."

Eamonn turned on the stereo, and started singing along to the Grateful Dead.

Jack leaned over the seat.

"You know, James," he said as quietly as he could, "This is nuts. But I'm glad you're here. It's fun to hang out with you. Kind of like old times, you know? Don't mind Eamonn, he's okay."

I nodded. "No problem. Eamonn is okay. This is crazy, but, what the fuck?"

Jack laughed. Eamonn veered the car from side to side of the road, like a sailboat tacking upwind. He was oblivious to our conversation, humming to himself.

I watched the roadside pass by out the window. There was nothing out here, just the half lit form of the occasional sleeping house, empty black fields under a bright half moon. The mountains loomed straight ahead, like giant black cumulus in the night.

Jack climbed over the seat to sit next to me.

"I love driving around up here at night," he said, "it's like being on the moon."

"How did you end up here, anyway?" I said.

Jack paused for a long moment, almost as if he would not answer. He took a long drink from his beer and lit a cigarette.

"I don't know. Something about the mountains. I wanted to get away from the ocean. I was in Colorado. Then I left, thought I'd try someplace new, and somehow I washed up here. But I stuck around. These towns, this countryside seemed very old, permanent. I got a job as a teacher and a basketball coach, you know, traded in on my old college basketball glory. I rented a house. I quit gambling. I stopped drinking, except for the occasional special event. I like it here. I go up to the mountains a lot."

"That's all good," I said firmly.

"James," he said, turning away from me to look out the window, "I would have screwed up that alcohol program in Jersey that Michael had me signed up for. I wasn't ready. I know I'm doing this ass backwards and I'm sure I've burned some bridges. Like Frances. Maybe even Michael. But I feel like I'm getting somewhere. I have to do it on my own. I shouldn't have run off on you all and I should have called you in the past year, but it wouldn't have meant anything. I wasn't there. I think I'm coming back to earth."

He spoke strongly, as if practiced, non-apologetic. He looked at me.

"This isn't helping, is it?"

"You don't have to say these things, Jack, that's not why I came here, to hear those things." I took a deep breath. A lot of feelings came up at once and not all of them were good.

"Yeah, I was pissed off for a while. We all were. Some of them still are. Frances is not going to forget, not ever. And maybe I'll never feel the way I did about you when we were kids. Maybe that's just something I've got to get used to. Maybe it was good you ran off; let everyone get on with their own lives, stop trying to fuck around with yours."

"Don't be bitter, James."

"Don't tell me what to feel. I spent too much of my life thinking about you, trying to figure you out. The whole family has. They've all got a complex about you. Me, I just never understood any of it. I'm kind of a simple person, Jack. I see things in black and white. Part of me just thinks you fucked things up and there's no reason for it. But we were friends. I missed you, Jack. I had to get over that."

But then I had to let up, I couldn't be that hard.

"But I tracked you down, right? So it can't be all bad, I guess."

"Maybe if I came back north with you, James, came back home. Maybe I can get things together."

He looked at me and I nodded. Okay, I thought, let's see what happens.

Ahead of us on the road, the lights of a 24 hour gas station/food mart burned brightly.

"It looks like a space station," Jack said, "Hey Eamonn, stop here, we need some provisions."

"You got it, Jack, you're the captain of this ship."

A white lit neon sign in front said:

PRODO'S TEXACO
COLD BEER
AMMO

"Maybe we should pick up some firepower to go with our beer, eh, boys?" Eamonn said.

Jack laughed. We all fell out of the car and walked into the store, Jack draping his arms comfortably over each of our shoulders.

"Hell, yeah," Jack said in a mock backwoods accent, "Drink some beer and do some shootin'."

We pushed each other into the garish light of the convenience store and wandered the aisles beneath the scornful gaze of a middle-aged matron.

"You best be careful, Jim," Eamonn said, "She's probably got a twelve gauge under the counter. They shoot wiseasses from New York down here."

We bought beer, chips and Hostess Snowball cupcakes and stumbled, whooping, into the parking lot. Jack and I got into the back. In the car, Jack unwrapped the Snowballs with glee.

"These," he pronounced, "are the finest food product ever devised by man. You have all your basic food groups here: sponge cake, chocolate, fake coconut, fiberglass coating." He peeled the pink coconut-dotted coating off the cupcake and flung it at me, sticking his tongue out.

On Jack's direction, Eamonn drove up Carter Sells Road, towards Big Walker Mountain, and then turned up Route 58 to the top of the mountain. The road was pitch black and ancient trees hung, exhausted, over the road, turning it into a cave.

"Take you for an interesting ride, James," Jack said, "Up here in the mountains; some funny things go on, poaching, mountain gangs, regular Deliverance stuff. I drive up here sometimes at night, all the way up to the top of Big Walker. See groups of men travelling without lights by the road, armed to the teeth, like a regular war zone. And the hills, there are lights hidden in them, I think people live in the hills, under ground, waiting for the end of the world."

"Sounds dangerous," I said. "Why are we going there?"

"What the hell?" Jack said, laughing, "Right, E?"

"End of the world is coming, boys," Eamonn yelled, "Damn soon, too, I feel it every day. Better get used to it. Better get your ass ready."

I gazed worriedly down into the darkness of the ravines dropping away from the side of the narrowing road. The road grew steeper and the car swerved up the curves into the night.

"Angela okay?" Jack asked quietly.

"Yeah, she's fine, great."

"You know, I called Frances," he said, lighting a cigarette. "We talked. I mean, I know it's not much, but I'd like to make things better somehow, someday."

"It's not going to be easy," I said, not trying to disguise the edge in my voice. Jack's treatment of my sister-in-law, who I was fond of, was yet another thing to get annoyed about.

Jack nodded, but I'm not sure he even heard me. He stared absently out the window.

"I think about her every day. It's almost embarrassing how I think about our early times now, our good times; it's like a fairy tale. Live happily ever after and like that. I daydream about it."

There was silence for a moment, just the sound of wind and rushing tires on the pavement.

"But that's my problem, right? I'm the one who blew it."

"That's right."

Jack looked over at me, his eyes narrowing.

"You know, James, life isn't as fucking easy as you think it is. Not everyone sees it like you do. It's not so simple for some people." He looked like he was about to say more, than held his tongue, shaking his head.

"Simple. You think life's simple for me, is that it? Old simple Jim." I stared out the front window. I was mad, but I wasn't comfortable being mad at him, I didn't want to be mad at him, I felt like we were losing him somehow and I didn't want that. So I held the rest of it.

"It wasn't an insult, James. I'm sorry; I meant it as a compliment. I wish it looked simpler sometimes. Just wake up one morning, just once, and know what has to be done and how to do it. Look, I know I screwed up that marriage. My drinking and partying and staying out to all hours…"

"Frances thought you cheated on her."

He looked at the floor of the car steadily and did not speak for a few moments.

"I know she did." He looked at me.

"I came home one night and she had moved out. Do you have any idea what that felt like? I felt like the world had ended. It was totally my stupidity, but I did not know it was that bad for her. And that was it, it wasn't a warning. She told me she was done. I felt like part of me died. After that nothing really mattered."

"You're punishing yourself, Jack."

"I deserve it." He drained a can of beer and tossed the empty to the floor.

The road turned uphill every half mile. The trees on each side of the road appeared and disappeared in a moment in the gleam of the headlights. The unseen expanse of the valley could be felt occasionally in a clearing, distant lights floating far away like ships at sea. We sat in silence for a good five minutes. Seamus sang along to the radio in a surprisingly good voice, deep and sad.

"How's Mom?" Jack said after a time.

"Good. Okay. Well, not great. She knows I'm here. You know her; she's saying her prayers, hoping for the best. I took her to the cemetery a couple of weeks ago, to Pop's grave. Someone's been sending flowers up there, fresh ones every week. Mom said, 'I bet it's Jack.' I never argue with her, not about you, anyway, you rank slightly below God with her, so I kept my mouth shut. But I was thinking, not Jack. I mean, you couldn't stand him."

"Wasn't that," Jack said, "that wasn't all there was to it." He shrugged. "We had our problems."

"But you know," I said, "when he got sick, we still used to go out on the boat, or we'd go down to the Fisherman's Net so he could talk to a few of his old fishing buddies. And we talked about you a lot. Sometimes Mike would come, he got a kick out of that, you know, the sons taking the old fisherman out fishing."

Jack shook his head angrily. "What is this, James, am I supposed to feel like shit? He's dead and I missed it. So what? He never gave any of us a break and he cheated on our mother. I'm supposed to care about him? He was such a great guy? Like being a fisherman is such a goddamned accomplishment and I didn't do it. The only reason you took that boat is because you got forced into it and you're too proud to back out. Nobody would care if that boat sank."

I looked at him. I tried to digest those words. He looked like a stranger, hard and mean.

"Why do you say things like that? It's not even true. But even if it was, how could you talk to me like that? I don't understand you."

"You don't have to fucking understand me," he hissed, slumping into the seat.

"Maybe you're right, Jack. Fuck it, right? That what you want to hear? Fuck you, I don't give a shit about you, I'm going home tomorrow, is that what you want to hear?"

I took a deep breath. The beer can in my hand was shaking.

"You know, James," Jack said softly, then paused. "You know what the stupid thing is? You drive me crazy, more than anyone I've ever known, like you always know what the right thing to do is, like you never made a mistake. I mean, you think I don't respect you, but I'd trade places with you. I missed you, more than anyone."

I did not know what to say to that. I did not know if I could trust what he said. I missed him, too. I missed Pop and Catherine, gone for good with no chance for amends. I missed Seamus. I missed Angela. I needed her help.

"You and Patrick, I miss Patrick." Jack said distantly, staring out the window. "He's the only one there's hope for." And I suddenly had the strangest realization that I missed Patrick, too. How was that possible? Why was I even thinking about the boy at that moment? How could I miss his endless daydreams and his millions of questions and those eyes, those earnest eyes, fixed on me, unrelenting.

Eamonn turned the car slowly around a particularly tight corner. The car hung on what felt like the edge of a cliff. It looked as if the sky was draped in front of us, from the stars above to the houses hundreds of feet below us.

"You know," Eamonn called to us, "these mountain people, they know everyone who comes up here. They watch everything. You can feel it."

"Hey, Jack," I said softly, "why don't we head back?"

"Eamonn is right, James," Jack said, looking out the window. "I always feel like there's someone looking right at me up here, aiming at me."

The road flattened out. There was a feeling that we had reached the top of the mountain. We came around a bend and ahead of us there were lights shining by the side of the road. It was a van, its back doors wide open, the interior brightly lit. Seamus slowed the car to a crawl as we approached it. There was a dead deer lying in the back of the van, its head dangling over the bumper, the dead eyes glowing straight at us in the headlights. A pool of blood glimmered on the ground below it.

"What the hell is that?" I said.

"Poachers," Eamonn muttered ominously, turning off the radio. He looked around up into the black hills to his left. "It's off season."

"Let's get the hell out of here, Jack," I said.

"Wait," Eamonn said, stopping the car just past the van, "What if someone's in trouble? It's weird to leave your van wide open like that. I'm going to take a look."

"Don't be stupid, Eamonn," I said. "The only things that are in trouble are that deer and us. You said there were crazy people up here. Let's go."

"Just one second," Eamonn said. He opened the door and turned to look at Jack. "What do you say, Jacko, up for a little adventure?" He smiled broadly, the light gleaming oddly off his eyes. Jack looked at Eamonn, then at me. Eamonn stepped out of the car, stumbling. Jack opened the door.

"Jack, don't," I said, my voice rising.

He smiled as if he didn't have a care in the world. He drained his beer. "I'll just keep an eye on him. I don't have anything to prove to anyone, I just feel like it. What are you afraid of?"

"I'm not afraid of anything." I said, too loudly.

"I know you're not. If you'd been on the *Daybreak*, Seamus would still be alive, right?"

"What? What does Seamus have to do with this?"

"I should have saved him, that's what you all think. You could have saved him, that's what you think."

"Nobody could have saved Seamus, Jack. I was out in the same storm, remember? Nobody's ever blamed you."

Then he was out of the car and walking towards the van confidently.

"Take the wheel," he called over his shoulder.

"My brother the fucking hero," I muttered to myself, climbing over the front seat.

I looked into the rear view mirror. The van was lit up along the front like a cruise ship, white lights running across the top of the windshield. Eamonn moved around the side of the van, carefully touching it as if to see if it were real.

With a shocking crash, the glass of the car's rear window exploded in a cloud of glass fragments, covering the front seat and me with shards. I sat hunched over in the seat for an instant, stunned, then slowly felt my face and legs for wounds. I sat bolt upright and looked about frantically.

I couldn't see Jack or Eamonn by the van. Two flashes appeared in the woods uphill, accompanied instantly by two loud explosions, the shots sounding like huge firecrackers. The car rocked with a heavy thud, once, then again. I heard voices yelling, then more shots, further down the road behind the car.

No more than thirty seconds had passed since the first shot. I slammed my foot on the gas. The car careened down the road. Lights flashed in the dark behind me and I heard more shots. I stopped the car after a quarter of a mile, standing on the brakes and skidding wildly to the side of the road. I clutched both of my hands to my chest and struggled to catch my breath. I looked over my shoulder through the shattered rear window. For a moment there was silence, just the night.

I felt as if my head was exploding and I slammed my hands on the wheel.

"Jack, you miserable fucker!" I yelled, "Why are we here?" I drove on slowly, looking straight ahead. I hated him. Hated him, hated him, hated him. He had me trapped on top of fucking death mountain. I had lost my connection to everything that I cared about and all of it was that fucking bastard's fault. The cool mountain air blew through the shattered rear window. I sat back and took a deep breath, then another. I felt as if I was suffocating. I gripped the wheel with both hands as if it would fly out of my hands. I coughed out a hoarse sound, sounding partially like a wild laugh, partially a gasp of fright.

"I'm not stopping," I said, "I'm not. That's enough."

Then there was another volley of shots, far behind me.

"Goddamn it," I said in a whisper. I turned the wheel violently, ramming the car into the side of a hill, and then I backed away and raced the car back from where it had come.

I saw Jack in the headlights, staggering forward, gasping for breath. I stopped the car and pushed the front door open. Jack fell into the front seat. I reached over, pulled the door closed and pushed the pedal to the floor. The van appeared out of the darkness ahead. I stopped the car.

There were shadowed figures ahead of us on the road. Closer to us, a body lay on its back by the side of the road, its arms and legs folded underneath it at an awkward angle. I recognized Eamonn's yellow shirt.

"Stay down, Jack," I said urgently.

Jack lay on his side on the seat, silent. I drove hard up to the spot where the body was and slammed on the brakes. The car skidded violently to the left, my stomach rising into my throat. I leaned down behind the wheel and peered out. There was only darkness outside of the bright headlight beams. I saw dark figures moving up the incline to the right. I slowly opened the door. I crouched and stepped out, opening the back door. I put both arms under Eamonn's jacket and dragged him into the back seat. It felt as if those actions took an hour, I waited for more shots, but there was only silence except for the wind in the upper trees. Then suddenly there were three more gunshots, loud bangs! I heard a loud thump, as something hit the back fender of the car. I folded Eamonn's legs into the back seat and slammed the door shut. I crawled into the front seat and floored it and drove ahead, the back tires shrieking, not bothering to shield myself. My headlights lit up the front of the van. I was driving directly towards it.

There were two more shots and the front windshield blew apart on the right side, dropping glittering pieces onto Jack's back. The car weaved crazily towards the van. The headlights shined on several figures, all of whom scattered at the last moment. The car slammed into one, the body bouncing off the hood and to the side of the car. The car banged off the side of the van and skidded back to the center of the road. I made two turns down the road at dangerous speeds, tires screeching, then slowed to a manageable speed. No one followed us.

I drove for fifteen minutes, then pulled over, rolled down the window and threw up. I sat back, panting and coughing. I looked over at Jack, who was still curled in the seat. Slowly he sat up, his arms clutched to his chest.

"Where's Eamonn, James?" His voice scraped from his gut.

I motioned with my head to the back seat. I felt as cold as death. I did not care about anything or anyone except getting home.

I heard a cough in the back seat. I turned and looked. To my utter astonishment, Eamonn was sitting up, his yellow jacket splattered with blood. Eamonn turned and looked back through the rear window.

"What the fuck was *that* all about?" he muttered.

"We are going to get the fuck out of here," I said. "We've got to get you to a hospital."

"I'm okay," Eamonn said, "I'm not shot. I cut my side when I hit the ground. I learned how to hit the ground fast and hard in the Gulf, man. This ain't nothing."

I drove on, winding down the mountain, back towards Jack's home. We drove for a long time in silence.

"James, you saved my life,' Jack said, "My stupid fucking life. That was crazy, what the hell happened up there?"

He held his head in his hands, his voice rising hysterically.

"You said there were dangerous people around, Jack," I said, my voice shaking. "I guess you were right."

"That's crazy," he yelled, "You think I believe that shit?"

"Crazy is right, man," said Eamonn, with a relaxed laugh, "that was some real crazy shit. Let's not come up here again any time soon. What's your plan, Jim? Police might be coming."

"We are going to do nothing. Nothing! This is not part of my life! We are leaving you at your fucking car in the bar parking lot and we are driving home in Jack's car and Jack is never, never going to talk to me or anyone else about this again."

"James," Jack said, reaching his hand over to my shoulder. I shrugged him off.

We left Eamonn by his car in the empty parking lot. He walked around and leaned into my window.

"Don't be so hard on your bro', Jim. He's all you got."

"Mind your own fucking business," I snapped. "You almost got our heads blown off."

"Jim," he said quietly, "that was just bad luck, and you can't avoid bad luck, you know? You're a fisherman, right? Sometimes you go out on the water and some bad shit happens and you get blown all over the place, right? You can't control how it happens or what it does to you. All you can control is what it makes you become. You can become an angry, bitter man, Jim. Or you can put your head down and drive through that shit and thank God if you get through. And then just try to be a happy man. You know?"

He stood up straight. "But you're a smarter man than me, Jim, maybe I'm way off on that. Maybe I'm just full of it."

I looked at him. He was watching me with his eyes wide open in curious childlike anticipation. I nodded at him and held out my hand, which he took with a big smile.

"Take care of yourself, Eamonn. Stay out of the mountains." He smiled and shook his head. We drove in Jack's car back to Jack's house.

Jack stood in the driveway. I sat on the lawn. The sun was rising behind the mountains, the sky turning pink and the clouds streaked with grey and gold.

"James, we should call the police or something?"

I shook my head. No. The police would keep me here, I thought. I had to go. I wanted to be as far away from here as possible. I didn't care about anything else. I had the clear feeling that nothing in this life was going to feel like it had before. Because I realized up on that mountain that I couldn't do anything about Jack or what he was going to become.

"I guess I owe you my life or something, huh?"

"Forget it," I said. "You better get some sleep, Jack. You go in. I'm going to hang here for a second."

He ran his hands through his hair. The morning sun glistened off the broken glass sprinkled on his shoulders. He stood in front of me, swaying slightly.

"Go to bed, Jack." I tried to make my voice sound soothing. "Rest easy. You're home."

"But what about us, James," he whispered, "are we okay?"

I nodded. "We will be, Jack."

"Right," he said, "You're right, James. You're right. We'll figure this out. You and me."

He stumbled inside. I sat on the grass and looked up at the sky. Clouds gathered to the west. The air held a sweet promise of rain. Overhead a jet's engines streaked the highest part of the sky. I lay back and close my eyes. In my head I saw lights in the hills and heard gunshots.

The screen door opened and I heard Jack coming to my side. I didn't open my eyes.

Jack spoke in a strange, punished whisper.

"You okay, James? For real?"

I shook my head. No.

"You should have driven off and left me up there, too, James. I don't know why I do things, why I hurt everything. You're a rock, James."

He leaned over. I smelled his alcohol breath. He kissed me on the forehead.

"I'm going to go back with you, James. Enough's enough, right? This time I'm going to get it together."

I heard him stumble back up the stairs into the house. I moved my back up and down so that the cool grass tickled the back of my neck. For a moment, the air held not a sound, and the world just hung in the morning sky.

After a time, I got up and walked into the house. I looked into the largest bedroom, where Jack slept on his back, breathing loudly. I walked into the kitchen and sat at the table. I stared out the window for quite a while. I picked up the phone book and looked up a cab company. I called.

"I need a car to the airport," I said quietly, "As soon as possible." I gave the address.

I was about to hang up when the operator asked me another question.

"What? No, just one passenger. I'll be out front. Please hurry. I'm ready to go right now. I don't know how long I'll be ready."

*   *   *

I came home alone and I have not told anyone about what happened. Those close to me, Angela, Michael, my mother, assume that things did not go well between Jack and me. But they know me well enough not to press me for details if I haven't volunteered them. There has been a lot going on in my life since I got back and I bury myself in those things and stay busy on the water. But the memory lingers, of that dark road in the hills, the gunshots and Jack's desperately sad voice in my ear just before I left him.

I miss him and I hate him. He is haunting me. And now Patrick has moved in, on a trial basis my mother says. It is difficult to welcome someone into my life when everyone else seems to be slipping away.

My life is becoming full of goodbyes. I have tried to say my goodbyes to Jack. I wait every day for my wife to say goodbye, I feel myself losing her. And I must say goodbye to my father.

I have had his ashes sitting on my mantle for weeks. I just know that's not where he wants to be, so I got this idea we should drop them at sea. I talked to Michael about it and he said he couldn't do it. I did not understand what he meant. I asked him, you *can't* do it? Or you *won't* do it? I know what this is all about. He must have told Anne, his wife, about it. And she has some fucking twisted psychobabble take on why it's not good for him to do it. I ended up yelling at him on the phone. Loud enough for her to hear on the other end; I was sure she was hovering there, listening. I knew what would happen, Michael would call the next day and we'd make up. Which is what happened. I feel kind of shitty about how low I feel about him sometimes. But I love him and we'll work it out, some day, some way.

Angela says I should take Patrick and it should just be the two of us. That sounds right. Patrick and Pop were very close, closer than he was to his sons. It was kind of a mysterious relationship, neither one of them ever shared it with anyone else. It drove Catherine fucking crazy. Just crazy. She had gotten so mad and bitter at Pop over the years, about the shitty way he treated Mom, the cheating and the drinking. And then he took her husband's side in her marriage. She thought he was just being nice to Pat to get back at her. I wasn't so sure, though. There was a connection there, no denying it.

So today we're heading out. I look to the stern of the boat. Patrick is running lines out, clearing gear; doing everything he is supposed to. He is actually a pretty good mate for a fourteen year old. He's been living in our guest room and is never any trouble. But there is something different about that boy, something truly mysterious that I will never understand. He reminds me of Seamus on the boat. Not yet moving with Seamus' ease, but they're about the same size and they look alike. He makes me think of Seamus, with the enormous wave of regret and loss that comes with that.

But he's not Seamus. Seamus was free, open, funny, crazy. Patrick is closed, guarded, and deeply intelligent. If Seamus was the riotous surf at shore, Patrick is the deep sea fishing waters over the canyons, black deep and unfathomable. He can be funny, in a very dry, offhand way. He is forgetful and clumsy. He thinks of things that no one else would and he is very kind. I don't know who he's like. Not like any of us. He's a little like Angela.

"Pat, come here."

He comes and stands next to me. I hand him the ceramic container that holds the ashes. He takes it without saying anything and stares out to sea.

"These are Pop's ashes. He told you he wanted them scattered at sea, right?"

Patrick nods.

"Well, let's do it, then. Is there anything you want to say?"

Patrick looks down, then away. I realize he is crying.

"What's wrong with you?" he whispers, "You should say something. You should want to say something. Is this what happens at the end of your life, you just die and nobody cares except some stupid kid that nobody listens to anyway?'

I put my hand on his shoulder and he shrugs me off, stepping away.

"Give me the ashes," I say.

He holds them out without looking at me. I open the top and hold it out over the water. It starts to rain.

"Here's my father," I say loudly, speaking to the open water, "Take him back, he's all yours now. He wasn't perfect. None of us got along a lot of the time and he didn't help. But he tried in his own way to be a father and to work hard. He taught me a lot. And he was a very, very good grandfather." I look at Pat, whose eyes remain fixed on the sea. "I guess mostly because of him we have a good young man standing here saying goodbye with love. That's a hell of a lot more than most of us are going to get. Thanks."

I look at Patrick who is now watching me, a slightly puzzled look on his face.

"How's that," I say, "want to add anything?"

"I found something I want to read."

"Oh," I say, attempting a smile. "I could have saved the speech. Go ahead." I still hold the jar out, my hand poised over the water.

He takes out a crumpled piece of paper from his pocket. He holds it in front of him, his hands shaking. In a surprisingly strong voice he reads:

Full fathom five thy father lies
Of his bones are coral made
Those are pearls that were his eyes
Nothing of him that doth fade
But doth suffer a sea-change
Into something rich and strange.

"I will remember you always, Grandpa. I miss you. I miss Mom. I miss Jack. I wanted to say goodbye to all of you."

Then he begins to cry and he cannot stop, sinking to the floor and holding his head in his hands. I sprinkle the ashes over the water. I take one big handful and lean over and hold it out in front of Patrick. He takes it and stands and throws it gently out over the water. He walks back and sits in the stern of the boat and we do not speak for a long time.

I take my time heading back, thinking about Pop and Seamus and Catherine, and trying not to think about Jack. After a while Patrick comes to the bridge and offers to take the wheel, which I give to him. I sit down and start sorting through the pile of charts that are jammed into the cabinet on the bridge.

"Is Jack coming back, James?"

I look at him and then look out over the wake behind us.

"I doubt it."

Patrick winces when I say this. I remind myself how much he admires Jack.

"I don't know, Patrick. Maybe when he gets his head together."

"What happened down there? In West Virginia? Something bad, right?"

"Who told you that?"

"No one, but I can tell with you. You don't talk much, but you don't hide things, either. You're hiding something."

"Smart boy."

So I tell him the story. I start slowly, but then I offer all of the details, I tell him everything. About Eamonn and the drinking and the ride into the mountains. And I tell him how I left Jack there.

"You left him like that?" he says hesitantly, looking off into the sky. His eyes are watering.

"Yeah," I say quietly, "I left him like that. My brother. I just took off."

He does not say anything for a while, then he whispers, "I don't understand how you could do that, leave your brother in that kind of condition. Don't you have to take care of each other? Don't you have any feelings for people?"

I look at him and I bite my tongue. I can tell he really thinks less of me. I try to think of something to say, I want to say something to make things better. I lean forward and put my head in my hands. The only sounds are the dull rumble of the engine and the rush of the water on the side.

I remember Seamus, Jack and me sleeping in the yard on a summer night when I was 11, Jack was 10 and Seamus was 9. Roughing it with no sleeping bags, only blankets that we shared. We were pioneers, explorers. We were sleeping in the Sahara, or on Mount Everest. We had all our childhood daydreams together.

In the middle of that night I was awakened by Jack shaking my shoulder. He said; look up, Jimmy, quick, look up. I opened my eyes and there were meteors overhead. Burning white streaks in the pitchblack sky. Jack turned around and put his head on my stomach, so we could both look up.

Should we wake up Shay? He whispered.

No, let him sleep, I said.

Jimmy, he said, how far away do you think those shooting stars are?

I don't know, Jack.

Jimmy, do you think they're going a million miles an hour?

I don't know, Jack.

Jimmy, do you ever want to go far, far, away from home?

I didn't know the answer to that question.

I do, he said. I want to go to the end of the universe.

Hey, Jimmy, he said.

Yes, Jack? And now I was groggy.

We'll always be together, won't we?

Yes, Jack.

Jimmy, let's not ever tell anyone about this. Let's put this on our list of JJ secrets.

We had a list of secrets, our JJ secrets. Just for us. We stopped keeping the list as we got older. Then when we grew up and time battered us, we started keeping secrets from each other. And then we got older and older and ended up in the middle of the night on a road in the hills of West Virginia that I would never be able to stop thinking about.

I start to cry. I look up and Patrick is watching me, his eyes open in cautious amazement.

"You think I don't fucking care about him? I grew up side by side with him. You think this is easy? What the fuck is wrong with you people, you think I don't have feelings?"

I immediately feel embarrassed for the outburst. I get up quickly and move to the stern, picking up gear that doesn't need to be moved and moving it to another place. Patrick turns to face forward. I wait a while and go to the cooler and take out a beer and a Coke. I walk to the wheel and hand the soda to Patrick.

"I need to say goodbye to him, Pat. Just like we said goodbye to Pop. He's tearing me apart. I have to do it. I don't expect you to. Maybe he'll come back someday. But we have to live our lives without him in the meantime."

"Would you ever give up on me," he says quietly, "write me off?"

"God, no. Of course not."

"Why is Jack different?"

"You'd have to know the whole story, Patrick. I don't trust him. That's what it is, really. I love him, I guess, but I just don't trust him. I used to, but not anymore."

Patrick looks at me, shaking his head.

"I don't believe that, James, I don't think you can stop trusting your family. It's all we have, each other."

All we have is each other. The rain starts to come down harder, but I don't cover up. I get wet, leaning against the cabin and looking out past the wake to a darkening horizon. I realize I don't want him to come back, not unless he changes. I guess I'm jealous of the pull he has on Mom and Angela and Patrick. And me. If I thought he needed me I might feel different.

I walk to the wheel and stand next to Pat.

"I like those lines you read," I say.

"It was Shakespeare. The Tempest."

"I know. Ariel's song. Sea-nymphs hourly ring his knell."

Patrick looks at me as if I have suddenly sprouted an extra head. I shrug. He left the book on the kitchen table and I read it one night. I didn't get all of it, but it was interesting, particularly to a sailor with a drowned father. But I don't tell him that, I let him think what he wants.

I say, "Too bad you don't come across more sea-nymphs out here."

Patrick smiles broadly, which really startles me. It is like the sun peeking through what you thought was solid cloud cover.

"What do you suppose they look like?" he says shyly, "Sea nymphs?"

"Oh, beautiful, I'm sure. Beautiful enough to lure you under the waves."

"Like Angela," he says, to himself but out loud. "Except she would never lure anyone to danger. I could see that, though. Meeting some beautiful sea nymph and following her to some watery world where you can live forever." Then he frowns. "But I'd miss everybody at home."

"You need a land nymph, Pat," I say, lightly placing my hand on his shoulder. "Just a regular girl."

"Do you think?" he says hopefully.

"Oh, sure. Hey, if I could marry Angela, anything's possible."

"That's for sure!" Then he grimaces and looks at me, embarrassed. I laugh. He quickly scrambles to correct himself.

"I mean, meeting someone like her is really lucky, not that you don't deserve…"

"Forget it, Pat. I wonder myself sometimes."

We are starting to hit some chop near the harbor mouth, the boat rising up over the waves and crashing down on the other side. Even after all these years I still find it exhilarating. I watch Patrick's face as he carefully steers our way home. It is open with undisguised emotion, hopeful, excited, and yet a mystery to me. He has no idea how important he is in my life at this moment.

My wife longs for a child. When we pass a mother and small child on the street, her walk slows and her voice trails off in mid-sentence. We were told in a cruelly offhand way by a doctor several years ago that we'd have a better shot at winning the lottery than conceiving a child. He actually said that. I briefly daydreamed of reaching across his desk and crushing his smug face.

I am angry about it, angry that Angela cannot have this one dream of hers. I guess that's one of many things I'm angry about. Everyone thinks I am so calm all the time, but Angela knows better. "You'll never be happy, James," she says, "Until you figure out what you're really angry about."

I know Angela is thinking about Patrick, about how alone he is and about caring for him. I see how Angela and Patrick are with each other, their private conversations, and their need for each other. But I am struggling with the whole idea. I am still hurt and, yes, angry, that Angela lied to me for all those years about drinking. She offered to come on the boat with me shortly after that confession and I told her no, I needed to able to trust my mate on the boat. It was a cruel and angry thing to say. And as we drift along together on this uncertain current, Patrick draws her affection and confidences. Am I jealous of him? Certainly.

I think Angela wants Patrick to stay with us, forever. I don't want it. I care for the boy, he's family. He's strange, but oddly interesting. But I do not want him coming between me and Angela. And more than that, I do not want to be his father, I don't know how. I am afraid that I will be no good at being a father. My father wasn't much good at it, why would I be any different?

But what if Patrick is what she wants, if that is what will make her happy? Then what can I do? I think about her every moment of every day. With fear and hope and anger. I don't know about Patrick. I don't know what's going to happen to any of us.

Patrick suddenly turns to me, his face serious.

"James, promise me something?"

"Sure."

"Don't ever leave me anywhere, not just because you're mad at me?"

I look at him carefully and I nod.

"I promise, Patrick."

"And I won't ever leave you. Okay?"

I nod. I like that idea. That this boy, this hopelessly dreamy, impractical boy, is going to look out for me. I think of the people I know who've sunk under the waters or fallen out of my life. I think of Angela, who feels as tenuous sometimes as hanging on to a piece of driftwood in a raging sea. And then I look at Patrick, gripping the wheel, as he always does, as if his life depends on it.

"I'm going to start to stow everything, you bring us in. Okay?"

"All the way in? To the dock?"

"All the way, captain."

He nods eagerly. He has never done it, never negotiated his way through the currents and crowded lanes leading to City Island. He might wreck the boat. He really might. But I squeeze his shoulder and walk away.

CHAPTER FOURTEEN
Angela December 2008

I thought I really was working my way free of my past, free from alcohol, even, regretfully, free from Jack. But I should know enough from being out on the ocean with this family that there is sometimes bad weather just over the horizon and it can come on fast.

One day, Mary and Padmina, two of my fellow teachers, ask me to join them for a small birthday celebration. I say sure, but then they tell me they are going to Hurley's, a bar I visited a few times when I was drinking. I am very reluctant, but I don't want to disappoint the birthday girl. I sit with them for a couple of hours, drinking coke. After some initial uneasiness, I feel relaxed and comfortable. James is out on a night charter and Patrick is sleeping over at a friend's house. I am looking forward to reading my book at home and making myself a small dinner. I like to cook, it relaxes me. We leave at 8:15 and stand talking for a few minutes in the parking lot. After my friends drive off, I realize that I have left my umbrella in the bar and I go back inside to get it. I stand at the bar holding it in my hand, staring absentmindedly at the news on the television, when the bartender says, "Can I get you something, miss?" He is older, almost distinguished looking. He looks vaguely familiar.

"Oh, no thanks, I'm just going home."

He smiles at me. "Special on Apple Martinis, you used to like them, didn't you?"

"You have a good memory; I haven't been here in a while."

"I doubt too many people forget your face. Hey, the first one's on me." He walks down the bar before I can respond. I stand there, watching him mix the drink. Thoughts creep into my head, but I scare them away. There's nothing happening, I'm just standing here.

He places the drink in front of me with a theatrical wave, bows slightly with a smile, and moves to another customer. It is a lovely sight and he's right, it is one of my favorites. Served in an extra wide martini glass, the apple colored liquid sits as still as ice, shimmering in the bar light. I pick it up and take a sip. I am shocked by the feeling, a warm electric plunge down into my center. I put the umbrella down and sit on the stool. I'll have one, just one, and then I'll go home. I've been good. I can have a little treat.

When I used to drink a lot I could sit at a bar for hours, staring into my drink, disappearing into elaborate fantasies of different lives. A life where I had a warm and loving mom and dad, or brothers and sisters. A place where I was rich or famous, a great doctor or musician. I would forget where I was or what I was doing. And so it goes today, a fog quickly surrounds me and carries me away.

Several hours later I sit in my car and try to decide if I am going to be able to drive home without crashing into something or getting arrested. I stupidly decide to risk it. Although I am able to pull into the driveway, my hands are shaking with fear from the two near accidents I have on the short ride home. I stumble into the house and get into the shower. I need to sober up a little or I'll wake up puking.

James won't be home until 2 or 3, but he'll smell it for sure. In the shower, I sit on the floor and hold my head in my hands. I am overwhelmed by grief, my sobriety is gone, and I have destroyed it. I feel like I am in the grips of something that I can never escape. After a while, I put on a robe and sit in a chair in our living room. I look at the clock on the wall. It is eleven o'clock, it seems so much later. I have done so much damage in such a short period of time.

The phone rings. It is Jack, of all people. He has been calling every once in a while since James came back from West Virginia. He calls on Friday nights because he knows that is James' night for charters. I tried to keep the calls short at first, knowing how upset James was at him. But the conversations got longer and longer. He knows how to pull my anxieties out of me and it feels so much better to have them out in the open.

"Hey, Jack."

He is instantly alert. "You okay, Angie?"

My voice is a croak. I am starting to feel nauseous.

"No, Jack. I'm not. I got drunk."

"Tonight?"

"Yes. I am such an incredible, stupid jerk, Jack. I was doing great. So great! I am such a loser."

"Hey, Angie, you listen to me. Stop with the self-abuse. Right now. You are trying to do something that's really, really hard and you're not perfect."

"I'm not perfect? The bartender at Hurley's said I am."

"Who, Sydney?"

"Yeah, that's him. Serpent-tongued devil."

"Apple Martinis?"

"Yes, they were having a special."

"They became a special as soon as you walked in the door. Sydney could get Mother Teresa drunk. He's the best alcohol salesman in the world. You gotta stay out of those places. Angie. For a while, anyway. Live and learn."

"Oh, Jack, I don't know if I can do this. I really don't."

"Maybe I can help."

"Oh, sure, the blind leading the blind."

"Hey, I'm trying to get sober, too. I have had a few slips, but I am going to do it. We're doing the same thing. We can help each other out."

"Well, if you expect me to move to West Virginia, you can forget it." I feel bile rising in my throat.

"Jack, hold on, okay?" I barely make it into the bathroom and spend the next fifteen minutes barfing violently. The room reeks of vomit and alcohol. By the time I feel clear of it, I am sweating and shaking. I sit on the toilet and lean over the sink, shoveling water into my mouth. Then I remember the phone. I stagger out into the living room and pick up the phone.

"Feel any better?" he says.

"I can't believe you're still here."

"Do you think I'd desert you in mid-puke? I've decided, Angela. I'm coming back. Not just for you, I should anyway, you know? I need to be home to get back on track. But let's keep it between us for now. We can help each other out."

"James would be seriously displeased if he thought we were meeting. He's very unhappy with you."

"Well, does he have to know? If I get better, he won't have any reason to be unhappy with me."

"Sydney's not the only serpent-tongued devil. Well, if it's going to help get us sober, I guess it's for a good cause. I can break it to him later and tell him how much it helped."

Deep down, I know there is an attraction between Jack and I, a very complicated connection driven on his end by loneliness and jealousy and alcoholic idealizing of who he thinks I am. And on my end? He is everything James is not: open, sympathetic, he seems to understand me without my having to explain myself. It is a powerful thing, to feel like someone is attracted to you, no matter what the reason. Good sense would keep me apart from him. But I tell myself there is good that can come of it and that I can handle the rest. An alcoholic can rationalize anything.

I clean up that night and pretend I'm asleep when James gets home. Somehow I do not get caught. And then I start to meet Jack at different times, our own private AA meetings. We meet in different places. He calls me at school and we make a plan if I can get away without James or Patrick noticing. It's generally not difficult. We frequently meet at the Larchmont Diner. You can find it not too far north of the Bronx on the Post Road, bright, garish and anonymous. Plates clatter, children scream, it is totally without a trace of intimacy. This lack of ambiance is a conscious but unspoken decision on both our parts, to avoid any possibility of any appearance of impropriety. But in the chaos it is possible to talk about anything, no matter how private. No one is listening but us.

This time we decided to try the Galleria Mall in White Plains. I had been dragged there by a friend to go shopping and immediately recognized the value of its hideous attributes: lit like a Vegas Casino, shockingly noisy, teeming with misbehaving families and clusters of churlish teenagers, but with countless walkways to stroll anonymously without a destination. An endless conversation.

Jack tells me he has found an apartment in the Village. Greenwich Village is not where I would put a person struggling with drinking, but he is not going to listen to me on that score. I am not going to go live in a cave, is how he puts it. Each of our visits together has the slight thrill of being surreptitious. A platonic affair. James would be furious if he knew, he has angrily written Jack off. But I could imagine a legitimate defense. I'm just helping. That's what I do.

But I have been wondering exactly why I am doing this. Is this a betrayal of some kind? What do I really want and where is this going? The fact that I cannot settle on an answer suggests to me that subconsciously I do not trust what the answer might be.

We stroll along the second level of the Mall, past Wilson's Leather and Banana Republic. We start by talking about our day, but then, as always, we quickly settle on a topic or person that is dear to both of us: Patrick, or Catherine, or Pop, or sometimes drinking. Never James, though, he never brings up James. And he never talks about Seamus.

"You and Catherine were birds of a feather," Jack is saying with a smile. He is eating an ice cream cone, with sprinkles. We tend to eat quite a bit during these visits. He could use it; he still looks drawn and underweight. He says he still drinks occasionally, but has it under control. I've been going to AA meetings for a while; I have no faith in anyone's ability to keep it under control. Ever since my hideous falling off the wagon, I have stayed straight. But it is always on my mind. Still, he is always sober and clear-eyed when we meet.

"Catherine and I are totally different," I say. I always talk about her like she is still alive. "But I do understand her. I really love her."

"She loved you too," Jack says, looking at the ground, the smile disappearing. "More than anybody." We turn a corner and head for Nordstrom's.

I fell in love with Catherine the first time I met her. She felt the same about me, I could tell. I know that sounds weird, but I don't mean it that way. It wasn't sexual or anything like that. It's just that we were kindred spirits and when you find that, you know.

Whenever there was a family gathering, it always deteriorated into men acting like men. James and Pop and Jack and Michael, and frequently other miscellaneous cousins, all being loud and arguing. And Nanny floating above it, having voluntarily disconnected from all of it to avoid her husband's nastiness. Michael's wife, Anne, would sit in a corner and glower at everyone. "Well, fuck her," Catherine whispered to me, "If she thinks she's so much smarter than all of us why doesn't she just get the fuck out of here." Catherine and I would sit together and talk quietly through all this, talking as easily as you'd talk to yourself. I say that we were kindred spirits, but we were opposite personalities. She was intense, fierce. Still, the only thing we ever disagreed about was Patrick.

"He's going to be a loser like his father, Angie, I'm sorry to say that, but he is. He's a space cadet. He already is the person he's going to be, I can't help him." But I saw something in Patrick, a startling sweetness that you were never going to find in another person. And I noticed that despite Catherine's apparent hardness towards him, they still never let go of each other. There was a connection there that couldn't be severed, no matter what she said. I decided even before Catherine died that I was going to look after him.

I see in the reflection of a store window that Jack is watching my face as well stroll along. "She would be very happy that Patrick is living with you," Jack says.

And there it is. He can read my mind. Corny, but true. He usually knows what I'm thinking and that makes it so much easier to say it to him. Things I can't say to James or Patrick or anyone.

I am on my fourth cup of coffee since we got here and my hands are starting to shake a little. I think about the day stretching out ahead of me tomorrow. Sometimes the days seem very, very long. Antabuse, Nicorette and caffeine are my sustenance, the things that get me through. I still sneak a cigarette every once in a while, but that only makes it harder not to smoke all of the time. I miss drinking and smoking so, so desperately. I feel about both like you would feel about a lover who up and left you without any warning. I mourn their absence, every moment. I can easily imagine grabbing a pack of Marlboros and a twelve pack of Heineken as soon as I get up tomorrow. Seven o'clock in the morning and it would taste just fine. I could feel the guilty pleasure of drinking early in the day, the relaxation of just giving up, giving in. When you lose control you lose all the pressure of responsibility. There's a song that goes "I like a nice beer buzz early in the morning" and I know exactly what that means.

But I look at Jack walking next to me, depending on me to help him through all of this, and I shake those ideas out of my head. I tell myself to go to the 7:00 AA meeting at St. Peters and be at school by 8:30, ready for my third graders. Once I get there I will be fine. Just say that to yourself, over and over. Once I get there I'll be fine.

"Catherine's last words to me, the morning of the accident, were take care of yourself, kiddo," I say to Jack, "she always called me kiddo or pal or sweetie. She spoke to me differently than anyone has ever spoken to me. She was not at all soft and fuzzy, but it was intimate, in a way. Or maybe exclusive, maybe that's the word, like I was different. I miss her."

I do miss her. I miss many things. I miss drinking. I miss the dream I had of being a mother, with a swarm of kids to care for. I miss the dreams that didn't happen. I miss James, as I remember him, when we were younger, when his affection for me broke through the walls he had built around himself.

Jack and I split up to move around a group of teenagers, shrieking like a flock of birds taking flight. When we come back together, we bumped shoulders ever so slightly.

"She was as hard as a nail," Jack says with a laugh, "she was unforgiving and rigid and tougher than you and she let you know it. But in her own strange way she cared very deeply about the people around her. Even Patrick, as merciless as she was with him."

Jack points into the window at Dalton's Books. A self-help book for addictive personalities. "Five steps to a better you," he says. He looks at me with a mischievous smile.

"See, it can be done in less than twelve steps. Who needs all that apologizing?"

I scowl at him and poke him in the arm.

"Nothing's as easy as those books say it is."

"I wish I knew why Cath was so hard on Patrick," Jack says, suddenly serious.

"Patrick reminded her of Pat's dad," I say. "She just ended up despising Roger, she hated herself for marrying someone she decided was weak and not amounting to anything. But you know what I think; the interesting thing is that Patrick is totally different from his father. He is a dreamer, but he will not settle for anything less than everything he's dreaming of. His father settled for less, and that was his curse. Patrick will never settle for anything less than the world he dreams of. And that's his curse. I tried to explain that to Catherine, but she couldn't change her mind on things."

We step on to an escalator, up to the third level. I watch the faces of the people moving down on the other side. Do they look happy? Are any of them so sad that they feel like they have to sit down and curl up and stop moving? What if your feelings floated above you like a cloud so that everyone could see them?

"Catherine accepted me, for some reason," I say, "and after that I could do no wrong. She confided to me about everything, about her hatred for Pop and how bad that made her feel, because she desperately wanted to love him. She didn't say that, but that's my theory. And we talked about everyone else, about all of you."

I motion towards a pretzel stand.

"I'm seriously over-caffeinated," I say, "I need some solid food."

I take my pretzel and we stop in front of Foot Locker. We lean against the glass and metal railing that looks down on the main floor.

"You know," I say, "when I identified her body; I expected to be shocked, because they said she was really torn up. But when I saw her, I was not revolted for some reason. Her face was untouched, her eyes were closed and she had just the slightest smile on her face. I actually think of her that way when I think of her, lying on her back in a morgue with a smile on her face and a sheet up to her neck. And all I could think about was Patrick and me and you. We had each just lost something that would take years to figure out. And we were now thrown together. I suddenly felt this feeling in my heart for Patrick, you know?"

I look at Jack, who is watching me intently.

"I felt something for Patrick ever since then, ever since that moment that I looked at his dead mother, this feeling for him that is like no feeling I've had for anybody else."

"You always sound like you're trying to talk me into thinking it's a good idea for Patrick to live with you. You know I think it's a good idea. Who are you trying to convince?"

"Me, I guess. Honestly? Sometimes I feel like I'm avoiding my real life, my life with James. Taking in somebody else's child. Meeting with my brother-in-law in secret. What the hell am I doing?"

"You're looking, Angie. You're looking for who you are. And you should continue. If you ever stop looking, you're dead. Hey, I want a pretzel, too. Or maybe some chocolate chip cookies, let's go down to the main floor and get cookies."

Later, as we prepare to leave, we stand on the sidewalk in the rain. I have to go back into the lot to get my car and his is across the street. I have an umbrella, but he stands under the rain with no cover, his head tilted back, letting it run across his face.

"Is James out on the water tonight?"

I nod.

"Where's Patrick?"

"He's staying with Nanny."

"So you go home and sit and stare at the walls?"

"No, I get ready for class and read and listen to music and walk around in circles. I would be drinking and smoking, but..."

He nods. "Me, too," he says, "I'm trying to walk in circles and not drink. Sometimes it works."

"Come to an AA meeting with me."

"Maybe. Maybe. But only because it's you." He smiles and winks. For a moment I think he is going to hug me or something, he leans in a little, and then he turns and walks away.

"Do you think Patrick would see me?" he calls across the street.

"Soon," I say. He waves and drives off. But how soon, I do not know. Patrick has been deeply hurt by Jack's abandonment. We have not talked about Jack. But I bet he hasn't given up on Jack. I am learning that Patrick, like me, is a romantic and always dreaming.

As I watch him walk across the street to his car, I feel very attracted to him in so many different ways that it confuses the hell out of me. I tell myself a lot of it is okay, that I like him because he is a drunk, because he is a friend, because Patrick used to adore him, because Catherine had adored him, and I honestly do not identify lust or love in that list of reasons, not at all, but I feel very uneasy about the whole thing. And I am still mad at him, for running off, for exposing Patrick to his dangerous trek out west.

I spend a lot more time thinking about Jack than I do my husband. That does worry me, because I do not know my sober self that well, and I am not sure I trust that person.

*   *   *

There was a day not too long ago when Nanny came down to the docks with Patrick and the two of us watched the *Daybreak* go out, Patrick waving at us from the stern. Nanny asked me if I wanted to get a cup of coffee.

We sat at the dockside diner. I have always been uncomfortable around her, very different from how I was around Pop. I understood Pop, his flaws and vices and anger. I did not understand Nanny, or Ellen as she told me to call her. I thought she was the opposite of me, devoid of vices and addictions, almost saintly. But saintly in a threatening way, an archangel of judgement. Or maybe that's just me being oversensitive.

"Why do you tie your hair up like that?" she asked as we sat down, "You have such lovely hair. When you pull it back it makes you look so severe."

"Oh, I just didn't have time to brush it. I didn't expect to run into anyone."

"You should always expect to run into people," she said, offering a thin smile, "That's why they call it running into people."

"I'll try to keep that in mind."

"So what's going on with Jack, anyway?" she said gruffly.

"What do you mean?"

"Oh, come on, I know the two of you talk, you meet, he goes to your alcoholic anonymous meetings with you. He's not an alcoholic, you know. What do you talk about?"

"He tells me how he's doing and I listen."

"Did you ever wonder why he picked you?"

"Because I had a drinking problem, I suppose."

"Oh, maybe. The fact that he's got a crush on you wouldn't enter into it?"

"What difference does it make as long as I'm helping him?"

"Maybe you like it that he has a crush on you."

"I'm married." My voice was a flat as I could make it. Her voice was a study in nonchalance. She spoke her questions softly, but each one hit me like a wave.

"How is Patrick doing with you two?" she said, carefully watching her cup as she stirred it.

"Okay, I guess. He was just with you, have you asked him?"

"He wouldn't tell me if he was unhappy there. He wouldn't complain to me. He is a very troubled child; he's had a very rough time of it, losing his mom and Pop and now Jack. Does he talk to you at all?"

"A little."

"You're not going to tell me if he does, are you?" she looked up at me steadily. "Do you want to know what I think?"

I looked at her and did not answer. I was getting very angry. Her tone was annoying, but there was something else behind it and without even knowing exactly what she was thinking, it was pissing me off enormously.

"I think he bares his soul to you. Like no one else. And you're keeping it to yourself."

"And what if he did? Am I supposed to tell everyone what he says? Do you think that's a good idea? Do you think that's what he expects me to do?" I kept my voice calm and low, but it was trembling and my heart was pounding in my ears.

"I just think," she said in a very low voice, "that maybe he shouldn't be relying solely on someone who has a number of, I don't know what the right word is, problems? Problems she is dealing with."

There were tears welling up in my eyes, but I squinted and would not let them out. My ears were ringing like I had been slapped. I stood up and walked towards the door, just barely resisting the urge to say fuck you to her.

I stepped outside and walked to one of the docks. My hands were shaking and I jammed them into my pockets. I started to cry but squeezed my eyes shut to stop it. It was a lovely day, cool and breezy. Masts and lines rattled in the wind, the incoming tide slapped against the bulkhead. I stood there for a few minutes.

"Do you want to know what's hard?" Ellen was standing on the dock across from me, separated by twenty feet of water. Her voice was carried slightly away by the wind, giving it a mysterious disembodied quality. I just looked at her.

"It's hard to watch every man you care about fall in love with someone else. First James, then Jack, Patrick, even Pop. Michael, too. They all just fell head over heels for you."

As she spoke, she walked around to the dock I was on, her voice getting closer and closer. Until she was standing five feet from me.

"They would do anything for you. All of them. Patrick would follow you to the ends of the earth. I wanted to take care of that boy, but he only wanted to be with you. And do you know what the worst thing of all was?"

I shook my head.

"It was absolutely right for him to be with you. You can take care of him better than me. I can see that already, he's snapping out of this daydream funk. Between working on the boat with James and having you to talk to, he's getting better."

"We're trying." I said tremulously.

"Well," she said, looking out to sea, "it's not easy to admit it when you know your time has passed."

"Your time hasn't passed, Ellen."

"Oh, please!" she waved one arm at me furiously, "I'm not stupid! I'm an old woman. I want you to tell me something, Angela."

I nodded.

"Are you going to give up on James?"

"No," I said quietly, "No, I'm not."

She looked at the ground thoughtfully. "Because no one would blame you if you did, he is the biggest pain in the ass I ever met. He's stubborn and pigheaded and impossible to understand."

"Tell me about it."

"But you are right for each other, I suppose."

"I'm not sure that's a compliment."

"I didn't come here to give out compliments. I don't know if we're ever going to like each other, but you're a damn sight better than Michael's wife, she's heartless." She looked at me curiously. "Yes, that's it."

"What?" I said cautiously.

"I better go. Take care of the boys."

She turned quickly and started walking away.

"What's it?" I said suddenly, calling after her.

She stopped and turned, looking at me expectantly.

"You said, yes, that's it," I said, "What did you mean?"

"You've got a good heart, Angela. That's it. I guess that's enough."

She gave me a small wave and walked down the dockside. As she moved away, I noticed that she walked with a limp, pushing one hand into her right hip. She looked small. An old woman, walking home alone, everyone she'd ever cared about either dead or gone.

CHAPTER FIFTEEN
Jack
December 2008

My father used to ask me, what happened to Seamus, Jack? What happened out there? He asked me in an offhand way, like a question about the weather, but he asked each time as if he hoped the answer would be different. The answer was always the same:

"I don't know, Pop. We got hit by that rogue wave and the boat tipped all the way on its side. I fell into the hold. When I came out, he was gone. It was really, really rough, out there, twenty foot waves, you know how those summer squalls blow. I went to the side with the life preserver and a line. But there was no sign of him."

Pop would shake his head, and look at the ground or the line he was tying. And he would sigh, in a deep, inconsolable way. He never got over that, losing Seamus, he just never did. And he never talked to anyone about it, except me. It was always the same conversation. What happened, Jack? Like it might change one day and have a better ending.

Seamus had this girl he liked, Annabel Sorrentino, whose father ran the Lobster Pot on City Island. She was very pretty. I mean really, really pretty. And she liked Seamus. He was always happy, Seamus, so that sometimes people didn't take him seriously, but he quieted down when Annabel was around and when he talked about her. He said he thought he was going to marry her. I said what, are you crazy? You're fourteen years old. But maybe he would have, who knows? You couldn't have a sweeter smile than he had on his face when he saw her, so maybe she was the one for him.

Patrick asked me once what was the last thing Seamus said to me.

"I have to think about that, Pat," I said.

"Was it right before he washed overboard?"

"No, once the storm hit it was too loud to talk, all we could do was look at each other and laugh. When it started to rain he said that he wanted to be a teacher when he grew up."

"A teacher?"

"Yes. Seamus was possibly the worst student in the history of Our Lady of Mount Carmel School. He repeated fourth grade, how many people do you know who repeated fourth grade? And he decides he wants to be a teacher." I laughed.

"Could he have done it?" Patrick asked in his sweet, singsong voice.

"Yeah, he could have. He was a lot smarter than he let on. I was the smart one and James was the tough one, so he had to be the funny one. But he was smart. You would have liked him, Pat. You had a lot in common."

"I'm not funny," Patrick said mournfully, "I wish I was. I would have liked him, I bet. I bet I would have. Somebody else I didn't get to know. All these people who aren't here."

Seamus has never left our family; he hovers over us, the ghost of what might have been. We talk about him all the time, when we are reminded of him, but often for no reason. Angela asked me once what happened to Seamus. Out of the blue at a family party, she brings up Seamus. We were standing alone in the kitchen.

"Didn't James ever tell you?" I said, looking away.

"A little bit,' she said, "He doesn't like to talk about it."

"You think I do?"

"Why are you so testy around me, Jack?"

This was back when she and James were just going out, before they got engaged and she quit drinking. We were all pretty toasted at these family parties. And I was a little testy with her, a little hard on her. I didn't know why, she was nice and James was crazy about her.

"You know what a full blown squall is like?"

"No," she said quietly.

"Like a hurricane in a small room," I said, "here one minute and gone the next and God help you. It'll blow you clear out of the water. The wind sounds like a jet taking off, the rain blows sideways so hard it feels like gravel. You can't think, it is such a terrible commotion. You hang on to something and you pray. Even if you don't ever pray, you pray then. It hit us hard and knocked the boat on its side. Seamus got washed right over; I didn't even see him go. He was just not there. I wanted to go in after him. But he was gone."

"I'm sorry," she said. Her eyes were a little wet and she touched me gently, quickly on the elbow. "I shouldn't have asked."

I looked at her. Have you ever looked at someone a hundred times and all of a sudden notice how they really look? Angela's eyes were a little bloodshot from whatever it was she was drinking, but they were deep, deep blue and didn't have a trace of meanness in them. I felt a little woozy.

"I've got to go check on my Mom," I said.

"Momma's boy," she said lightly, with a smile.

I nodded. I looked out of the kitchen window.

"Maybe I am testy," I said, without looking at her. "James and I have had this competitive thing going on forever, this brother thing, and I thought I had him beat hands down with me being married to Frances and him looking like he was doomed to spend the rest of his life with only bluefish for company. Now Frances and I are on the rocks and that knucklehead never leaves the Bronx and somehow manages to find this lovely person to hang around with. So maybe I'm jealous. Maybe. Maybe that's why I'm testy."

This all came out in a quiet stream, almost a mumble, but she caught all of it. She looked at me with those deepwater eyes, slightly widened in surprise, her forehead wrinkled in puzzlement. Then she gave me a kiss on the cheek and a squeeze on my arm and whispered in my ear, "Thanks, Jack, better go check on your Mom."

Some people are like a squall, the way they hit you all of a sudden.

I got Seamus drunk for the first time when he was only the age my nephew Patrick is now. Getting my nephew drunk now would be utterly out of the question, an unthinkably ill-advised thing, but somehow back then with Seamus it seemed like a good idea. We stole a bottle of Southern Comfort from Jay's Liquors while we were there with Pop one afternoon. Just slipped it under my jacket. A few years later I was in there and Jay said he saw me do it but figured I'd be a good enough customer one day. We drank it on the *Daybreak* while it was docked, hiding in the cabin. We got silly and eventually both threw up. Pop figured it out but strangely left us alone. We sat up in the room we shared until four in the morning, making up impossible stories about what we were going to do with our lives. I cannot think of growing up without thinking of him, I just cannot get away from the memory of him.

So now, years and years later, I start hanging around with Angela while supposedly trying to get sober. I am not getting sober; of course, I just want to be near her. I found out about her secret drinking, but never told anyone. Now she is actually clean.

One day, we are walking in a mall, talking about nothing, when I look in the book store window and see a new edition of Tom Sawyer. Seamus was reading Tom Sawyer the summer he drowned. He loved those books, that one and Huck Finn. He thought he <u>was</u> Huck Finn. I sit down heavily on a bench right in front of the book store.

"I'm getting a pretzel," Angela announces. She brings it back and sits down next to me. She turns to me with a smile, but I am crying, trying very hard to keep it in, but my shoulders are shaking and I am starting to let go. She suddenly looks alarmed.

"Jack? What is it?"

"I lied. I've been lying all this time," I say quietly.

"About what?" she looks around.

"Seamus."

She takes my hand and holds it tightly.

"How?"

"It's about how he drowned."

She shakes her head, not understanding.

"The wave hit us and the boat went over. I fell into the hold. I climbed half out, so I was on my stomach on the deck, but since the boat was on its side, I was looking right out over the side. And Seamus was hanging on to the side of the boat with one arm, he was off the boat and only his head was out of the water. And he looked right at me and said, 'Jack, get me, get me, Jack.' I couldn't hear him but I could read his lips. And he held his hand up a little. I tried to get up but the boat was leaning farther and farther over and I couldn't get on my feet. The wind was howling, it wasn't raining anymore, it was just water top to bottom, water flying everywhere, you couldn't see or hear or think. But I could see him, I saw his face. Then he said Jack, he said my name one more time and then he slid into the water. Then the boat tipped back over and I was able to get up. But he was gone."

"How is that a lie?"

"I could have saved him."

"Jack, you told me what a squall is like; you couldn't get up and get over to him. And you couldn't have gone in after him, that would have been crazy."

"Maybe I didn't want to save him, maybe I wanted to be on my own, not always Jack and Seamus. Funny Shay and Jack, cute Shay and Jack. Maybe I just wanted to be alone."

"Why are you doing this to yourself?"

"He wanted me to save him. And I didn't do it. I was the only one who could have saved my brother. And he's dead."

"It wasn't your fault, there's nothing you could have done." She puts her arm around me and for a moment I daydream that touch is a common thing. That she will always put her arm around me, even when I'm hurting.

"Maybe you're right, Angie," I say to her softly, "Maybe we're all too hard on ourselves."

But I do not really believe that. Because there are other things I do not tell Angela. I do not tell Angela this: The night that I took off from Mom and Patrick, when I ran away to go to Denver, I went into Patrick's room after they were both asleep. I sat on the edge of his bed for two hours, watching him. I knew that if I stayed, he would end up with me and I would be responsible for him. And I was afraid. I did not think I could do it. I did not want to stop drinking, give up my alcoholic fantasies. I did not want to live a real life, where people need you and you can fail them, where people hurt and die. I wanted to go far, far away, to a place where nobody needed anything from me. So I left. I betrayed Patrick. And he understands that, I can tell, and he has given up on me. That's even worse than what I did to Seamus.

As for my dead little brother, there is nothing that can change the way I feel about Seamus. I feel like I could have saved him and that I was always jealous of him and that those two things must be related somehow, somewhere, deep down. And there are other things about what happened that day that I do not tell Angela, that I cannot even bear to think about. I feel like I can't go on that boat ever again. My father and my brother drowned off the *Daybreak*. It is cursed, a ship of doom from a pirate story.

Every night before I fall asleep I see Seamus' face hanging on to the side of the *Daybreak*, wide-eyed, hopeful, and terrified. Thinking his big brother is going to pull him out of the raging sea. And every night I try to sleep and I am trapped on the *Daybreak*, tossed mercilessly in rough seas, white capped with dark angry rollers underneath, unforgiving and grim. Then the *Daybreak* starts to go down, bow first. I want to sink into the waves with it, just get it over with, but the sea will not take me. Every night I am thrown back out, washed up through crashing surf to an empty shore; the cold, dark early morning beach lined with barren trees and littered with the broken wood and glass of a thousand sunken ships.

Chapter Sixteen

Angela
December 2008

Two weeks after our walk in the Mall, Jack and I decide to go back to the Diner. Jack is distracted when he arrives, ordering only coffee. He looks like he might be hung-over. He gets right to the point.

"I'd like to figure out a way to see Patrick," he says, "Do you think we could do that?"

"I'd have to talk to him about it."

I realize as I speak that I do not want him to see Patrick. Am I jealous of how Patrick might feel about Jack? Or do I want Jack all to myself?

"Patrick's all yours now, Angie, you know that, right? All I'm getting is visitation." He spreads his hands out, as if in surrender.

He has read my mind again; but only half of it. I have seen the other part of him now, the drunken part, and those dark clouds are scudding across my sunny fantasy. I am accessible to Jack and so I become a means of getting things that he wants. He may not think that consciously, but that's how we think, us alcoholics.

He sighs and looks at me intently.

"You know what, forget I said that. You okay, Angie? How are you doing with your resolutions?"

Here is where Jack is different from how he's supposed to be. The problem with AA meetings is you walk out of them thinking everyone who ever had a drinking problem is exactly the same. And they aren't, or Jack certainly isn't. Alcoholics are supposed to be utterly self-centered and lack empathy. But this question from him is real, I know him that well. I shrug.

"Tell me about it. Forget Patrick. Talk about you. I want to hear it." He sits up straight and waves at a waitress.

"Can we get some coffee here? Actually, bring us a pot; we're going to be here for a while." He leans forward to listen. So I tell him some things. But not everything, I never tell anyone everything. My dreams, for instance, I keep those to myself.

I have always dreamed about drinking since I stopped. I dream about romance, too. Maybe I don't see romance in my real life, only some affection and reliance and more mundane emotions. I've been having one dream a lot. In it, I am at a wonderful, dark, lively bar. Music blaring, people laughing. Sitting on a stool belly up to the bar with a martini in one hand and a Marlboro in the other. Jack is there and we are telling each other secrets and having such a time. I am very happy. I love that dream, I look for it every time I close my eyes.

I leave Jack in the parking lot with a smile and a wave and I go home from the diner. James is on a night charter and Patrick is up watching television.

"How were your friends from school?' he asks absentmindedly.

"Good," I say. "You need to get to bed."

"It's Friday, Angela," he groans.

"It's still 11:30. Go."

When I go to bed, I have that dream. The one with me drinking with Jack. I wake up in the middle of the night parched and stagger to the kitchen. It is pitch-black. Then the light comes on in the hall. The front door closes. James is just back from his night charter. I really do not want to see him, I want to climb back into sleep and continue my dream. I lean on the wall in the doorway and close my eyes.

He walks up to me and holds my shoulders. He smells of salt water and fish.

"Dreaming?" he says.

I nod.

"Go back to your dreams." And he sweeps me off my feet and carries me up the stairs. I nestle my head into his smelly shoulder. His coat is scratchy and damp. I think that there is nothing sexy or romantic about any of this, not the way I think of romantic. He tucks me in and kisses me on the cheek.

"Sleep in tomorrow, love. I'll get up and get bagels."

I do not dream again that night. When I wake up, I hear James and Patrick in the kitchen. When I hear their voices I realize that I never dream about either of them. They only occupy my waking life.

I hear the unruly clatter of plates and silverware. I know they are trying to get breakfast together and that it will be a charming disaster. I hear James laugh. Very unusual, to hear that. I sit up quickly, eager to get down to them. I stand at the top of the stairs and listen.

"I'm no expert, Pat, but I don't think the pancakes are supposed to be on fire."

"Aaaah! What is that? What's happening?"

"Those are flames," James says dryly. "Oh look, they're almost reaching the curtains."

Then I hear a crash as a large metal object hits the floor.

"Well!" James says, "Throwing the oatmeal on the fire is unorthodox. But it worked!"

"James!" Patrick says loudly, "I'm so sorry."

"Forget it, Pat," James says warmly, "We are doing the best we can. We're a little lost on dry land, us sailors."

"Yeah, if I was trying to catch a swordfish I wouldn't be this klutzy."

"Nope. You're smooth as silk on the water."

"Do you think so?"

"Yes I do. Let's try scrambled eggs, we can't mess that up."

"She'll be excited to get breakfast in bed," Patrick says loudly.

"Ssssh. She'll be very happy. We want to keep our Angela happy."

I run back to our room and climb under the covers and pull them to my chin. I wait, warm electricity rippling through me. What is this? What do you call this? It's not in my dreams. It's not dangerous or exciting. I search my drunken fantasies for what it might mean, but it's not there. For a moment I feel like that drunk, lost girl is gone forever and someone else has dived under these warm covers. It is quiet and I can hear them whispering. "Don't drop it!" "Sssshhh. I am not going to drop it!" I kick my ragged slippers off my feet under the covers and listen for steps on the stairs, almost giggling. And for a moment, a moment that feels like it will last if I let it, I do not have a care in the world.

*   *   *

I come downstairs one Saturday morning and just catch Patrick as he is heading out the door, pulling his coat on as he goes.

"Hey, where you off to, Pat?"

He turns and glares at me, a look of such totally uncharacteristic hostility that it stuns me. He pushes out the door and runs down the street. I grab the door before it can close and walk out on the porch in my bare feet.

"Pat?" I call, "Patrick, where are you going?"

But he is gone.

James is sitting at the kitchen table, reading the Daily News and drinking a cup of coffee.

"What's going on with Patrick?" I say, pouring a cup for myself.

"A friend of his happened to mention to him that he saw you and his Uncle Jack walking around at the Mall."

He does not look up as he says this. I get a sudden sick feeling in my stomach, like a sudden drop on an airplane.

"Oh." I sit down. The kitchen is deafeningly quiet. I look out of the kitchen window. It feels like spring is coming. Birds sing and buds appear on the trees. The sun reflects off of the window glass and bright light streaks the floor.

James stands up and walks to the sink.

"I'm taking a charter out today, remember?" There is nothing unusual in his voice, but his tone is always cryptic.

I nod.

"Explain whatever you're doing with Jack to Patrick, I'm sure he'll understand." He pauses.

"Are you guys drinking?"

"No, James. Never. Never again."

He nods without looking at me and he walks out the door.

I sit there for an hour in a daze, trying to figure out what the hell that means. He isn't angry? He has no questions? Doesn't he care? I would be furious except I feel so guilty and uneasy.

James calls that afternoon and says he has gotten a night charter and will not be home until late. I think of bringing up the subject of Jack, but I am afraid of what he might say. Patrick calls in the early afternoon and asks if he can sleep over at his friend Peter's house. He is polite and not outwardly angry on the phone, but he is not himself either, not friendly or confiding.

I am home by myself. I tell myself I should eat something, but I am very tense and can't sit still. I want to drink, to smoke, to talk. But there is no one. I leave the house and walk for miles, up and down the main drag on City Island, past all of the tourist restaurants, out to the end where the fishing boats are, then all the way back to the bridge.

In front of The Castaway Tavern stands Captain Ronnie, who runs the Shamrock, an old 70 foot boat that takes charters in the summer and traps lobsters in the winter. James was a mate on the Shamrock for a while, but jumped boats because Ronnie was a bully and a drunk.

"Angela!" he yells at me from across the street.

I wave halfheartedly at him.

"Come on over here," he bellows, staggering across the street, "I'll buy you a beer." He stops in front of me. "Or a soda. You quit, right? Make it a soda. Where's James?"

"Out on a charter."

"Wouldn't catch me out at night with a pretty lady like you at home." He smiles, and then holds one hand up. "I don't mean that like it sounds. But that husband of yours is the most mule headed man I know. What's he got against me, anyhow?"

He suddenly sits down on the sidewalk and puts his head in his hands. I walk over to him, curious.

"You okay, Ronnie?"

"Oh, sure, just tired and drunk and alone. Just fine."

He looks up at me. "Well, nothing another beer won't solve, right? Give a man a hand, will you, love?"

I grab his hand with two hands and help him up.

"You okay getting home, Angie?"

"Sure, Ronnie. Thanks." I smile at him, suddenly feeling an unexpectedly deep kindness for him. He smiles back.

"You're one of us, ain't you, Angie? Everyone knows that you been visiting Mrs. Reeves. Playing hearts with her."

Mrs. Reeves is the widow of one of the oldest Captains who died just this past fall. James had worked with the man when he was just a boy. I thought it would be decent to stop by and she became so partial to our card games that I kept going back. I wondered how Ronnie knew about that.

I look at Ronnie and shrug. "She's a nice old lady."

Ronnie nods and turns to walk back to the bar. "How's your brother-in-law, Jack?"

"Oh," I say, surprised, "He's fine."

"He crewed with me when he was a teenager. Great guy. He's not James, though."

"I thought you and James don't like each other."

Ronnie leaned unsteadily against the Castaway's wall.

"Correction. James doesn't like me. He likes to be in charge but he won't admit it. Didn't like me giving him orders. But I was okay with him; I'd work on his boat any day. You can count on him. That Jack, he's a great guy to have a beer with, but I don't know how he'd do in a storm."

Ronnie puts his hand on my shoulder and looks at me with surprising clarity.

"I know Mrs. Reeves very well, Angela, since I was a boy. What goes around comes around. You're okay. Old King Neptune's gonna look after you." He turns and disappears into the bar, shouting and laughter bursting forth when he opens the door, then fading into quiet when it closes. I look around. I am alone on the street.

I want to go into the bar, just for a couple of beers. Just to relax for a few minutes. They would be nice to me, make a fuss over me. I could disappear for a little while. I take a step towards the door. Then I clench my fists and stop, force myself to turn and quickly walk away.

I finally find my way home and force myself to go to bed. I try to fall asleep, tossing and turning as a foghorn calls mournfully into the night.

That's the sound I hear when I wake. The foghorn in pale, pre-dawn light. Not another sound in the world. James sleeps next to me, his hair wet from a shower he must have taken a couple of hours ago. He smells of fish. No matter how hard he scrubs, he always smells of fish. I think he is self-conscious about it, but it is really impossible to tell, he certainly wouldn't say.

I watch his face as he sleeps; even asleep it is closed, impenetrable. Not a man who wears his heart on his sleeve. But I see something there that I have not looked at in some time. The face is strong and yet peaceful. I know that he is sometimes not at ease with the world and sometimes not even at ease with himself. But looking at him I remember what I feel about him: that he would do anything for me, anything except open himself up. And I think of his brother, who is an utterly charming open book; who has this undeniable pull on me, but who cannot be counted on in any sense, tearing through our lives like a Midwestern tornado.

By sneaking around with Jack I have caused mistrust in James and Patrick. I have the curse of wanting things I should not have, I know that. I am beginning to understand that I cannot trust myself, not yet. Just because I stopped drinking doesn't mean my head's on straight. I thought getting sober would clarify everything, but it has only clarified one thing: that I do not understand the hearts of anyone around me, or even my own.

*   *   *

Peter's mom calls a few hours later and we make a plan for me to pick up Patrick. I stop by their house on the way home from an AA meeting.

I attend a meeting at a church in Pelham, so that I don't run into anyone I know from City Island. Peter's dad is a fisherman, but he doesn't have a boat, he crews on whatever boat needs a hand. Sometimes he joins James on the Daybreak. He isn't James' favorite, though, he is unreliable. Sometimes he is too hung-over to go out in the mornings. Their house is a small, worn Cape on the other side of City Island.

As I walk up to the house, Peter's dad comes out to greet me. He is a bear of man, but quite nice. He has a sheepish smile on his face. He motions me off to the side.

"The boys had a great time and Patrick was very good," he says.

"Okay," I say.

"Ummmm, I should tell you that the boys seem to have gotten into a little beer." He coughs.

"What?" I say in a whisper. "What do you mean, got into?"

"Well, I got a lot of beer here, you know? I buy Pabst Blue Ribbon at $10 a case from this distributor guy I know, so I got piles of the stuff around here. I was taking out the garbage and I saw a few cans stuffed into the bottom of the bag. I cornered Petey this morning and he said they stole a six and split it."

He chuckles, "Not the first time Petey's done that, neither. He's a little ahead of his time." He shakes his head with a smile. "But I'm gonna talk to him about it," he adds, "It won't happen again. Anyway, I thought you should know."

I look up and Patrick is standing on the steps of the house. He regards me warily, and then smiles.

"Thanks," I say to Peter's dad. I nod towards the car and walk over and get in. Patrick gets in and we drive off.

I do not speak on the way home. I do not know what to say. I feel sick to my stomach, but my head tells me not to panic. Seventh grade boys do this kind of thing, I think. I have heard about it from the parents of another friend of Patrick's. But I still feel sick to my stomach. I had been prepared to apologize and try to make up with him over the Jack situation, but now I feel like I need to scold and lecture him. But he's probably still mad at me about Jack. I'm mad at him, he's mad at me and I can't lecture him about drinking because I have a drinking problem. I do not know how to raise a thirteen year old.

When we stop in front of the house, I turn the car off and put my forehead on the steering wheel. I hear him move forward in his seat.

"What do you and Jack talk about?" he asks.

"You, mostly," I say, without looking back. "Drinking, we talk about that sometimes. We both have a drinking problem, you know. You do know that, right, you do know that I'm an alcoholic?" My voice is rising, but I do not look back.

I try to lower my voice. "Are you out of your mind to be drinking at your age? Haven't you learned anything from this family?"

He is quiet for a full minute.

"I hate him. Jack."

"Don't. He can't help himself."

"Everyone can help himself. Everyone has control of his own life. Pop told me that when my mom died."

"That's funny coming from a man who had nothing but regrets when he died. I loved your grandfather and he treated me well, very, very well. But he was very sorry about how he handled the rest of the family. Especially your Mom."

Then he starts to cry. I can hear it. So now I turn and look at him. He is hunched forward, his head in his hands, sobbing. Of course, that gets me to crying as well.

"Why did he run off? Why didn't he want to stay with me? Why does everyone leave me? And then I thought I had you and James and now you're going to leave James."

"Hey!" I say, startled, "What the hell are you talking about? I'm not leaving James."

"He thinks you are."

"Who thinks I am? What are you talking about? Because of Jack?"

"James said," but then he stops and takes a deep breath and sits back. I hand him a tissue and he blows his nose.

"We were on the boat one day and we were talking about stuff and we started talking about you and I said I thought you are the prettiest girl in the world and he said you mean the universe. He said sometimes the two of you will be sitting on the dock watching the sunset, that you love sunsets, and he said he'll just watch you watch the sunset. That he never gets tired of watching you. But then he said someday that woman's going to wake up and realize she's married to a fisherman from the Bronx and off she'll go."

"Wait a minute. I thought you guys never talked about anything."

"What?"

"You both always complain about how you can't talk to each other."

"We hardly ever talk," he says.

"Well, what you just said is like three months of conversation from James."

"Really? Well, we kept on talking, too. He asked me if there were any girls I liked. You know the way James is, he said it like he was annoyed when he wasn't really. He said, aren't there any girls your own age that you like, or anyone besides my wife?"

I laugh. I can hear it exactly.

"Did you tell him?"

"Yeah, there's Donna DiFrenzi."

"Donna DiFrenzi? Didn't she call the other day?" I turn around. He is beet red.

"Don't even start," he says with a smile.

"What's with the beer, Patrick?"

"A lot of kids my age have tried it. I just wanted to be able to say I tried it."

"Is that it?"

"Well, unless the other beers taste better than Pabst, I'm not heading in that direction."

"Actually, almost anything tastes better than Pabst. Will you promise to be careful?"

"I'm not going to be like Jack," he says, "I won't."

I am still worried, but there is a long road ahead on that score and I force myself to drop it.

"Angela, why are you meeting Jack?"

"He needs my help. We can help each other. We both need help with drinking."

"You're not going to leave James?"

I turn around and look at him seriously.

"You don't think James actually believes that, do you?"

Patrick looks at me steadily, his eyes as dark and still as his mother's and his grandfather's.

"I think James is afraid he's not good enough for you. That's what I think. That you're perfect and he's just a fisherman."

"What? That's crazy. He knows I'm not perfect, I'm a total mess."

"He doesn't think so. It's hard to explain. I think he worries about how cool Jack is. He doesn't have any faith in himself when it comes to you."

"Did he say that?"

"No, but if you spend enough time on a boat with someone, I think you start to know what they're thinking about most of the time."

Patrick leans forward. "When did you guys meet?"

"James and me? Oh, a few years ago. It's a long story."

"Tell me?"

"Okay. I guess I can do that. I went on a fishing trip with three really obnoxious stockbrokers and two of the teachers I worked with. They dragged me along because they needed a date for the third guy. He was a real jerk, he starts putting his arm around me as soon as we get out of the car. The charter was James and the Daybreak. He took us out by himself because his mate called in sick."

I turned around to look at Patrick, "You know, he usually prefers to go out by himself, you're the first person that he's been taking out on a regular basis."

"Really?"

"Yeah. Anyway, I was really intrigued by our captain, he was very quiet. I don't want to spoil your impression of me, Patrick, but I got a little drunk, that's when I was drinking. And I started teasing James a little, calling him Captain Ahab and pretending to want to steer the boat. He barely reacted, you know, a little smile. He must have thought I was totally obnoxious. Then on the way back, everybody's been drinking and my date, Mr. Charming, comes up behind me and wraps his arms around me and then he won't let go. I'm saying, let me go, and he won't. Then all of a sudden, he lets go and I turn around and James has him by the scruff of the neck, lifting him off the ground. He looks at him and says, 'When she says let go, you let go. Or you're swimming home.' Everyone was very quiet. He seemed very, very imposing. Mr. Charming's friends teased him the whole way back and as soon as we got to shore he stormed off. I was going to say something to James, but he really didn't seem like he wanted to talk."

"This doesn't sound like a very romantic meeting," Patrick says.

"Pat, like I said, I hate to burst your illusions, but I was a drinker and there is nothing romantic about that. But listen, while we were fishing I was telling one of my colleagues that I had this old car and I couldn't get it to run. I was going to junk it. As we're all leaving, I'm standing there and James wanders over to the side of the boat, so he's within earshot and he says, real quiet so no one else hears, 'I can fix that car of yours.' I said, Oh! Okay. And I told him my address and he said he'd come by one day."

"Did he?"

"Yes! To my total surprise, he appears at nine the next morning. I look like hell, all hung-over and bedraggled. And James, he was dressed up a little, khakis and a sweater. I don't want to embarrass you, Pat, but I have always thought he is so handsome, so striking, in a way that he is totally unaware of. That's what makes him so attractive, that he's so unaware of it. He could have swept me off my feet right there."

I look at Patrick and he is looking at the floor, blushing a little. So I don't tell him all of it. James has always had an effect on me like no one else. When you are a drinker, you're numb, after a while you feel nothing. I never really felt much with men before, I went through the motions for the occasional company. And I didn't think I cared. But the first time James held me I felt this electric current of warmth flow through me. It was like waking up on a beautiful day without a hangover. I got so carried away I was a little embarrassed later. Our attraction for each other was a strong part of our connection to each other; since he didn't know that I kept drinking, he couldn't know that he was my one connection to real feelings. But as the days and then years went by, that part of it, the physical part became a little subdued as we became more tentative around each other. My lying about my drinking was separating us without him knowing why or how. And after I told him that I had been lying to him for years, he became harder and harder to feel connected to. I wondered if we ever would be able to get back to those first feelings.

I try to stop worrying and I smile and say to Patrick, "Sorry to embarrass you, Pat. So anyway, we barely talk, but he fixes the car, which was a miracle. Then he says, 'I'm sorry for that Neanderthal behavior on the boat yesterday.' I say you don't have to apologize for that jerk. He says, 'no, I'm apologizing for me, grabbing people and threatening them, I can't imagine what you think of me.' I say I think you are a gentleman. Then he says, 'well, I gotta run. But here, I thought you might be interested in this.' And he hands me something wrapped in brown paper."

"What was it?"

"I told people on the boat that day that I had done my Masters on Zen Buddhism in America. I didn't realize how much he was listening. I open the wrapper and there were two books there, by Peter Mathiesson."

"Oh, *Men's Lives*."

"Right. That book about fishermen on Long Island. But the other book, by the same author, is called *Nine-Headed Dragon River*. It's about Buddhism in America. I had heard of it but I hadn't actually ever read it, because it's not a scholarly treatise, it's more like a memoir."

"James is so weird!" Patrick exclaimed. "He reads all these books in secret and then tries to convince everyone he's this dumb fisherman."

"Totally weird. But I read a lot of the book and then a couple of days later I went down to the docks and he took me out, just the two of us. And I have spent every minute of every day ever since trying to figure out what he's thinking. He's so different from Jack."

"But you can trust him. You can't trust Jack. You can always trust James," Patrick says.

"You don't think you can trust Jack? I don't know. But I do trust James. And I'm never leaving him, Patrick. Can you forgive Jack, Patrick?"

"I don't know. Maybe."

"He wants to see you."

"Maybe. Maybe later. Are you going to tell James about the beer?"

"Yeah, but it won't be a problem. He trusts you."

"He does?" He sounds completely surprised. "What do you mean?"

"He said you're a little absentminded but you're the one person he would take out in bad weather. He said you are at your best when things are worst."

"Really? He said that?" He looks out the window and smiles.

"So anyway," I say, "tell me about this sunset thing that James said about me?"

"Why don't you ask him yourself?" He nods towards the front of the house, where James stands, holding the door open.

We get out and walk up to him, each holding our secrets. He raises his eyebrows.

"What are you two grinning about?"

"Nothing," I say.

Patrick laughs. "I told Angela you *like* her."

"I told Patrick you said he could be your first mate."

He squints at both of us without a trace of a smile and shakes his head, turning to go inside.

"I think you're both nuts," he says over his shoulder, "But I'm glad you're both home. I can't stand this place when you two are gone."

CHAPTER SEVENTEEN
Jack
December 2008

I am a hopeless dreamer. I pass absentmindedly through my days, all the time imagining other lives, other places, other versions of me. Of course, that's what being an alcoholic is all about. Escaping into another world, wherever it might be that day, the world where you can be anything other than what you really are.

I am what you call a dry drunk now. I stopped drinking a little while ago, after years of torturing myself to quit. One day I woke up in an unspeakably foul mood and I realized as the day wore on that my despair was because I was going to stop drinking that day. Angela says she misses drinking like a lost lover, she thinks of it with great fondness and longing. I don't, I hate it. I think of my drinking self as a miserable hateful person who I wish was dead. I'd kill that guy with my bare hands if I could. I'm a dry drunk because I stopped drinking, but I'm not better. At least I don't feel better and I still mistrust my instincts in every decision I make.

So here is how I think this story ends: I prey on Angela's insecurities, vulnerability and frustration and convince her to run away with me. A terrible thing to do, but one that would make me very happy. I love her, in my own twisted, self-absorbed, completely destructive way. I love everything about her, the way she sways when she walks, the way her eyes wrinkle up at the sides when she smiles, her blunt sense of humor, the way there are curves to look at no matter which way she turns. Running away with me would break James' heart, but I am past the point of caring about that. It would ruin any chance of reconciliation with Patrick, but it would be worth it. It would be awful for Angela, who is forever teetering on the brink of sobriety, but I just don't think about that.

I stopped by her school today to visit again, but she was engaged in a deep conversation with a boy in her class. She shook her head, which I took to mean that she would not be able to talk, so I left. I call her later that night.

"I went down to the docks to see James," she says.

"How come?"

"That boy, Gerald, was telling me things about James. James and his father were friends. His father just died. It's terrible."

"That is tough for a kid. But as Pop used to say, we all got to die sometime. So what does Gerald know about James?"

"James has been very kind to him. He said James was funny."

"Funny?"

"Real funny and silly, actually."

"Funny? James? Huh. Guess that shows you just never know people the way you think you do.""

"Has James helped you in the past, Jack? You seem so independent of each other, but have you relied on each other sometimes?

I do not answer. Have there been such times? Oh, yes. Many, many times. But I don't want to think about those times.

"I don't know. We helped each other out, the way brothers do. What brings that up?"

"He's helping this boy, this family."

"So, what, is everything okay with you guys now?"

"No. No. We've gotten pretty far apart. We've come a long way together, but we've grown apart in a way that kind of shocks me. Mostly because I was too busy drinking to discuss anything. I think we lost a lot along the way, I don't think he really trusts me to talk to anymore. I think we're kind of lost. But now we've got Patrick to take care of. I want to see if we can figure it out. At least today I do. You know how it is."

Yes, I think, I know how it is, but I don't feel like confirming that to her. This conversation is not going the way I want things to go.

"Is that what you want, Angela? To piece together a broken marriage? To salvage something? You're sober, you have a chance to start a new life. Don't you want a fresh start?"

There is a pause on the phone, a long pause.

"What do you want, Jack?"

"Me? Oh, I don't know. How the hell should I know? I'm even more lost than you are. I'm way behind you recovery-wise."

But she interrupts me.

"Don't bullshit me, Jack." She adds softly, "It's me, Jack, what do you want?"

I wait. All the bullshit answers get stuck on my tongue.

"You," I say, "you and Patrick. A house and a yard. Kids that run up to me and fight over who gets the first hug when I get home from work. Friends. Happiness. Not to feel like I wish I was dead." I take a deep breath, suddenly shaky. "Mostly you."

"You could have some of those things. Most of them."

"Not you, though, huh?"

"No, Jack, not me. Not that way."

"Yeah, I guess the part of me that isn't mentally deranged knew that."

"You don't want me, Jack. Not the real me. That would be for all the wrong reasons, wouldn't it? You need to find what you really want out of life, now that you can start to see it more clearly."

She is wrong about that, though. I do want her, it isn't just because she is a drunk, or because of James and Patrick. It is exactly because I am starting to see more clearly. It is her.

"You might get everything else you want, though. And things you didn't even think of. And you could have me, but in a different way, if you can get used to that."

But I don't think I can get used to that. For a shocking moment I do not feel like a drunk, or a hateful, damaged person. I feel like an ordinary young man, not someone who has torched his entire environment; just a guy who might have had a reason to think that life is going to work out the way he wants it to. A guy who then finds out that the most important part of what he wants is not going to happen. This has gotten all flipped around. I thought I was pursuing Angela because I felt like it, but that I didn't really care. I thought I didn't really give a shit about anyone or anything else. But why is it, then, that I cannot get a word out and the hand holding the phone is shaking?

"Jack?"

So this is how I see this story ending: Everyone who I really care about in this world, Patrick, James, Michael, Angela, has completely lost faith in me. And there are others who are lost forever: Seamus, Catherine, Pop. And I have lost at least one of them myself, in a way I cannot even bring myself to think about. The world is drifting away from me; I have no hold on it. After years of fiercely pushing people away, now I cannot stand being alone. So maybe I go home one night and blow my brains out. I don't see any other end to this miserable fucking story.

I hang the phone up and walk to the apartment window. I lean my head against the glass. This is bad, I think, real bad. I thought I was cold and manipulative, I thought I had gotten rid of my feelings, drowned them, leaving me with nothing left to hold me back. But a drunk can fool himself even better than everyone else. I am not cold, I am desperate. Desperate for love and a connection to something or someone.

The phone rings.

I answer, suddenly very tired, "Yes?"

"Jack."

"James?" I sit down, startled. "Hey, James."

"What are you doing tomorrow?"

"Tomorrow," I repeat, confused. "I don't know. I don't have any plans. Why?"

"Feel like fishing? Patrick and Angela are coming. We're taking out Gerald and his mom."

"On the *Daybreak*? You sure you want me?"

"Of course. Hey, it's partially your boat, you know. Pop left it to all of us."

"That's your boat, James. Always has been."

"Do you want to come? I'm asking."

"Why are you asking? Don't you hate me?"

"Nah. A little annoyed, maybe. But I'll get over it."

"Don't bullshit me. Why are you doing this?"

"Oh, pick your reason. Patrick misses you. My wife is making me do this. She has a thing for you. I miss you. You're a good fisherman."

"This must be the delirium tremens part of getting sober kicking in; I could swear you just said you missed me."

"I would never say anything of the kind. And if I did, Angela made me. But it's a new me. I'm getting sensitive."

"Fuck you. You're just trying to impress Angela."

"Well, of course I am. Wouldn't you?"

"Yes I would, I surely would. But you beat me to her. Apparently you have all this secret charm that no one knew anything about. What time are you going out?"

"6:00. None of this late start charter crap. We're not amateurs. I want to get thirty, forty miles out. Catch some real fish."

"Okay, okay. Jesus, lighten up, you sound like Pop. I better go to sleep. I'll see you in the morning."

"For sure?"

"Yeah."

"You okay? You want us to come get you?"

"No, I'll be fine."

There is a pause on the line and it occurs to me that he is worried about me.

"I'll be fine, James. I'll be ready."

"Okay. I'll be looking for you. I'm coming to get you if you don't wake up."

So now maybe this is how I see this story ending: I get up in the morning and buy a large coffee and drive out to City Island at five fucking o'clock in the morning. I like City Island; I know it better than anywhere else. I'll drive by the closed restaurants and pass a few pick-ups backing up to their boats. And James will be on the boat, pulling lines and loading gear. Patrick will be a little stiff with me at first, still mad, but he'll break down and we'll be fine. Angela will look glorious and I'll spend the rest of my life sneaking looks at her and getting a grip on that.

It will be cold and damp. We will cruise past the docks, very quiet that early in the morning, just the sound of gulls and the clatter of tackle. I'll get used to the feel of the boat, that gentle rocking, a different earth. And James will let me take the *Daybreak* out, he always does. It will feel good to take her out, under the Verrazano and out to sea. And as the shore disappears, my ill will can slip away with it. It will be okay. So I won't blow my brains out, not today.

I will just hang on to the wheel, follow James' gentle directions to where the fish are, feel the pitch and the swell increase, and push the boat into it. And I will think of the people still alive who I care about, most of whom are on this boat, and then I will think back to the dead, to Catherine and Pop and Seamus. Catherine will be easy, I never betrayed her, she was the one person I stayed loyal to. Seamus I have to skip over, still. Then it's on to Pop. Drowning himself off this same boat. Bastard. Leaving me with a lifetime of guilt.

As soon as I stopped drinking, I started going to the beach early in the mornings. I like it better when the weather is dirty, cold and wet. I strip down and wade in, swimming out and sinking headfirst like a stone into the bottomless black. I try to imagine what Pop felt like as his boots filled up and he sank into the dark. Was there a last second of regret or love for me? I feel a release while I am submerged, hidden from the world, brushing up to death. The sea could take me in, swallow me up and let me rest. I open my eyes sometimes under the water. I hear voices and I see faces. I try to feel what Pop felt when he realized that the sea was not going to let him go. Was he really ready for that, after spending his whole life on it? I push down into the black until my lungs are bursting and there is nothing but darkness. And there the last face I find floating up towards me is my father's, wide-eyed with surprise that after everything he'd done, the sea had taken him back.

CHAPTER EIGHTEEN

Angela
January 2009

Gerald Peavy is a small, quiet boy in my third grade class. He is no trouble, except that he sometimes needs help keeping up academically. He told me three months ago that his father was home sick and had stopped going to work. I asked him every once in a while how his dad was doing and he said fine. Getting better, he said. Gerald never smiled, but he was always a somber child, so I did not wonder too much about that. With twenty-six children in my class, it was difficult to pause and dwell on a particular child.

This past Monday Gerald did not come in. That afternoon the school's assistant principal came by and told me Gerald's father had died, of cancer. I have never taught a child whose parent had died, but I have discussed the topic with other teachers and I quickly developed a plan for informing the kids and addressing the issue of death. I think it went well; they were frightened, but very attentive. I tried to be organized and very careful about how the subject was discussed in class.

I went to the wake and the funeral. At the funeral, I patted Gerald on the head and leaned over and whispered to him that he should talk to me if he ever thought I could help with anything. He nodded, showing no emotion. As I drove home, I wondered if there was anything else I could do for him. It occurred to me that I was being very detached about the whole thing. But I did not want to change that, I honestly did not want to share Gerald's pain, I was feeling shaky enough as it was. I let my mind wander back to my own problems.

Jack has been dropping by the school recently. I think he has figured out that James never visits. I sometimes wonder why James never comes to visit me. I never ask James about it or suggest that he come by, but you'd think it would occur to him to visit me at some point. But he doesn't. I must have mentioned it to Jack. Jack sits in my classroom once or twice a week and we talk. I find myself unburdening myself to him more and more, about my preoccupation with drinking and smoking, about my anxiety and feelings of emptiness, and I tell him about this distance between James and me that I cannot seem to close. Jack says he has stopped drinking and has been working as an analyst at a small investment company in Manhattan. But he does not volunteer much more about himself. He seems calm, composed, understanding. Different than when we had first started meeting, when he would chatter on for hours.

This morning I sit across from James as he reads his paper. I suddenly feel very frustrated with the silence, although the mornings have been like this since we first met. I find myself comparing Jack and James: James physically larger, sometimes brooding, self-contained; Jack long and slender, bright-eyed, outgoing. I'd like to be outgoing, happy, fun.

"Are you going out on a charter tonight?"

He nods, without looking up.

"Are you doing these charters to avoid me at night?"

He looks at me impassively. "We need the money; we've got Patrick to take care of."

"You didn't really answer my question."

"There's something going on with you, Angie. I don't know what it is, but you're very far away." He looks at the table and plays absentmindedly with his fork. It is very uncharacteristic, to see a sign of nervousness from him. He looks up.

"It worries me."

"You don't have to worry, James. I'm still the same me, I haven't changed. I'm not going anywhere." I try to say this with feeling, but it feels flat, distant.

He nods and forces a smile. "I know, I know." He stands and picks up his plate. He pauses by the sink, looking at the floor as if he were going to add something, and then just says, "Well, I better get going."

He pauses at the door. "How's Gerald?"

I turn, surprised. "Fine," I say. I don't remember mentioning the boy to him.

"His dad used to mate on my boat. Good man."

"Oh!" I say, "Why didn't you go to the funeral?"

He looks down, scratching his foot on the ground.

"I was out on the boat. His wife understood. That's where he would have been."

In the afternoon at school I find myself wondering if Jack will come by. I realize that I am hoping that he does, quite strongly, and as I am standing in front of the class listening to them read poems about springtime I feel something in me start to unravel. Some basic assumption of who or what I am just comes apart and starts to float away. I am not sure I want to be with James anymore. I am not sure I want to devote my life to taking care of Patrick. I want to have some excitement, some fun. If I cannot drink or smoke and I have to live through these days in this endless cycle of work and loneliness I think I will die. I wonder if Jack and I could run away somewhere, just take off. The thought gives me a thrill. I think of talking to him about it, and the thought of that gives me a feeling like I used to feel walking into a crowded bar: excited expectation.

Then the 2:45 bell rings and the quiet room bursts into singsong chatter, like sparrows in a tree. I pick up some completed poems from the desks and walk back to my desk. Gerald is there, holding a piece of paper.

"Will you read my poem, Ms.Cabrera?"

"Okay," I say, surprised, taking the sheet from him. I sit on top of my desk. He sits down at a desk in the front row. The room is now empty except for us.

"My mom helped me, it's not all me. I didn't want to read it in front of the class." He sits hunched over, as if in pain. He watches me carefully. I read it aloud:

Spring is here
But my dad is gone
The flowers are coming
But first it rains and rains and rains
I have a dream every night
In it the sun finally comes out
And my dad comes back with it
I wake up every morning
And open the window
To see if they are here

He is trying not to cry. I walk over and sit next to him. I take a deep breath. If I start crying now there is going to be no stopping me.

"That's a beautiful poem, Gerald."

"But what good is it?" he says with sudden anger, "He's not coming back."

"Yeah, but Gerald, he was here! He was with you for eight years and he gave you everything that he had and you'll always have him that way. Always."

The words come out faster and faster and I start crying. "You'll never forget him and he'll be watching you. He can be the last person you say goodnight to and the first person you say good morning to and wherever you go, for the rest of your life, you can take him with you. Here." And I tap his heart. "Right here."

"Were you ever so sad you thought you would die, Ms. Cabrera?"

"Yes," I say, surprising myself with how quickly I answer.

"Really? What did you do?"

What did I do? Did I ever think I would die from how I used to be? I can remember standing in a parking lot of some miserable bar on Long Island, not quite remembering how I got there and being too drunk, too foggy headed, to even begin to think of how I would get home. It was cold and all I had on were a sweater and jeans. I started walking, shivering and staggering, down a brightly lit but empty two lane highway. I came upon a bridge over a surprisingly deep valley. I leaned over the railing and looked down. I felt a shocking and frightening loneliness that I cannot explain in words. I imagined just dropping over the railing, turning end over end until I hit rock. Then it would end. I tried to imagine what difference that would make to anyone. I don't know why I didn't do it. I wasn't afraid. But my head was starting to clear a little and it was a beautiful night, a thin black sky littered with stars. I could see my breath and it was starting to snow. I watched the flakes drift silently into the darkness below. I started to walk, not knowing which way I was going or where I might end up. But thinking that there was a trace of life left in me that might come out if I kept moving.

"Ms. Cabrera? What did you do?"

"I got up and went to work. I came to see you, Gerald. You kept me going."

"Me?" he says with a surprised smile.

"Yes, Gerald, you kept me going," I say, wiping my eyes and taking a deep breath.

"Will you tell me a story? My dad used to tell me stories."

"Sure," I say. I look up and see Jack standing in the doorway, an uncertain look on his face. I look at him for a moment. I could ask him to wait for me, but suddenly I don't want him to wait. I need him to leave.

I must be losing my mind. These feelings of running away, of leaving my life behind, are fading as quickly as they came. I feel something different, a kind of sorrow that I cannot run away, that my life has to be lived here in this pale and lonely place. I feel an empty longing that I have felt every day since I quit drinking. But I know that I have to get through it, that I cannot run away from it. Jack is not going to save me.

I shake my head silently at him. He looks surprised for a moment, then nods and walks away.

"Well, let's see," I say, "What kind of stories do you like?"

"Boat stories. My dad was a fisherman. He knew your husband. My dad liked him a lot. James comes over sometimes. He's real funny."

"He comes over? He's real funny?"

"Yeah. He's silly."

"He's silly?"

"Yes!"

"My husband? Are we talking about James MacAfee?"

"Yeah, Captain Mac. I went out on the *Daybreak*. Three times!" He holds up three fingers. "He let me steer. I caught a sea bass. He taught me songs! Do you want to hear *What Do You Do with a Drunken Sailor?*"

"No, no," I say, laughing, "I've heard that song many times. That's a shower favorite in our house."

"He has a really bad voice," Gerald says in a conspiratorial whisper.

"Yes, he does. But you know what? He doesn't care!"

"Nope!" Gerald says with a big smile that I have never seen before. "He came by last night."

"He did? James? Came by your house last night?"

"Yeah, he brought me a fishing rod and a cap that says "*Daybreak*" on it, so I can come and be a mate on the boat. A new deep sea rod."

I sit, stunned. "Well," I say slowly, "how about a *Daybreak* story, then? I know that boat pretty well."

He nods.

So I tell him a story. I put him on the boat, with his dad and James. Stormy seas and giant whales and heroic rescues. I put Patrick and me on the boat, too. I toss Gerald and me out to sea, hanging on a broken mast, riding waves the size of skyscrapers. I have James and Gerald's dad rescue us. As I tell it, and watch Gerald, he nods contently.

And it was totally believable, that Gerald's dad would save him and that James would save me. I knew that James could do that, if it ever came to it. I knew he would dive straight into the beautiful, unforgiving ocean to save me, without a thought. I give my story a happy ending. Just as I am finishing, I see his mom in the hallway, she must have been waiting for a while. She nods at me, her arms folded, clutched to her chest. When it is over, I tell Gerald to come back anytime. He nods with a smile.

"You can keep the poem, Ms. Cabrera."

"Won't your mom want it?"

"No. She says she's memorized it. Can I come again tomorrow?"

"Definitely."

He runs out into the hallway and hugs his mom. They walk down the hall, her arm on his shoulder. I can hear his voice down the empty hallway, no words, just the sound rising and falling like a bird song. I watch them from the door. Just as they turn the corner, she looks over her shoulder at me. She raises her hand in a shy wave and smiles.

One thing I expected when I got sober was that things would change. But I thought that everything would change all at once and that would be it and then I could get on with my life. It doesn't work that way. When you get sober, reality keeps shifting as you emerge from your alcoholic fog. And as the world tilts away from me on a daily basis, my emotions, freed from years of self-medication, run amok.

So I do not run away with Jack. Not today, anyway. That fierce urge floats away in the breeze that carried Gerald Peavy through my life. I go home and take a bath and think about the grateful look on Ellen Peavy's face. I do not deserve her gratitude, Gerald has revealed himself to be a child of uncommon strength and hidden gifts, but it makes me feel just fine all the same.

I dress up a little bit, in something that I know looks pretty good, and I go down to the docks. It is 5:30 and the day boats will be settling in for the night. The night boats will be gearing up, with all of the clatter and cursing that comes with that. I have grown to love the sound of the docks, I have even gotten used to the smell, and all of these things will always remind me of my husband. I walk down to the *Daybreak*'s usual spot, realizing that I have not been there for weeks. James is working on the roof of the boat's cabin and spots me from a distance. He stands up as I approach, eight feet over my head, and looks down, puzzled.

"Hey, everything okay?"

I nod. I smile at him.

"Haven't been here in a while," I say lightly, "you saw me coming."

He looks at me carefully. "I guess I always have my eye out for you."

"Mind if I come aboard, James?"

But he surprises me by quickly jumping down, stepping off the boat, taking my elbow gently and leading me down the dock.

"How about I buy you a soda at Jimmy's?" he says. He sniffs his hands and wrinkles his nose. "I reek of fish."

"What else is new? You smelled like fish the first time I met you. Didn't bother me then."

I turn and watch him. His face is troubled; I can tell from his expression that there is something on his mind, something he wants to say. But knowing him, he might not say it. He looks at me.

"You look nice," he says quietly.

"Thanks," I say, "I told a story about you today."

"Oh, who to?"

"Gerald Peavy."

He smiles, looking down. "What was it about?"

"Fishing. The ocean, the boat. All the things we care about." I lean over and kiss him on the cheek. He looks as surprised as I've ever seen him.

The docks stink of fish and oil and low tide. Seagulls shriek overhead. Everywhere there is the rattle and banging of boats getting ready. Men shout orders to each other, with every other word an obscenity. It is a strange, unromantic place. Until now, if I was making up a story with a happy ending, in a million years it would not have ended here. But now I can think of a good story that takes me right here, right now.

I take a deep breath and try to relax, try to get things to hold still. I feel some fear, even in this quiet moment. I know there are other versions of my story, ones that could end elsewhere, some with an uncertain ending, and some with a very bad ending. I have no illusions about my own strength or willpower. I am afraid that I will not know which way my life is heading until it is too late to turn back. I do not trust myself to choose the way.

The wind suddenly picks up off the water, rattling the lines and masts on the boats in a chorus of anxious clanging metal. Clouds have gathered, dark underneath, shrouding the sunset and promising a storm. Lightning flickers directly overhead and a dull rumble promises something worse. Hundreds of sea birds take off as one and fly wildly in different directions. The world could be unraveling. But James looks up at the storm, unafraid. Then he looks at me with a slight smile and that unfailingly calm gaze that opens for a moment to show tenderness and something more. I feel the back of my neck tingle. I put one hand in his and wrap the other arm around him and I hang on for dear life.

CHAPTER NINETEEN
James
January 2009

There's a Nor'easter blowing in and I'm not going anywhere. The *Daybreak* is tied up and I'm down in the basement trying to rebuild an old outboard engine. Like always, I've got the ship-to-shore radio on, listening to the chatter. That's where you hear where the fish are running, although no one's on the air today. Nobody in their right mind would go out in this howling mess.

Then a scratchy voice comes on that I recognize as Bob Cullen, captain of the *Port Royale*, a charter boat out of Port Jefferson.

"Anyone interested, I've got a secondhand Mayday from the *Olivia May*. Sounds like the Coast Guard can't get a fix on her. Anybody knows the boat, maybe you can help. Distress call from *Olivia May*."

Olivia May. Why did that name sound familiar? I work for a few minutes longer, chewing on the name. Angela comes down with a load of laundry.

"James, can you throw these in the dryer when you hear the machine stop?" she calls from the back room.

"Sure. Hey, what's the name of Audrey Mackey's sailboat, the one she just bought?"

"Oh. Olivia something. *Olivia May*. Why?"

My stomach sinks. I feel slightly nauseous. "Nothing. You know what? I just realized the *Daybreak*'s back hatchway isn't down. I'm going to run over there. And I might stick around for a bit if anyone needs a hand."

"Of course you will," she says cheerfully, walking into my workroom. "Hey, want to watch Pride and Prejudice when you get back? It's the old one." She smiles. "I know that's your favorite."

"Yes," I say. "I would like to watch it." I give her a kiss on the cheek and hold her head to my chest.

"Huh?" She looks at me. "Really? Everything okay?"

"Sure. Gotta run before the boat floods."

I call Jack from the car.

"James?" he sounds surprised.

"Hey, meet me over at the boat?"

"You know, I was just listening to the howling wind and thinking about going fishing. It's lovely out. Are you nuts?"

"I need your help, Jack."

"Oh?" suddenly serious, "Okay. I'll be there in five."

It is a quiet Sunday in January, the summer crowd is long gone and there isn't any traffic. I drive as fast as I can to the docks, rolling through some stop signs and red lights. I call Audrey Mackey on my cell.

"Hey, Aud."

"James!" The affection in her voice always makes me a little embarrassed. Her husband Stan went down six years ago with the rest of the crew of the *Belle of the Ball*, when it sank out on the Banks. Like everyone, I have just tried to help out, but she has always seemed to think I've done more than my share.

"How are you, Audrey?" I try to keep my voice flat, calm, but my heart is racing.

"I'm just fine. Are you looking for the kids? They went to the movies."

"Oh, yeah?"

"Horror movie double feature. They won't be back for hours. Patrick is so sweet, but he's awfully shy around Cynthia. Tell him to speak up, she likes him!"

"Doesn't take after his mother that way, does he?" Audrey and Catherine had been great friends.

"Ha! No, but we wouldn't want him to. There was only one Catherine. And Patrick is who he is. He'll be fine, he's smart and kind. He's got my support!"

"I keep telling him Cynthia's way over his head, she's got to be the prettiest girl in the class. But he won't give up."

"James, you're awful. You should be encouraging him."

"Oh, he gets plenty of encouragement from Angela. Hey, Audrey, is that new boat of your tied down, it's getting pretty nasty out there."

"Oh yes. Actually, the kids volunteered to go down and check it out before going to the movies."

My heart sinks again.

"Okay, I'll track Patrick down later, nothing important."

By the time Jack tears into the parking lot in his old Corvette, I have the lines off the *Daybreak* and the engine running. He runs over and jumps on deck.

"Hey, are you really going out? What's going on?"

I start backing her out as I talk. Jack looks out into the harbor, where the sky is deathly gray and the wind is shrieking.

"I heard a Mayday for the *Olivia May*, Audrey Mackey's boat. Patrick and Cynthia Mackey are supposed to be at the movies. That's what Audrey thinks, anyway. But someone's in distress on that boat and I think it's them. That's the only explanation that makes sense."

"Holy fucking shit," Jack says, barely audible over the wind. "Holy fucking shit. Patrick wouldn't go out in this, he's not crazy."

"He's a MacAfee and he's Catherine's son. You had to figure that would all surface sooner or later. I figure they can't be more than a couple miles out. That's why the Coast Guard couldn't find them. If the boat turtled and they have their life jackets on, we could get there in time. Water is freezing though, they won't last long."

"Is Patrick out of his mind?!" Jack yells as the boat turns into the wind.

"He's trying to impress Cynthia. We've both done worse."

Jack looks thoughtful for a second. "Yep," he says, "We sure did. Cynthia Mackey, huh? Pretty good, Pat. So what's the plan? We take a fishing boat into the teeth of a full blown Nor'easter and find a sailboat in a haystack?"

"Something like that."

"Okay. Just want to be clear."

"Why are you smiling, Jack?"

"I'm really glad you called me."

"I need a good sailor. This is going to be rough."

"I have to give it to Patrick," Jack says, sounding worried, "this might be as crazy as anything we ever did."

"Keep your eyes open," I say. "Why don't you get up in the bow. I'll sweep the stern."

Even in the flat shoreline seas the water is treacherous. The swell is ten feet and the current is vicious. It's all I can do to keep the boat on course. The wind is accelerating with every passing moment and the boat is heeling 45 degrees, the wake on the port side washing over the railing. This close to shore, if we get turned around we could get smashed up on shore before we can do anything about it. Ordinarily I would never be this close to shore in any kind of weather, much less in a howler like this. I am praying for the first time in twenty years, praying that Patrick and Cynthia have somehow stayed afloat. I think of Angela. She's going to figure something's up. I don't know if she could stand it if anything happened to Patrick.

I look up at Jack, who is leaning on the rail and watching the shoreline as we emerge from the harbor and head down the coast. He looks worried. I'm not sure why I called him instead of several other more reliable hands I know. I guess I thought it would mean something to him and it clearly does. I feel myself softening towards him. I remember some of the crazy things we used to do when we were younger. We stole the harbormaster's boat one time and ran it aground off Ingram's Point. I was thirteen. Jesus, was Pop mad.

I turn the boat away from the wind and follow the current and the wind up the coast. If the *Olivia May* is adrift, this is the way she'll be going. I am feeling very, very bad about this, the wind is picking up and the water is terrible, a boiling cauldron of current and wind-driven waves. The current has already started to pick up some storm debris: a small Sunfish mast with a sail still attached to it floats by, blown right off a boat on shore.

Jack is waving, pointing towards the shore. I pull the boat up a little and I see the hull of a boat. I don't see any figures on it and I start to panic. Jack looks back and he is crying. He waves me towards the hull. I look at the shore and try to remember the charts for this area. It is a bad patch of water; there are rock reefs that stretch out into the Sound. I could sink us, but I don't have time to go below and check the charts. I grimace and head straight for the hull, bracing myself for the crash when the boat hits bottom.

We pull right up to the hull and I slow the engine and let the boat drift right next to it. There is no one in sight. They could be under the hull, either dead or maybe in an air pocket. Jack pulls himself back towards me, hanging on to the side rail for dear life. He climbs up to me and shouts in my ear to be heard over the wind and rain.

"Should we run up and down once, maybe they're hanging on to something, still floating. Maybe they stayed up on their preservers."

I look at him and shake my head.

"If they're not under that boat they're gone, Jack."

He looks at me in shock, then outrage, then acceptance. He looks desperately at the hull.

I yell, "I'm going to take a look. I'm going under."

Suddenly, the *Daybreak* rears up on a huge swell and nearly rolls on top of the sailboat's much lower hull. There is a grinding sound as the two hulls crash into each other.

"No way," Jack shouts, "I cannot handle your boat in this storm, James. And I'm a much better swimmer. I have to be the one who goes in. You know that."

Jesus Christ, he's right. The tide is now creating havoc with the water, causing the waves to break into each other, an explosion of water like an overflowing pot on a stove. I don't know anyone else who could handle this boat in this weather, except Pop. Without saying more, Jack goes down below. I try to hold the boat in position. He emerges with a snorkel and two life jackets, stripped down to shorts, a tee shirt and a life jacket. He waves at me with a nervous smile. I wave back and push the boat forward, then turn it hard so it nearly stops into a wave. Jack slips over the side and disappears into the water. I pull the boat away and try to maneuver around the hull, so I can see every angle. It should not take long for Jack to figure out if anyone's under there. I am worried about Jack. I shouldn't have let him go in like this. We should have waited. I turn the boat around and start coming up on the hull downwind. I gun the throttle to get up over the next wave and lean forward to see over the crest.

That's the last thing I remember clearly in this world for a while. There is an enormous crashing sound and everything stops. After that there is only darkness.

CHAPTER TWENTY
Seamus
August 1993

It starts as a beautiful day, pale blue skies and distant wispy crowds. It is breezy, even gusting at times. *Daybreak* is sturdy on the water, as always, cutting through the choppy waves.

But today it is just Jack and me and that is so, so great. Pop isn't feeling well today, the "Irish flu" as James sourly calls Pop's frequent hangovers. And James got a late call to first mate on the *Mrs. Pearl.* Jack and I have never gone out alone, but Pop says sure, why not, without checking with Mom. We run off to the dock before he comes to his senses.

"You okay with this, bub?" Jack says with a smile, as we scramble around pulling the lines and casting off.

I shrug as nonchalantly as I can.

"Sure, why wouldn't I be? Ain't nothing we haven't done a hundred times, bro," I say.

"Yeah, but James and Pop aren't here."

"I'm cool. You can do it, Jack. Dad says you could skipper this thing through the gates of hell."

"I think what Dad means is he *wishes* I would go through the gates of hell."

I shake my head and laugh. "You're his favorite, Jack! Don't you know that? Why is everyone in this family so weird?"

"Whoeee!!!" Jack yells, as we clear the last dock. "We're gone, baby!" He pushes the throttle forward and the engines roar.

"I love this shit!" he yells, "Nobody to tell us how to do anything!"

He points us straight out from the Verrazano, heading for deep water. We chatter happily about everything. I laugh at his teacher impressions. I have the same teachers this year, my freshman year at St. Raymond's high School, that he had last year. He tells me which of the sophomore girls he's gone out with, an impossibly gorgeous lineup of cheerleaders and party girls. But I am waiting for a quiet moment to ask him something that's been bothering me.

"Jack, can I ask you a question?" I say hesitantly.

"Shoot!"

"I found a bunch of empties in a bag in the basement back home."

"Yeah?" he says, carefully studying the horizon and not looking at me.

"Are they yours?"

He is quiet for a moment. "Yeah, I've had a few beers. It's no big deal, Shay."

"But you're okay. Right?"

"Of course I'm okay," he says, turning and slapping me on the back. "Don't I seem fine? I'm cool, right?"

I nod. "Yeah, of course." He does seem okay. A little louder than usual, but nothing too strange.

"Hey," Jack says, "Dad was drunk before lunch most of the time in the old days."

I must have a funny look on my face, because he suddenly gets serious.

"But that's Dad. We're not going to be like Dad."

"Why not? He's a good skipper. You or he or James are the best on the Island."

"You don't want to be like him. Or me. Be like James."

"Who? Mr. Cranky? I don't think so."

"James means well, Seamus. He just worries about you."

"He's no fun, Jack! He's like Annabel's dad. 'Life's not a game, Seamus. It's time for you to grow up, Seamus.' Yuck!"

I grab Jack by the shoulders from behind. "I want to be like you, Jack! You're the man." I shake him.

Jack laughs. "So what's the deal with this girlfriend of yours, anyway?"

"I'm not telling!" I say, moving down the steps. The wind has picked up and white foam is blowing off the top of the waves. I have to step carefully and yell to be heard.

"A gentleman never talks! I'm securing the seat covers and stuff, in case it really starts to blow."

"Get back here," Jack yells. "I want details!"

"Never!!" I yell. I skip across the deck to the stern. I am smiling as I think of Annabel's face and how she kissed me, just for a moment, the last time I walked her home. I turn around to yell something to Jack, but stop when I see the horizon behind us.

"Jack!" I yell.

He turns and I point directly astern. There's bad weather following us.

"Holy shit!" Jack yells.

The storm is a beautiful thing, a tidal wave of dark clouds rolling along the ocean five miles behind us, kicking up spray and white caps. Jack turns the wheel and glances with worry over his shoulder, following the line of it.

"It's going to cut us off from the shore, Seamus," he yells down to me.

I climb up to the bridge and watch the line of clouds approach. I can see Jack had an idea about beating the storm to shore, but it's going to get in front of us.

"Pull out," I say, "Let's run straight out. Maybe it will pass behind us."

Jack nods. "Yeah, that's our best shot."

The wind is picking up, snapping our two flags, American and Irish, over our heads. Jack turns hard and the *Daybreak* starts to roll with the swell the storm is pushing ahead of it. In moments the wind is howling, so that we cannot hear each other even standing next to each other.

Jack struggles with the helm. He points back to the stern and motions down with one hand as he grips the wheel with the other. I nod. He wants me to tie everything down, this could get bad. I turn to head down the steps, but he suddenly grabs my arm. He smiles calmly at me and winks, then pulls me closer and rubs the top of my head, like he always does when I'm doing well. I'm always trying to be as good as him. I smile right back and climb down the ladder carefully. The boat is listing 45 degrees with each wave and I start to think this seems like a bigger storm than we've been through in a long while. I fix the engine hold door, which has blown open, then turn to work my way back to Jack. And then I stop, frozen in fear.

Ahead of us the sky is strangely calm. But there is nothing but black swirling clouds on either side and behind us. Jack is hunched over, looking straight ahead, holding his hat on with one hand and one hand on the wheel. Trying to hold his course.

He does not see the huge surge of water looming over us on the starboard side, a black wall with a white crest, coming with a roar that I just now hear over the wind.

"Jack, look out!" I yell. I start to run across the deck to the bridge. And then there is crushing water and no air and darkness.

I reach out slowly to grab the side of the boat, but I sink quickly under the weight of my foul weather gear. Everything is receding away from me, the clouds and the boat and Jack and Annabel. The last light fades on the surface far overhead and I am pulled down and down and away.

CHAPTER TWENTY ONE
James
January 2009

A long time passes. I slowly wake up to a searing pain in my chest and a throbbing ache in the back of my head. I open my eyes and there is Jack, who is holding both of my hands together in his.

"Hey, hey, Jimmy," he whispers, "Take it easy, bud. Just lie still." He has not called me Jimmy in twenty five years. I slowly remember the ride out and Jack going under the hull, but nothing else. I am lying in the cabin of a boat, but it's not the *Daybreak*.

"Where am I?" I try to look around, but my head hurts so badly I close my eyes.

"The *Anna Marie*. Charlie Sorino's boat. She picked us up."

"What about Pat and Cynthia?" I say, barely getting the words out. My chest hurts so much. I realize it must be because I swallowed a huge amount of sea water. I almost drowned.

"Relax," Jack says, "we got them. They were under the hull. They're up top."

"What happened to me?"

"You hit a reef. You got thrown clear over the bridge. You must have bounced off the deck and hit the water."

"Did you pull me out?"

Jack watches me with the strangest expression, expectant, almost happy. "Yeah, Jimmy, I did. I pulled Cynthia out from under the hull and Patrick came out and took a hold of her. Then I went down and got you. You were pretty deep, man, way down there. I almost couldn't find you. The *Anna Marie* was nearby. Cynthia and Patrick climbed on board and Patrick yanked you back in. It was touch and go for a bit. It was really hard for Patrick to get over to the *Anna Marie* with Cynthia, she was panicking. But we got you in."

"Did the *Anna Marie* tow the *Daybreak* in?"

Jack looks at the ground steadily. I get a very bad feeling.

"She went down, James. She flipped and she must have busted a hole in her upper hull when she hit the sailboat. She went down before anyone could get to her."

I still feel very woozy and this information only sinks in part way. But still, I start to feel this cold hole in my gut, this shock of regret. I sank my boat. She's gone.

"James," Jack says, "You did it to save the kids."

I look at him, lost. Yes, he's right. But I have broken my own heart with this.

Patrick and Cynthia come down a little later. There is a great deal of whispering in the cabin and then Patrick sits down next to me. Cynthia stands slightly away, a deeply worried and frightened look on her lovely face. Patrick looks fearful, still shaken by the experience.

"I'm so, so sorry, James. I almost got you killed."

For a second I do not know what he is talking about. I must look confused.

"We took the boat out without telling anyone," Patrick says with tears in his eyes, "We shouldn't have done it, it was so, so stupid."

He looks at me, crushed. "I sank the *Daybreak*, James."

"Oh, that. Forget it. You helped save my life, pal. I owe you one big time. That means I have to keep you as a mate forever, if you want. As soon as I get another boat. I'm not the first captain to lose his boat and I won't be the last. What happened to Audrey's sailboat?"

"It looks like it's going to wash up on Shane Beach. The mast didn't break, it'll probably be okay."

"You're okay? You and Cynthia?"

"We're fine. We swam out from under the hull and Jack saw us. Jack says you probably have a concussion. We should let you rest."

"Thanks for getting me, Pat. Somebody better call Angela if I'm coming into port with a concussion."

"We'll call her," Jack says softly from the door. He flips off the light. "You rest."

"Pat," I say as I close my eyes.

"Yes, James?"

"I've been hard on you sometimes."

"Forget it, James."

"No, I won't. You were very, very brave out there. We're going to change things, you and me."

"Okay, James." He sits back down. I open one eye. He is crying. I take his hand. I hold it up and kiss it lightly. Then I fall asleep.

When I wake up, I am home in my bed. It is pitch dark, inside and out. The window by my bedside table is open. I hear the murmur of voices on our back porch below. I am unbelievably thirsty. I stand up, feeling dizzy and very shaky. I go into the bathroom and drink several glasses of water. I work my way down the stairs and walk into the kitchen. No one is there, the lights are piercingly bright. I suddenly feel like I am going to collapse and I stumble into our den. I drop into the small couch and put my head back. The window in this room is open as well, only now I can hear the voices quite clearly. Jack and Angela. Angela's voice sounds so lovely, floating into the room.

"I still don't understand how Patrick got Cynthia to the boat. He's so skinny! That's like one those stories you hear about a mother lifting a car off her child."

"Angie, I'm serious, it was a miracle. He stayed calm, he kept his head. A lot of people would have lost it. I think the life jacket helped, you know, he was kind of bobbing along there."

"Was James conscious when you got to him?"

"No, he was out cold. *That* scared me. Really scared me."

"They'd all be dead if it wasn't for you, Jack. Jesus!"

"I was just in the right place at the right time. Patrick could have panicked, headed for the boat. He stuck with Cynthia and kept an eye on me. That's what courage is, isn't it, when you have a choice about what to do and you do the right thing?"

They are quiet for a moment, then Angela says, "So, what's the plan, Jack?"

"You mean tonight or long term?"

"Long term." Her voice is a little clipped, surprisingly so.

"I don't know, Angie." There is a long pause. Then an audible sigh. "I have a major problem with you, you know that. I tried to tell you this before, but I was all fucked up, excuse my language. I doubt I was clear. I mean, you said that we wouldn't know what I really felt about anything until I got sober. Well, the fog is lifting and I'm in love with you, there's no two ways about it. And I understand that's impossible, I really do. But I don't know what to do about it."

"Me neither." She sighs. "Look, Jack, I love you, I do."

I cringe a little when I hear this.

"But it's like the way a mom loves a particularly difficult child, you know? You drive me crazy. Sometimes I feel like I'm climbing out of a bottomless hole myself and you're hanging on to my ankles, dragging me back. And up until today, James was fed up with you; Patrick was fed up with you. I'm trying to get my life moving in the right direction with the people that I'm closest to and I want to help you, I really do, but it's killing me."

"Did you ever tell James about what happened that night outside of B&B's? When I kissed you?"

"When we kissed each other. Yes, I did."

"How pissed was he? Why hasn't he killed me?"

"I had to tell him everything. If he can go forward with me, I want it all out there so we can start over for real."

Neither of them says anything after that, for a little while. Then Jack says, "Angela, I have to tell you something I've never told anyone else."

"Yes?"

"When Seamus drowned, that day in the storm? I was drunk. I had started drinking with my friends and I liked it, so I started doing it a little on the side. It never mattered on the boat because James was always around but then one morning James got another call and Seamus was bugging Pop to let us go out. I had already been drinking beer in the shed that morning and I got that stupid bravery you get from drinking. I should have been too scared to go, deep down I was, but drunk I was too proud to admit that and I let Seamus nag Pop into letting us go."

I hear his chair scrape back as he gets up quickly.

"Jack, take it easy," Angela says.

"I was too drunk to handle the boat. I should have taken us into shore, where James was. I should have turned the other way. I should have made Seamus get below. My drinking killed him!"

Drunk? I can't believe it. He was at the helm drunk? Goddamn him, that bastard. If I could get up I'd slug him.

"Jack, didn't Seamus know all that?"

"All what?" His voice is still loud, agitated.

"Sit down, Jack. Sit." There is a pause and a quiet push of a chair on the floor. "Take a deep breath. Now listen. Seamus was fourteen, just a year younger than you. He was already a good deckhand, you said so, right?"

"Yeah," he sighs.

"He knew that boat, he knew his way around the Sound, right? He knew as much as you did. He would have known where the storm was coming from, whether or not to hug the shore, where to position himself on the boat?"

"Yeah," A whisper.

"Were you even giving him orders? Or were you doing things together?"

"No, I wouldn't give him an order. He wouldn't listen to my orders anyway."

"He thought you were okay. He thought your boat could handle anything that came up in the Sound. Drunk or not, that's what you thought. You probably would have done the same thing sober, wouldn't you?"

"I don't know, Angie. I don't!"

"C'mon Jack, think! Stop feeling sorry for yourself. Seamus knew what was going on. He was with you and he didn't say anything. If he thought you should head in, would he have said so?"

A long pause.

"Would he have told you to head in, Jack? Did he know enough to do that?"

"Yes."

"Why didn't he?"

"I don't know."

"He thought you were going to be okay. And you thought you were going to be okay. And you could sail a boat through a hurricane drunk, I know you. It's in your blood. It was a freak accident, Jack. You wouldn't have run to shore sober and you wouldn't have known that wave was coming sober. Stop killing yourself. What would James have done?"

I tried to think. What would I have done? The *Mrs. Pearl* headed into the channel that day, close to shore, but that was her skipper's style. That wasn't my call.

"I don't know what James would have done," Jack says. "I don't know James anymore."

"Who's the most stubborn person you know?"

"James."

"Ever see him run home ahead of bad weather?"

No way. She's right.

"He would have done what you did. Seamus was okay with what you did. Pop would have done what you did. They would have ridden it out and gotten hit by that wave. There's nothing you could have done. Jack?"

"What?"

"You're punishing yourself because you need an excuse to drink. You have to let this go if you're going to get better."

There was a long pause, and then Jack said, "Let me get you some more tea."

"Wait."

"Yes, Angie?"

"Do you believe me?"

"Yes, I think I do."

"Honestly, Jack?"

"Yes. Yes, I think you're right. I never thought about it that way before."

I hear him walk into the kitchen. I hear her follow him.

"I guess I better start thinking about where I'm going next," Jack says, as glass and silverware clink.

"I'm not telling you to go, Jack."

"But you don't think it's a good idea if I stay?" he says, a little sourly, then quickly adds, "Sorry."

"It's not my decision to make," she says quietly. "It's up to James."

"Why James? I care what you think; I don't have to care what he thinks." He sounds angry and I am getting a little pissed off myself.

"You have to care what he thinks and deal with it, Jack. Because I'm not splitting my heart up anymore. I have to let go of drinking, I have to let go of you, I may even have to let go of Patrick. I need James. He's my family. I have put everything I have into that."

"Sorry, Angela. I am sorry."

"It's okay. It will be okay. C'mon, sit down, let's work on this. Tell me some ideas about what you can do."

I lay my head back and let out a deep breath. Part of me wishes Jack would just go away; I will never get comfortable with him near Angela. I do not trust him, I cannot trust him. But another part of me could not bear it if he left. Seamus would have wanted him here. Patrick will want him here.

I hear the scrape of chairs as they settle in at our small kitchen table. I am fading out. I close my eyes and things start to go black again. I stay awake for a moment and listen to their voices, the murmured sounds of two alcoholics consoling each other in the night.

Goddamn Jack. He could ruin everything. I feel like Angela and I are getting close to maybe being able to make it. But he could mess it all up. And there's something that feels doomed about him, like he'll pull all of us down the way he did Seamus. Seamus would still be here if it wasn't for him. Their voices swirl softly around the quiet night, a conversation that has taken place countless times over countless kitchen tables, as people try to pull each other in from the storm.

Then just as I am falling asleep, I have a sharp and sudden memory. I am drowning. Water is filling my lungs. I cannot tell if I am under or over the surface, the water is so rough. I do not have my life jacket on and I am going under. I catch a glimpse of the head of a swimmer moving towards me. It is Jack, stroking furiously with a desperate, determined look on his face. But I do not think he will make it, not this time. The water is around me, in me, over me. I cannot breathe any longer and I start to spiral to the bottom of the ocean. Then I feel a strong hand catch my collar and pull me up, out into the air.

I wake up with a start, gasping for breath. Voices in the kitchen suddenly stop and I hear a chair fall over as people rush into the room.

"James!" Angela says with alarm, "How did you get here? You should be in bed!" she sits next to me and puts her arms around me. "James, love, take a deep breath, nice and slow."

I realize I am still gasping uncontrollably.

"I'll get some water," Jack says and he hurries from the room.

I hate him. I love him. I want him to stay but I want him to go. My head is too foggy to figure anything out, except to mutter, "Fucking Jack."

I am sitting up, my head on Angela's shoulder. She is gently stroking my hair.

"What, James?"

"Nothing," I whisper.

"Why don't you go back to sleep?" Angela says.

She hands me a tall glass of water, which I drink in one long gulp.

"Where's Jack?" I say.

"He's going to sleep on the porch. He said he was going to leave us alone. Let's go upstairs."

I nod and lean forward to get up. Then I stop.

"Wait," I say, opening my eyes and looking at her carefully for the first time since I was saved. She looks tired and deeply concerned. She places a hand on my cheek and smiles. She shakes her head and kisses me on the forehead, then on the lips.

"Please, James," she whispers into my ear, "please be careful out there. I can't make it without you."

Outside it has started to rain, a soft rushing sound as the water brushes on the leaves outside. There isn't another sound, inside or out. I lean my head back and close my eyes. She cannot make it without me.

"Angie, I lost my boat."

"I know, love," she whispers in my ear. "I'm so sorry."

My head is splitting; I have never hurt so much. I feel myself fading away. There is a jumble of thoughts in my head, many of them fearful or sad. My *Daybreak* is gone. Now what will I do?

"But I still have you, Angela," I say in a croak, "Do I still have you?"

"Always," she whispers. "We came through our storm. We sailed right through it."

"You'd make a hell of a sailor, Angie."

I close my eyes and think about my boat, sunk to the bottom of the sea. Down there at rest with Seamus and Pop. I imagine her sitting straight up on the bottom of the Sound, as pretty as the day Pop bought her, fish swimming in and out of her portholes. I'd have to find another one or go to work on someone else's.

But I was still alive. Jack saved me. Of course he did, he's my brother. And yet, he must have acted with extraordinary quickness to get to me before I went all the way under. He must have been looking out for me. Why couldn't he have done the same for Seamus?

"Fucking Jack," I whisper.

"James!" Angela says with concern. "Why are you mad at Jack?"

I look into her eyes and remember that day that she told me about her lies, about her drinking. And I think how hard and brave it was of her to have given up the truth without knowing what I would do about it.

"Angie," I say, trying to get the words out quickly before I fade out, "I heard what Jack said about Seamus, about what happened out there that day."

"Yes. And what are you going to do about it, James?" she asks.

"I don't know." We hear a noise and look up. Patrick is standing in the doorway.

"This is all my fault," Patrick says softly. He is standing in the doorway, watching us, tears on his face.

Angela stands up quickly and goes to him.

"Pat! What are you doing here? Jesus, what is wrong with all you people? Everybody needs to go to bed, to get some rest." She puts her arm around him and leads him to the couch next to me.

"I caused all this, James," he says.

"Well, yes you did, sort of. But it's okay."

"I thought you'd be so mad at me," he says with a grimace.

"Why would I be mad at you?" I grumble, "You take a sailboat out in a typhoon, flip it, endangering yourself and Cynthia, cause dozens of adults to panic and nearly lead me and my boat to our watery graves. I'd be overreacting if I got mad."

"Now, James," Angela says, patting me on the leg.

I look at Patrick, who is sitting upright, his eyes wide with concern.

"So, now what?" I say to Angela, "I've got to let everyone off the hook? Forgive Jack, forgive Patrick?"

"Up to you, James," she says. "But you might as well forgive Pop, too, while you're at it. And your mother. And me. Be nice to everyone. Jack pulled you out of Davy Jones locker. Maybe that's the exchange."

"Oh, Jesus Christ."

"C'mere," I say to Patrick. As he leans towards me, I wrap my arm around him and pull him toward me firmly. "I've done worse, so has Jack. But you can't take those kinds of chances, Patty. We love you, we're family. I just painted your room, for Chrissakes. We're roomies. You have to take care of yourself and Cynthia, you understand?"

"But the boat, James. The *Daybreak*..."

"Forget it." I lay all the way back on the couch. "Nothing lasts forever. Many a noble vessel has found her way to the bottom of the sea. She's in good company."

"Is that a sea quote?" Patrick says.

"No, I just made that up."

Angela nods, "Not bad."

"No, it's pretty good for a fisherman," Patrick says, "You know, not the literate sort."

"The bell is about to toll for thee if you don't get the hell out of here," I grumble ominously, my eyes closed. But I smile.

"Everyone out!" Angela announces. She leans over and whispers in my ear, "You just sleep here. We'll be quiet."

I lay back on the couch and feel myself slipping away.

"Angie," I say.

"Yes?"

"Jack needed to save someone, I guess, huh? This could be good for him. Tell him I know about Seamus. Now I've got to start looking for a new boat."

"A new boat?" she says, rubbing my neck gently.

"Yeah, a big one, 50, 60 feet. Something we can all fit on."

"What about Jack?"

"I don't know about Jack. I don't know if I can let him back in or not. I owe him now, but I don't know if I could work with him. What do you think, Angie?"

But I don't hear what her answer is, because I'm already gone.

CHAPTER TWENTY-TWO

Angela
March 2009

Every story has a beginning, middle and an end. So here is the beginning of one story and the end of another.

I am pacing in the yard of our little house. I have done this many, many times over the years, usually chain smoking, sometimes drunk and always wrestling with the monsters in my head. There was a day some time ago where I stood out here and thought about how to tell my husband something that I knew would break his heart. It was a day like today, gray, quiet and ominous. It is even more so today, a stunned silence, the only sounds float into the yard as if they are lost: a car horn, a birdcall, a child's cry. I glance at the kitchen window and I see James watching me, worried. He catches my eye and moves away, pretending to be busy.

I walk towards the house, looking up at the sky. It has no features, colorless from horizon to horizon. This same sky has crushed me in the past, gathered up all of the weight of my regret and my fear and dropped it on my shoulders. I have walked circles in this yard trying to convince myself there was a reason to stay alive. But today the silent sky does not crush me; instead I am floating up into it, flying through it like a bird. I see a seagull high over my head and that's where I am, dipping down for a look at the ground and then expertly turning a wing and moving straight up, through the dull cloud cover and into the clear sky above it, brilliant, sparkling, weightless.

I walk into the kitchen. James stops moving and looks at me. He slowly puts a dish into the dishwasher.

"You okay, Angie?" His voice, ordinarily deep and sure, is soft and hesitant.

I nod and I smile. I move around the kitchen, get a glass of water, take out some crackers. I put my hand in my pocket and feel the single sheet of paper there. A fax sheet with two sentences on it: "Dear Ms. Cabrera: This is to let you know that the reasons for your recent occasional lightheadedness are most likely related to the pregnancy our tests uncovered, which based upon your history we estimate to be in its seventh week. You should schedule an appointment with us to review your pre-natal care. Yours, Dr. Ann Reindel."

Underneath the typed name there is a smiley face drawn in pencil, with words in large letters: "Surprise! Yay, Angie! Call me, Ann. Woooopeeeee!"

Again I feel the rush of excitement, joy and fear. A lot of fear. I don't know how to be a parent. I had no mother, no father. No memories to cherish, no experiences to pass on. I was alone throughout my childhood. I might as well be stepping into a jet plane to fly it. I only know what I've daydreamed about, and what good are daydreams? I stop moving and look at James, who has stopped and is as still as an animal in the forest.

"James," I say to him, "I have something to tell you." He looks at me warily, frightened by prior experience but warmed by my smile, which I know has reached the beaming stage by now. I think to myself that this man can help me figure out all of this. He was my first real connection to any person and in return I wounded him terribly. But maybe that's why we have come this far, to do this together. He watches me.

I told Patrick the night before. I swore him to secrecy. I thought, I hoped, James would be thrilled. But I was not sure about Patrick. We had welcomed him into our home like our own child and now we would have our own child. I really worried about what he would think. He and I were driving to a swim meet. I had convinced him to swim for the team at the local pool. He was the slowest swimmer in his age group, but he was working hard at it and I went to all the meets. I just blurted it out after we pulled into the parking spot, "Pat, listen, I'm pregnant. If everything works out, I'm going to have a baby." I instinctively reached for his hand, which he gripped. His eyes widened and his mouth opened to say something, but for a moment nothing came out. I felt like I had betrayed him, lured him into this family and then left him without a place.

"Is it a boy or a girl?" he whispered, his face still unreadable.

"I don't know yet. What do you think, Pat? Are you okay?"

Then he smiled and said, "Holy shit." We both laughed. He leaned forward.

"I'll be a really good big brother, Angie," he said, "you'll see."

I held his hand to my cheek. For the first time in my adult life I felt like maybe, just maybe, I wouldn't need a drink again.

He said, "Oh, boy, I wish I could be there when you tell James. He's gonna freak! Is he out on the water?"

"Yeah, he's coming home tonight."

Now I walk over to James and stand in front of him.

"Sit down, James," I say, touching him on the elbow. He sits down slowly, his eyes never leaving me. His face is wrinkled in confusion, but something hopeful flickers in his usually impenetrable eyes. Yes, I think, sit down, here in our crowded little house. A place I used to hate coming back to and now never want to leave. Sit down so that I can mend your heart.

Angela
September 2009

I wait, playing nervously with my hospital name tag. It says "Mother:Angela – Child:Catherine." Her name is Catherine, but I don't think of her that way yet, as an individual person. She's my baby, still part of me. I haven't separated her yet. Today they left her here with me for a long time and just took her away a few minutes ago. She is beautiful and I wish she was here right now. I miss her already, her scrunched up little red face and tiny little fingers. My emotions are splashing around right now, happy, sad, nervous, worried, giddy.

Outside of my window I can hear the tattered edges of a full blown Nor'easter ripping at the awning over the entrance, which flaps angrily like a loose sail in a gale. I pull the covers up to my chin. I try to remember everything that happened in the past few hours. I should remember this, it will be important to remember this.

It was pouring when Jack drove Patrick and me to the hospital. Jack started singing *Jumpin Jack Flash*:

I was born in a cross-fire hurricane, and I howled at my ma in the driving rain.

I was sitting in the back seat with Patrick, who held my hand and smiled through his tears. He kept saying, "I'm sorry I'm crying Angela, I don't know why I'm crying." Jack was chattering a mile a minute and driving three miles an hour. I finally had to say, "Jack! Can you pick it up a little? I'm not going to break if you go over a bump and this baby is coming pretty soon." He looked over his shoulder in sheer panic and stomped on the gas, driving 70 miles an hour the rest of the way.

James was out on the *Islander*. The past few weeks he and Jack had been skippering her while John Hoppens considered retirement. Jack had stayed home to look at another boat this weekend. My labor started Saturday night, two weeks early. They raised James on ship to shore and he came flying into the delivery room with his dripping yellow slicker and boots still on.

When he burst through the door, I don't know what came over me, I sat up and threw my arms out and yelled, "Jesus fucking Christ I am so glad you're here!" He hugged me and got me all wet and I didn't care. The doctor and the nurses all laughed and everyone relaxed. The doctor said, "Well, we've got the captain here! It should be an easy voyage from here on in." I had been starting to panic but after that it was fine, everything was fine.

When they held her up in front of me for the first time a couple of hours later I started crying. A little later one of the nurses whispered "What's this little sailor's name?" And I said "Catherine, after her late aunt." That was a surprise for James. I hadn't told him I was thinking about that. I'd given him a few decoy names. I watched for his reaction.

He took her from me and held her and I thought he was going to cry, I really did. But he didn't, dammit. And neither did she. He sat on the edge of the bed, holding her up in front of him.

"Well, well, well," he said. "And I thought I'd seen everything. I guess we know the name of our next boat now, don't we? The *Catherine M.*" He brushed his nose against hers and said, "What do you think of that, little girl? How would you like to have your own fishing boat?"

He watched her, tentatively offering a smile, and our daughter looked right back, her deep sea eyes serious and unblinking.